ANSTEY'S REVENGE

Will Love be Enough?

Anstey's Kingdom Book Two

By

Susan Hancock

ISBN: 978-1-8381095-2-3

For Peter, he knows why.

CONTENTS

ACKNOWLEDGMENTS

Thank you to everyone who encouraged or helped me with this endeavour: The North Devon Records Office and the Landmark Trust for assistance with historical research; Yvonne for making me believe my books are worth reading; my publishing team at Kindle Book Publishing for their invaluable help in bringing this publication into being. And thank you, Peter, for unending patience and belief in me.

Author's Note

My author's note to *Surviving Anstey,* the first volume in this trilogy, explains the composite location of Anstey's Kingdom in sixteenth-century England (Lynmouth, Devon and Holywell Bay, Cornwall) and these details remain the same for *Anstey's Revenge.* As with the first of the 'Anstey' novels, I have tried to be true to the life and times of Elizabethan England throughout, though I have necessarily changed some of the dates and details (and language).

In this book, in particular, I have moved the horrific floods which occurred along that coastline in 1607 to an earlier date to fit the story. A poignant wood cut from the time, "Cover illustration of the pamphlet of the flood along the Bristol Channel, 1607" as reproduced in Todd Gray (ed.) *The Lost Chronicle of Barnstaple 1586-1611* (Devonshire Association 1998) shows the horror of the floods. In this portrayal the cot I refer to as being empty (chapter 10) has a tiny occupant being whirled to destruction.

As before, where I have mentioned significant places, I have used the names as they appear in the 1579 map which is reproduced in the same book (see above) – such as Barnstable for Barnstaple, Ilfraycombe for Ilfracombe, Lundye for Lundy Island (other contemporary variants that occur elsewhere are Ilfradiscombe and Lunday.) I again thank the team at the North Devon Record Office in Barnstaple Library for access to the North Devon Local Studies Library which located much of interest for me relating to the period and place.

The Lundy pirates are a more prominent feature of this book. Their exploits are well documented. See information held in the North Devon Record Office and also accessible on the page "Lundy-part 2." "A piratical past – Elizabethan times" on devonperspectives.co.uk accessed on various occasions, including 10th August 2019. Thanks are due to the Landmark Trust for assistance during my fact-finding trip to the island of Lundy (located roughly twelve miles off the Devon coast.) The extent of pirate problem there (dates changed), and official responses to it, is highlighted in *Lundy – Its History and Natural History* (Longmans, Green and Co, London: 1925). I have taken the liberty of including Mathias on the crew of the one of the ships authorized by the commission.

… complaints made to the Government by shipowners and local authorities concerning piracies in the Bristol Channel became so constant that in 1608 a commission was issued to the Earl of Bath to inquire into the matter. He sat at Barnstaple and took the depositions of three persons there to the effect that merchants were daily robbed at sea by pirates who used Lundy as a place of refuge. This action appears to have borne fruit for on March 20, 1610, a commission was issued to the Earl of Nottingham to give authority to the Mayor and Aldermen of Barnstaple to send out ships to capture pirates. And a month later (April 17) the deposition was taken of a William Young, who had been made prisoner by a pirate Captain Salkeld, and escaped (Lewis R. W. Loyd, pp116-117).

Other depositions detailed by Loyd include that of Nicholas Cullen (p.118) who claimed that "…Turks had taken out of a church in Cornwall about sixty men and carried them away prisoners. They continued in Lundy a fortnight." A variety of other sources exist detailing the taking of slaves by Barbary pirates; for further information a number of these are listed in the author's note in *Surviving Anstey*.

With regard to the Thornes' business interests in Barnstable, there were 25 merchants recorded as regularly exporting cloth in the year

1565-1566 and there is no reason to believe that the cloth trade did not continue to flourish throughout this period. Originally the trade was with Spain and Portugal, but, disrupted by the war with Spain, developed to include Ireland and the New World. Merchants were also given letters of marque to take reprisals against the Spanish and many made their fortunes between 1590 and 1592 (Source: Stone, Avril, *The Book of Barnstaple*. Wellington:2002, revised and reprinted 2012) I can imagine that appealing to the Thornes.

For general information on the life and times of Elizabethan and Stuart England, I am again indebted, in particular, to Ian Mortimer's *The Time Traveller's Guide to Elizabethan England* (Vintage Books, London: 2013.) As before, the names of characters are drawn from sources such as Chris Laning (SCA: Christian de Holacombe, claning@igc.org) "Faire Names for English Folk: Late Sixteenth Century English Names" s-gabriel.org

Lastly, Elizabeth Norton's *The Lives of Tudor Women* (Head of Zeus Ltd, London: 2016) offers compelling evidence that Thomas was very wise indeed to insist on Kat giving birth in the complex, with all the medical advances that an advanced alien civilization could offer, before her power developed sufficiently for her to protect the baby herself.

Susan Hancock

Foreword

This is the second book in the 'Anstey's Kingdom' trilogy.

The first book in the series, *Surviving Anstey,* tells the story of refugees fleeing through time and space to escape war on Domum-Orbis in the Auriga constellation only to find themselves trapped into slavery by a power-hungry and pitiless dictator – the Anstey of the title – in an underground complex in Elizabethan England. But it also speaks to the love of two of the refugees – one born far away in the stars, one born on Earth – and their fight to free themselves from an evil man's sadistic rule. The current volume, *Anstey's Revenge,* continues their tale.

Major Characters (alive at the start of the book):

The Wrenn-Alban Family

Katharine Wrenn-Alban (Kat): With a mother from the planet Domum-Orbis and a human father, Kat has lived most of her life in sixteenth-century England. She is hand-fasted (the Domum-Orbis equivalent of marriage) with Thomas Alban and is also married to him under human Church Law. Being born to an 'elite woman' Kat has greater power than the majority of the other exiles, being able to move and destroy objects and weapons using just her mind.

Thomas Alban: Born on Domum-Orbis from where he travelled to Earth when he was just five-years of age, Thomas has been brought up in the exiles' underground complex. His parents' failed attempt to escape Anstey resulted in their deaths. Throughout his life Thomas has been persecuted by Anstey and his guards in an attempt to discredit and destroy him. He is hand-fasted with Kat.

Bess Wrenn-Alban: Her human mother is dead and she has an unknown father from Domum-Orbis. Thomas encounters Bess when they are both imprisoned by Anstey. She is now Thomas's and Kat's adopted daughter.

Alice Wrenn-Alban (Lissy): Kat's and Thomas's baby daughter.

William Wrenn: Kat's human father – the man who stole Anstey's wife and kept her safe from him for twenty years.

Others

Adam: A former guard who has been banished from the complex for crimes associated with his work for Anstey.

Richard Anstey: Deposed despotic leader of the exiles, Anstey is responsible for countless deaths, both human and Aurigan. He has fled from the complex following the rebellion and continues to work with the pirates on Lundye Island.

Robert Darley: Human lawyer, William Wrenn's friend and partner to James Notfeld.

Alice Derricott: A powerful empath and medical expert, Alice originally travelled from Domum-Orbis with Thomas and is a close friend to both Kat and Thomas.

Stephen Derricott: Close friend of Thomas and hand-fasted to Alice.

Thom Derricott: Alice and Stephen's young son (Thomas's godson.)

Giles Donnett: Anstey's closest guard (enforcer) who helped him to escape the battle and Kat's attempt to kill him. Bess's abuser.

Anne Gomfrey: Librarian and contemporary of Richard Anstey.

Cecily, Edward, and their son Eddie (Gomfrey-): Anne Gomfrey's daughter, son-in-law, and grandson, who live in William Wrenn's old house after escaping from the complex.

Edith and Hugh Hawkins: Former friends of Thomas, Edith had hoped to marry James Notfeld's twin, Henry, and blames Kat and Thomas for his death during the escape.

Megs: A young human woman who, along with Bess, escaped imprisonment in the complex. She is expecting a baby with a young man from Domum-Orbis.

James Notfeld: Notary for the complex, James is the official responsible for hand-fasting. His twin, Henry, was killed during their attempt to escape from the complex with Thomas and Kat. Partner to Robert Darley.

Margery/Mathias Palmer: Margery, who grew up in the complex with Thomas, is now trying to live as the young man, Mathias, in the world outside.

The Thornes: Exiles who betrayed the families of Thomas and his friends. Parents to Richard Thorne, the traitor killed by Kat during her escape with Thomas.

Recently Dead

John Dinley: One of Thomas's close friends, died from an infected wound inflicted by one of Anstey's enforcers

Henry Notfeld: James Notfeld's twin brother, murdered by one of Anstey's enforcers.

Richard Thorne: Traitor killed by Kat Wrenn-Alban

Elizabeth Wrenn: Kat's mother, murdered by Anstey's paid assassin.

Prologue

The Aftermath

Thomas lies with his wife, kissing her, holding her close against him. Her fingers reach out, gently touching the swirls that curl down from his shoulders under his skin. He feels a surge of love and pleasure, and touches hers, following them slowly, fingers lingering, down to her breasts. Kissing them, her. He wants to make love to Kat so badly; he is roused, ready, and he presses her closer to him.

The memory of enforcers holding him, doing those dreadful things to him, mercilessly, over and over, possesses him. Threatening to do the same to her. Making him feel as if *he* is. And now he can't. His mind reaches out to the curtained inner room, flicks oh so gently at the mind of their baby, waking her. Baby Alice cries and Kat, regretfully, moves away from him, gets up and goes to tend to the child. He doesn't think Kat knows what just happened. He hopes. He pretends to be sleeping when she returns.

He wonders if it will be better when they can leave the complex and return to Kat's old home far away from here. Surely it will be. He was starting to recover there; it was where Kat conceived. The ghosts of his abusers only came back to haunt him when he was walking across the courtyard as he and Kat returned to the complex for her to give birth. He'd imagined himself safe, restored, with her beside him; instead he's lost and alone and he can't reach her anymore.

The Island

Anstey paces the room, regretting the absence of luxuries. His accommodation in the complex was so much more civilized, a replica of the richly furnished space he had dreamed of living in when he escaped from the war on his home-world. Here, on this lump of rock in the middle of the sea, the pirates do as he bids them when he puts his mind skills to work on their inferior brains, but oh, how he despises them and how much doing it wearies him. And, worryingly, he's running out of the drugs they've always bought from him. None of the rabble are anything like his hand-picked guards from Domum-Orbis, his enforcers … but all except one of that elite were captured or destroyed during the rebellion in the complex. These barbarous humans are just an uncouth tool, including their fucking self-important Captain, who imagines himself in charge. When he has enough gold once more, he will abandon them and return to the mainland. Re-take the complex, or, if it is too well guarded, buy somewhere else and train up an *obedient* army of human servants to do his bidding.

His shoulder twinges. An unpleasant reminder of unfinished business. That and his hideously burnt hand. The girl … Katharine. If his last enforcer hadn't been there to help him, her knife in his back would have finished him. And the pain, when she destroyed his mind-enhancing weapon and half of his fingers with it. Her mother is dead, he dealt with that bitch for the terrible thing she did to him so many years ago. He imagines Katharine's husband Thomas Alban will be dead too. No-one could possibly have survived all they inflicted on him. No more fucking self-righteous Thomas Alban. Now for the girl's human father and the girl herself. He would like to breed from her though … so powerful … imagine a child from her and his last enforcer. He could almost wish Thomas Alban alive to see and suffer such a day. Now that *would* be a fitting revenge.

Chapter 1

I couldn't believe the continuous bustle in the underground complex. It was almost like the story of *Sleeping Beauty*; a tale from a future-Earth book I had once found in the library here. Like so many others, it was a book that had been transported from Domum-Orbis, our planet of origin in the Auriga constellation. A book saved from the library in the capital city before the war was lost and these Aurigans, my mother included, had fled through an ostium, a momentary rift in time and space, across the stars to this moment and this place. As refugees, those who had travelled had sought freedom. Instead they had been tricked into a new kind of servitude, working for Anstey and his enforcers, with no hope of release.

But now all the exiles here were waking up to a newly won liberty, after more than twenty years of a virtual slavery … the gilded cage I once compared it to … so like the dormant castle of that fairy-tale narrative. We had vanquished our villain, Anstey, now we only lacked a knight, or was it a prince, hacking down the thorn bushes, which would have been all that separated us from the outside world if we lived in the make-believe story. Such a hero would do no good to us though. The world outside the complex was not a world that we, as exiles, could ever safely and freely inhabit – marked as we were by the strange blue mottled swirls that stained our skin and shimmered in sunlight. 'Serpent skin' the men who came to rape me called it. More than that, we were a race set apart from humans by the power of our minds and our knowledge of future ideas and technologies.

Yet, unlike the others, I felt as if I was still caught fast, trapped in the spell. Being part of two worlds – with a mother from Domum-Orbis, whose skin markings and mind powers I shared, and a human father from Elizabeth's England – I feared that I more than anyone else could never fully belong in either. I might have hand-fasted with an exile from Domum-Orbis and born his child, but I had grown up outside this subterranean community and it was not, nor ever would be, my true home. More and more now I was finding myself moving so slowly in contrast with the rest, inexplicably weighed down in this oppressive, artificially lit underworld.

All of the true residents were excited and busy as they worked for themselves for the first time instead of slaving unpaid on contracts that could never be completely legally fulfilled. I was the only one who felt unbelievably sad and tired. Or at least it seemed that way to me. Our baby, Thomas's and mine, slept well by day, but at night she always seemed to have a fretful time. Ever the wrong time for Thomas and me. I almost felt she knew when to disrupt us. But that couldn't be true, could it? Surprisingly, Thomas seemed able to get back to sleep quickly after she woke. Perhaps that was because I hurried to Lissy each time – preferring him to get the rest I was certain he needed. But later his nightmares unfailingly woke me. My strong, capable Thomas reduced to this. The bad dreams seemed unending, with him thrashing and crying out in his sleep in the early hours of the morning. At such times I couldn't even wake him to offer comfort; he was so worryingly fragile to me and frighteningly unreachable. More so since we had returned here. The shadow of Anstey and his ruthless enforcers remained all over this place for us both.

Oh, how I ached to go home, my old home, to be in more familiar surroundings once more. Thomas had been recovering there, I was sure. But we were – I mean *he* – was in such demand in the complex. Everyone had begged Thomas to stay – wanting him for his technical skills as he found himself in charge of developing the stun weapon. He was there now, working in the laboratory already, while I fed and changed our baby on my own, as always. Everyone applauded Thomas's invention of the new, more benign, mind-enhancing technology. Everyone agreed it was more in-line with our new ethos, yet still might save lives if the Barbary pirates landed and threatened us, or if Anstey returned. I remembered Thomas once asking me if I could use my mind power to stun rather than kill – the thought must have stayed with him. No-one appeared to remember what could be done with one mind alone – mine – that it had been me who had kept them all safe from Anstey's completely lethal Aurigan weaponry. But I was getting sour and bitter.

Thomas's work was important, vital even, I conceded reluctantly. We certainly needed something to protect ourselves from human marauders. Our friends James and Robert, travelling between here and Barnstable regularly, told us that pirates were raiding all up and down the coast at present, not simply attacking shipping. I always worried that they might come back for the human girls they had been promised by Anstey. It was rumoured that an entire coastal village of Iryshe people had disappeared. And sixty from a Cornish Church. Apparently, or so gossip told it, the pirates were supplying slave markets in somewhere called Salé: rowers for the galleys, women for the harem, men and women for the fields. According to our new leaders, it was a good reason to stay safely hidden in the complex.

There was always an additional unspoken thought: Anstey might have survived, together with the one who was the worst of the enforcers. It was possible that those two might have a hand in whatever was being organised from Lundye Island, the pirates' lair, off the coast near here. I felt responsible. They should both be dead, but I was the one who had tried, and failed, to kill them outright.

Then there were the banished enforcers too, any of whom might come back. When the new council, after deliberation, had decided that their crimes *could* warrant execution, despite my Thomas surviving all they had done to him, I had voted death for them. I hadn't been alone. James, my father, Megs, and many others had voted for their deaths too. We all had our own losses to mourn and revenge might be sweet. Thomas had hesitated, thinking of justice for the children, but, ill as he was himself, he was unable in the end to bring himself to support hanging. And there were too many others ready to stand up for the alternative sentence of banishment. Perhaps it was better not to give birth to a new community on the back of executions. But I feared we had just pushed our problems out into the human world. Could such men be capable of reform if they were away from Anstey's malign influence?

Preoccupied by my gloomy thoughts, I took longer than usual to get ready. It left me short of my regular playtime with Lissy; I had been sitting on the edge of the bed shelf alongside her for too long, ignoring her, other than absent-mindedly fastening her clothes. Lissy sensed my lack of full attention and gave a little wail, probably only wind. I kissed her, by way of apology, and she reached out to my mind (so precocious, my little girl) as I tucked her woollen shawl around her. The shawl wasn't a synthetic garment such as the complex provided. I was glad, and proud, of that. Another prejudice on my part. My father had found it tucked away in a trunk at home. He said it was once mine, my mother had saved it for me to give to a baby of my own. Seeing it wrapped around Lissy made me feel closer to my parents. I wished my mother had seen Lissy before Anstey had contrived her death.

"Come on, Lissy, time to get you to the infirmary. Your ever-admiring audience of Alice and her friends are waiting to take care of you, and I've promised to pick up Thom on my way to teach." Alice, my one real girlfriend from among those from Domum-Orbis in the complex, kept my Lissy (her namesake) in the infirmary with her during the day, while her son, Thom, though very small, attended my class. Thom was my newest pupil; a good exchange for his mother looking after Lissy during the day. He was *my* Thomas's godson, and a bright, cheerful child, a credit to any classroom.

I gave my baby another kiss and the tiniest 'home world' hug before we hurried off to the new day. Which would doubtless be just like the last.

Chapter 2

As it proved to be. Apart from one incident. Thomas's erstwhile 'friends' Edith and her brother Hugh had returned. Word of Anstey's defeat had somehow reached them. Anne Gomfrey had mentioned them to me, but this was the first time I'd seen Edith since her return. And she still hated me. Today, a brief confrontation in one of the corridors had left me in no doubt of that. She wasn't even consistent. With one breath Edith was accusing me of being Anstey's daughter, when she knew I wasn't. With the next she was abusing my daughter as a half-blood on account of my half-human parentage.

Make your mind up, Edith, you can't have it both ways, I'd thought, with resentment. What on this Earth had I done to incur such virulent dislike? It wasn't my fault that James's twin Henry had died during our earlier escape from the complex, and he wasn't going to marry her anyway, whatever she thought or hoped for, James had assured me of that.

"Thomas could have had anyone, why he chose to fuck you I've no idea," was her parting shot. I'd hurried away, saying nothing, I was glad she couldn't know that he didn't anymore.

Anyhow, eventually, yet another in a string of frustratingly tiring days was finished. I tidied away the books and sorted some out into the seamless, lightweight travel-boxes that were due to go back to the library. Anne Gomfrey would send down another set – I hoped they would be better choices than the last. I liked telling the children stories. Anne thought children were never too young to learn about the laws on Domum-Orbis in Auriga. Which none of them would ever be likely to see. There was something chilling and inflexible about those laws. While they were so much less fearsome in most respects than many, perhaps most, of the current human laws, they were emotionally barren, lacking any leeway to look at context and circumstances, to balance justice with compassion, to make any plea for mercy. Reading Anne's books on the topic – the products of a self-proclaimed superior race – it was upsetting to discover that time had not tempered Domum-Orbis law, it had made it ever more rigid. Just my view, of course. Which Anne never listened to anyway.

Helping in the new school for very young children, teaching them reading and writing, was my compulsory contribution to the life of the complex – not being much use at the scientific Domum-Orbis subjects and having none of the practical skills required to work in other areas. Or, at least, I had never learned any of these and no-one seemed disposed to teach me. Jobs were stringently graded and allocated on who you were, not what you might become. I was sure that many of those who were fully Aurigan regarded me as ignorant, only tolerating me for Thomas's sake. There was still a divide between the skilled elite of Domum-Orbis and all others. Humans came at the bottom of the scale and, of course, being half human, half from Domum-Orbis, I was regarded as 'tainted' in that way. Their word, I hasten to add. I felt differently – to me my human heritage was an enrichment. I loved and admired my father and all he stood for.

Given the general evaluation though, I sometimes wondered if Thomas regretted hand-fasting with me. Had he only wanted to fuck me after all, and had he seen hand-fasting as the best way to get his wish? Not that nowadays … There was that painful truth intruding again and I drew back, hastily, from such a sterile pathway.

It wasn't just Edith. Once I had overheard a couple of the Aurigan technical women whispering about me. I was concealed around a corner from them, not intentionally, their words had stopped me in my tracks. They were disappointed that Thomas had 'thrown himself away' on hand-fasting with me. According to them I had flaunted my naked body on the seashore and enticed his markings to respond to mine. Once our swirls had bonded, they said, Thomas was trapped by the power of mine. Everyone knew, they said, how mindless swirl-bonding was. I had stayed hidden until they left. It was all nonsense, of course. Just that slight fear, now that we didn't seem to be so close anymore.

Thomas's friend Megs, and the other vagrant human children he had helped to rescue, sat in on my lessons in the small school. They pretended to be assisting with the youngest complex-born pupils (there weren't many) but were actually avidly making up for the yawning void in their own access to education. Megs was pregnant herself, having formed a surprising liaison with a boy from Domum-Orbis (sorry, a young man) not unlike a younger Thomas. It made her doubly eager to learn all that I could teach her before her own child made an appearance. Being human, Megs was small, like me, so it made sense for her to stay to deliver the child in the safety of the complex. If it worried her, what had happened to her there, she didn't let on. Megs was the best sort of pragmatist. At least on the outside. Her young man, Anthony, was endlessly kind and gentle. Perhaps he helped her to forget Anstey and his sadistic ruffians and what they'd done to her and the other human girls for their 'pleasure.'

At first, I had enjoyed the teaching. I still found it rewarding. But lately I was just too bone weary to immerse myself in the classroom. True the school was a happy one, very different from the harsh place Anstey had founded when he separated a whole generation of refugee children from their parents, but it utilised the same surface buildings he had once designated for that purpose. I don't think anyone, whether from Earth or from our home-world, enjoyed trudging back down into the complex across *that* courtyard and through *that* manor house, where so many unspeakable things had happened to so many. Though at least the children saw true daylight.

Today I had hoped Thomas would volunteer to collect our baby daughter from Alice's, but he had said that he would be busy and not back in our rooms until later. Did he notice, did he even care, how tired I was? I felt bizarrely invisible to him. So, as I made my way back to the infirmary in his stead, I was surprised to see him in the distance, walking out of the narrow back-gate onto the clifftop path. I was about to call out silently to him, mind-to-mind, but something held me back. We didn't seem to communicate much that way anymore. I supposed there was no need; we had no secrets to keep from anyone. We were together in the evenings, we could say 'I love you' aloud as often as we needed to, though when said aloud the words somehow lacked full meaning, were kind of perfunctory. Thomas said it almost by rote, with a quick peck on the cheek, during the shorter and shorter periods of time he spent with me and with Lissy. But I missed the unique intimacy and truthfulness of mind-to-mind communication. Its absence made me miserable. Sometimes I took Thomas unawares when I spoke to him that way, and it seemed as if he held back for a split second, preparing himself, guarding himself, before he let me into his mind. Maybe it was just that he was taken by surprise.

I let him go. He probably needed time to himself. I wished he would spend some of it with the babe, his and mine. He was so good with our adopted Bess, another of the rescued children (one with an unknown father from Domum-Orbis). I had thought Thomas would be a great parent. If only we could just be a small family once more, not part of this giant, busy, somehow impersonal place. In a new setting, I was sure that he would hold the baby more, cuddle her more. It was almost, I hesitated to put words to the feeling, as if he blamed Lissy for the fact that I had nearly died giving birth to her. Which was ridiculous. I took a deep breath, trying to resist the tears that were always close to the surface lately. I *had* thought I was getting stronger. Evidently not.

Alice, with her usual empathic sensibilities, wasted no time in giving me a hug as I entered the infirmary. I would have been so lonely if not for her. Surrounded by noise but drowning in silent isolation.

"Here, come and sit for a while, Kat, have a rest and talk to me. Thom's already off playing with another youngster from your class."

I was pleased. It would give the two of us time to catch up with each other. Dearly as I loved Lissy, I looked forward to the time when she too would be old enough to have friends to play with. But here in the infirmary she would suckle peacefully in the early evening at least, and probably drop off to sleep in my arms. I sank down onto the bench beside Alice.

"I'm not busy and we don't have many chances to chat. I'm sorry it was so hectic when you came to feed her at lunchtime. Stay a while, you look worried and tired. Is there something wrong?" Alice looked at me with an anxious expression on her face. It was all I could do not to throw myself into her arms and cry as she took my hand and squeezed it sympathetically.

Why was it *so* impossible to hide anything from Alice? I felt disloyal to Thomas, but I couldn't help it, I needed to talk to someone. For some inexplicable reason, I began with seeing him just now, going onto the cliffs alone when he had said he was too busy to pick up Lissy. It seemed a petty, distrustful complaint to be voicing, but Alice was clearly alarmed by something. Her eyes glazed for a few seconds, as if she was somewhere distant. And then she rose, abruptly, and hugged me.

"Stay here, don't leave the baby, she's hungry. Feed her here rather than going back to your room. You shouldn't be disturbed, no-one else is due on duty. I've just remembered, there's something I need to check on urgently. Do. Not. Move. I promise I'll be back in no time. I really have to talk to you. Promise me you'll wait for me."

"I promise …"

There was no time to query anything further. She was gone, running, leaving me bewildered and worrying whether her abrupt departure had anything to do with Thomas, or whether she had simply forgotten an urgent task. I soothed myself by picking up my baby, my little girl, and hugged her, whispering in her mind: "*Your Dadde will love you soon.*" I hoped … prayed … wished … but I was afraid that I was lying to her.

By the time Alice returned, Lissy was sleepily full and I had her cuddled up against me. Alice's face was white.

"I'm sorry, Kat, there was something I needed to do."

I looked at her, a little fear tugging at me. "Thomas?"

"He's not in a good place, Kat." Alice didn't indicate whether her comment on Thomas related to whatever urgent reason had led her to leave the room so precipitously. Or whether it was simply in answer to the question implicit in the way I spoke his name. I was afraid to ask.

"I know that he's suffering." I tried not to let her see how much it hurt me to confess. "But he won't let me into his thoughts, not really in. Sometimes he seems fine, then, for no reason I can see, he's gone beyond reach to some dark place."

Alice looked at me, as if weighing up how much to share of her thoughts. She was my friend, but before that she was part of Thomas's surrogate family. I knew and accepted that her first allegiance was to him.

"A lot has happened to Thomas," she said slowly, as if weighing up what to tell me, "he's had to watch helplessly, twice, while you nearly died. And then there's what was done to him here, the very thing he was petrified they would do to you."

"I know Anstey and his men were horrifically cruel to him and that Thomas nearly died. He never talks about it and I'm afraid to bring it all back to him if I press him on it. He already has terrible nightmares."

I thought of Thomas, crying out night after night. After all that he had gone through, I felt ashamed of my selfish complaint.

"The state of him when I first saw him in that courtyard." I closed my eyes, speaking half to Alice, half to myself. "Almost unrecognisable, emaciated, covered in festering cuts and bruises. I shan't forget. I can only imagine the details of the abuse he suffered. He was such a long time in the operating room and then recovering in the infirmary here – I assumed it was his broken ribs, the punctured lung. That's right, isn't it? But he never shares anything about that time with me, just says he was beaten up a bit. And me, I was too out of things at that stage to know any more."

Alice looked at me, silent and thoughtful, then stood and fetched a folder from a cabinet set into the wall. I noticed that she'd needed to key in a code to release the touch pad that opened it. She put it down on the table beside me.

"I'm not allowed to show you this. It's confidential and deeply shocking. It contains details of everything that was inflicted on him and everything that had to be done to patch his body up, inside and out. May I take my little goddaughter for a walk? I won't be long."

I looked at Alice in bewilderment but handed my peacefully sleeping baby to her. There was a new dread in my mind as she walked out through the door and pressed the touch pad to close it behind her. Clearly the file had been left for me to read. Thomas's name was on the front.

As I'd said to Alice, Thomas had never given me a detailed account of his injuries, but I had been aware, though ill myself, that they had feared for his life for a much longer time than my own recovery had taken. They had kept me separate from him in the infirmary. Alice couldn't say so, but she obviously intended me to read the report, and I was aware of what it meant for her to betray the details of Thomas's own story, details he was withholding from me, or, at the least, saw no reason to share with me. For a moment I wasn't sure that I wanted to know. But whatever had happened to him then, it was still affecting him now. If I understood what he couldn't tell me, perhaps I could begin to understand what was wrong, why our closeness was so erratic.

I opened the file.

Part way through I had to put it down, rush to the sink, and throw up.

How he had endured all of this I would never know; but I could barely endure even reading the cold, clinical details. But I had to return to finish it. Alice was right; however difficult it was I had to know in order to understand. Oh! how I wished to God that I had killed Anstey for his part in it. I knew Anstey had promised that his enforcers would do the same to me as they had to Thomas: I knew that I would not have survived a hundredth, no a thousandth, of what they had done to him if Anstey had got his hands on me. No wonder Thomas always spoke of us ending both of our lives with a dagger if we were caught. He had already known of the depths of Anstey's depravity. Thomas! My heart felt as if it would break for him. How could those perverted bastards do such terrible things to him? How could he return to me from such a nightmare as that? My thoughts were consumed with an equal mix of fury at the perpetrators and compassion for my husband in the face of all he had needed to survive.

I finally closed the file and put it back on the table before walking back to the sink to clean up and rinse my mouth with the vile recycled water. I could rinse away the taste of vomit, but not the feel of the words in my head. They were burned into my mind. They could never be un-seen. I found that I was shaking uncontrollably. Yet I was grateful Alice had shared them with me. There was nothing I wouldn't do to help Thomas and knowing the truth had finally enabled me to understand fully and put aside my own petty and selfish thoughts.

But the first thing I had to do was to get him away from the complex. Find some reason to get him to my father's home, or anywhere but here, where it had all happened. I would pretend it was for me, or for the baby, I would invent something … anything. But I couldn't let him know that I knew. He would have to tell me himself, though I secretly doubted he ever would. How could you put something like that into words? Share such a thing with anyone?

Alice returned and laid Lissy back in the infirmary cradle. She looked at my face and poured me a beaker of wine. As I sipped it, gratefully, she returned the file to its cabinet.

"I'm sorry, Kat, I know it makes the most horrific reading. I have no idea how he survived. Anstey and his men must have been high on drugs, not that anything could excuse them … the level of bestiality. How could anyone do such things to another human being?" She scrunched her eyes shut for a moment at the thought, before looking at my face, doubtless as ashen as her own, and asking, hesitantly, "Did I do the right thing letting you see it?"

I hugged her and let her hold me while I sobbed, struggling for words.

"Yes," I managed to say at last, and I *was* sure. I loved him, impossibly much, and I needed to know everything he was going through. "I'll be careful not to let him realise that I know the whole truth of what happened, the appalling extent of it all. Maybe one day he'll feel able to tell me himself."

"I hope so, but I begin to doubt it. He really needs to talk to someone about it before he can begin to recover, but he seems to draw more and more into the darkness. Even before, it was always a tendency of his. I could offer him some drug to help him sleep, but to be brutal I wouldn't trust him with it. Talking would be better. Do you mind if I ask someone else, someone he's close to, one of the men perhaps, to try and persuade him to open up? In the meantime, spirit him away from here by any means you can manage and make him get involved with Lissy. She could bring something innocent into his life, something post-Anstey, to balance the shadows."

"Please, please do anything, anything at all that you feel will help. I trust your judgement. And I'll persuade him we should leave. Make him acknowledge Lissy. I won't fail him."

Chapter 3

Thomas walked out onto the cliffs, alone. The prototype of the new weapon was working well. He didn't feel they really needed him anymore. He was glad. He didn't want to be there. The creak of the gate closing behind him had something of a finality to the sound of it.

He wished their adopted daughter Bess was not away visiting – it would be better if she was with Kat, where she should be. It made him remember. They had all been happy in Kat's father's house, where Bess was now. He wished, fervently, that he had not made Kat pregnant. Selfish and stupid, he should have known better, given the risks. The baby had destroyed everything and endangered Kat's life. Without the child they would not have needed to return to the complex. Thomas wanted to do, always meant to do, more for his new daughter – for a horrible moment he couldn't even think of her name. But there was a frozen part of him inside somewhere and the baby was unreachable, on the wrong side of it. He tried to prevent Kat from seeing such thoughts in his mind – trying to stop her from realising how much he blamed the baby. It occupied most of the time that the three of them were together. And when it was just the two of them – Kat and him – there was a lot more that he tried to prevent Kat from seeing.

It was quiet and peaceful on the clifftop. No-one about. Air to breathe. The sound of the sea. A far distant horizon. He stood on the very edge of the highest point and looked at the rocks below, with the sea frothing around. Even the sound of it was distanced. A long way down. It made him think of Kat, all that time ago. He had felt so strong then, so confident, so invincible, swimming out to save her. Now he wondered how long he could hide from her, how long it would be before she suspected what he was doing … what he couldn't bear to do.

At some level he'd known that it would surface, was even waiting for it, and there it was. The dark thought which had been festering inside him had torn its way through the numbness, and had arrived, sharp and painful. Kat was so popular in the complex, everyone admired her. If he wasn't there, always in the way and dragging her down with him, she would fall in love again. Find someone less fucked up, remarry. He only had to make one final step forward and…

"Thomas," there was a quiet but breathless voice behind him.

He stopped, remaining motionless, the step not taken. The cold thoughts that had formed the intention chased each other around his tired head and spoke to him in a seductive voice. "Wait. Do it secretly in the night and they'll think it's an accident. Kat will mourn for a while. She won't blame you, no-one will blame her, and she'll be able to move on without guilt. Get through another hour or two. Soon it will be dark enough. Close your eyes, keep walking forward until there's nothing there. Patience, it will all be over soon. No more pain, no more shame."

"Thomas, come back here and talk to me." The voice was Alice's. He should have known.

With a twinge of guilt, he thought about how she and Stephen had been there for Kat and the child. Neglecting the house Kat and her father had found for them. Alice knew how much he had been worrying about Kat giving birth, and she had put aside her own well-being, insisting on staying on at the complex to help. He had been right to worry, he thought, morosely. The child had not arrived easily, it was just as he had feared, he always put Kat in danger. She would be so much better off when he was gone. But he owed a lot to Alice. There was no way he could do this in front of her or admit his intention.

"Don't stand so near to the edge! The cliffs crumble easily here, Stephen's always warning me about the dangers."

Thomas was aware of a guilty flush on his face. Alice was empathic, she was saving him from having to explain, but he was absolutely certain she knew exactly what he was contemplating. Alice had sensed the emotional turmoil in his mind – someone had alerted her to reach out to him and check – it was the price of being close to an empath.

He turned, carefully, and walked back to where Alice was eyeing him with considerable apprehension.

"Please, Thomas, you can't leave Kat, you can't leave the girls. Remember the last time you shut Kat out, how can you even think of doing it again?" Her rush of words confirmed his suspicions as soon as he was away from the edge and nearer to her.

Reluctantly, he turned to meet her gaze. The accusation. He couldn't lie. Closing his eyes to avoid seeing the look on her face, he confessed bitterly.

"Do you know I wake the baby up, so that she disrupts us, so that Kat isn't faced with the spectre of a husband who wallows too much in his own nightmares to love her properly. It started as soon as we returned here. Everything reminds me of the past." He choked on the words, trying to breathe steadily when his chest had a tight band crushing it. "It isn't so much what they did to me, just that everything they did to me they threatened to do to her. If I try to make love to her in this God-forsaken place it makes me feel like them. They've killed the link between love and sex. I desire her so much, I'm aching to be inside her, filling her with my love, but as soon as I start, I feel the indescribable pain of them in me. It becomes part of what they did. It destroys me, endlessly, and I'm letting it destroy us, her and me."

"Oh Thomas." Alice sounded so sad. "Why can't you share this with her? She loves you; she would understand, she would be patient. How can you hide it from her?"

He shook his head, consumed with misery at the thought of never making love to Kat again. What Alice was suggesting was completely impossible. How could he ever let Kat know the full shameful truth of what they'd done to him, and his own complete helplessness? For a moment his temper flared.

"You work in the infirmary; you *know* what those fucking bastards did to me on that final night. How could I ever possibly share such disgusting things with her, with anyone?"

"Thomas, I *do* know and I *do* understand and I'm way, *way* beyond sorry. I was there in the infirmary when Stephen carried you in. It's my job. I saw you; I saw your detailed personal Infirmary Records. Your recovery was amazing, no-one believed you would pull through."

"I wish to God I hadn't. I love her. I don't want Kat to ever have that living in her head, and I'm afraid she won't be able to escape it if I share it with her. Why did any of you want to save what was left of me? When you knew …"

Alice fished in her tunic pocket and brought out a crumpled piece of paper. She smoothed it out and handed it wordlessly to him. It was Kat's note to him, when he had nearly lost her, back in his angry days when he was so conflicted and had shut her out of his mind. He knew it off by heart, but he had somehow forgotten it in the bleakness of his current despair. He remembered her words too, spoken when he'd begged her forgiveness. He could feel them in his head, as they'd been then;

'I do forgive you, Thomas. I love you. I keep telling you I love you. But you must know that I couldn't bear it if you ever did that to me again. I would go if that happened, it's the worst feeling in the world, I wanted to die there and then; I couldn't believe you had abandoned our love, our closeness!'

And his own vow:

"… I'll never do that again. I promise you. I promise on my life never to shut you out again. It was unforgiveable."

"If you die, or leave her, it will be the worst way of shutting her out. She'll die inside too. You're bonded. It's irrevocable. *You* made that choice. You knew it when you hand-fasted. You knew it when you left those words for her when we thought she was dying. I can't believe you could even begin to think of doing this to her now. And to Bess, who dotes on you. And to your tiny baby."

Thomas found his legs didn't quite support him and he crumpled, to sit head in hands on the turf. Alice sat down beside him, staying silent, waiting patiently. Eventually he turned to her.

"The baby, it… she's part of the problem. I don't know if some of this is nearly losing Kat again when the baby was born. If we hadn't been here at the complex, if you hadn't been here, she wouldn't have survived. Part of Kat bows, willingly, to that knowledge – she's lived all her life in a world where death is an accepted part of living. There's no less grief or sorrow here on Earth, but death happens of itself. God's Will. All my life I've lived among home-world refugees for whom death is an affront. The war, our escape from it, the rage amongst our group when our parents were destroyed by Anstey. There's always someone culpable. With all the technology, the scientific and medical knowledge we have, no-one just dies. It's always preventable. A war, a killer, someone's fault, or someone's responsibility to prevent."

Covering his face in his hands, he stopped briefly then took a deep breath before admitting, "Now I blame myself and, illogically, the baby for putting Kat at risk. And when I flashback to what happened to me, I blame myself all over again because I know, I just *know*, I could have done nothing to prevent her from suffering the same fate as me – it crushes me – for some reason it isn't enough that she saved herself, it should have been me saving her. Fate made her *my* love; *my* responsibility; and I couldn't do anything – helpless, useless, waste of space that I am. Anstey was absolutely right about me. All I ever wanted, want, is to keep Kat safe and I'm completely incapable of it. I knew what they would do to her, but I had no plan, nothing. Someone else would look after her better."

"For fuck sake, Thomas," Alice shocked him by swearing. "She doesn't want anyone else, only you. Are you really saying that you can't bear anyone else to hurt her, but you're willing to do it entirely by yourself? It's *you* betraying her now as you did before. You're shutting her out from the truth of what happened to you, you're shutting her out by making your own decisions, imposing them on her. I'm not saying that Kat will kill herself if you walk off that cliff edge, that isn't her way, at least I don't think it is, though, who knows, maybe she would. At the very least she would look for a cause, the most dangerous one she could find, and she would abandon herself to it, hoping not to survive. You know how she intended to give herself up to save her mother when she thought you wanted to be rid of her before. How can you possibly imagine that she'd find someone else? Forget you so easily? Do you even know how arrogant your plan is – *you* deciding what's best for *her*?"

"Don't, please don't say that, I don't know what goes on in my head lately. All I can see sometimes is Anstey's satisfied face gloating over my powerlessness. I had every reason to hate him, but why did he hate me so much?" Thomas's hoarse voice broke on the words, picturing Anstey, remembering the times the director had tried, over and over, to break him.

"You mean you really don't know?" Alice sounded despairing, "I'm amazed – all the time – at the extent of your inability to see yourself. Anstey hated you because you were the opposite of everything he stood for. Because, even when you were a small child, he couldn't corrupt you. And more than that, you gave the rest of us, all of us, the strength to resist him too. You gave us the example we needed."

Thomas was quiet. Sad and guilty. When had he ever achieved anything? It was kind of Alice to try to cheer him up and he did appreciate it, but he couldn't let her see that she was failing. Whatever she thought he had given them, his own strength was non-existent, it had been absent for a very long time.

"I know you resist believing me," Alice sighed, "but at least promise me you won't hurt Kat and my goddaughter and Bess by killing yourself. They deserve better of you than that."

Thomas wasn't sure that he could make such a promise. The moment had passed for now. But how could he possibly guarantee that it wouldn't return? When the need for oblivion overcame him – swamping his soul with numbness and the hollow, aching shame of being who he was – it was the only way that promised rest, and an escape from sleepless hour after sleepless hour, nightmare after nightmare, the feeling of it being done endlessly, so that it *was* never … *would* never be over …

He turned to Alice and looked directly into her eyes. "I can't promise you; I won't make a promise I could break, but I will fight harder. For them, for you."

"If you won't promise me, then simply keep the promise you made to Kat. I'm trusting you." She gave him the piece of paper. He thought about how long she had kept it, saved it when he had rushed headlong after Kat. He hadn't known she still had it, but he guessed she had never trusted him not to need it.

Alice stood up and walked away. He did feel that she was trusting him now. But he wasn't sure if he could trust himself. It seemed a good idea to turn away from temptation though, away from the cliffs. He rose, reluctantly, and walked back inside, trying to avoid speaking to anyone, his hand clutching Kat's note, as it had once clutched his parents' final words.

Chapter 4

As soon as he came in through the door, I placed Lissy in his arms, not giving him a chance to think of an excuse and refuse. Despite feeling deeply guilty about making our daughter a pawn in this, I was on a mission to save Thomas. Helping him to begin a true relationship with his daughter was one of the steps on that route. As I looked up at him, willing him to meet my gaze, I prayed shock tactics would work. He stood bewildered, holding his daughter with a look of shocked surprise on his face. My words had a touch of desperation to them, and I think they fully penetrated his thoughts for once.

"Please, *please* help me, Thomas, I'm so tired, I'll be ill if I don't get some sleep. I'm going to bed now. Play with Lissy a while and then she needs to be bathed, changed, and tucked up in her cradle. I've fed her already."

Before he could reply, I walked straight into the cleansing-room to prepare myself for bed. He appeared not to have moved when I returned – but I avoided meeting his eyes. It wasn't easy to resist kissing him and giving Lissy a goodnight hug as I walked back across to our sleeping alcove. I had to keep telling myself that it was important for him focus exclusively on his child, just the two of them, for once. Thank Goodness we had managed to secure family accommodation rather than finding the three of us in Thomas's old single room – in fact four before Bess went back home with my father for a visit. Once in the tiny sleeping area I resolutely climbed into bed and turned my face away from the curtained archway. I did reach out to Lissy's mind though. He didn't even know we could do that, she and I – it would never have occurred to him.

"Love Dadde, Lissy. He does love you."

This would have been the ideal time to really catch up on lost sleep. But I couldn't. I thought I might drift off, but initially I found myself listening out for the murmur of his voice and Lissy's answering gurgle. Would he have any clue what to do? But it seemed to be going fine. Then the words in Thomas's infirmary file sprang up in my mind again and my head was filled with the most terrible images. I couldn't stop the tears from running down my cheeks. It was all I could do to keep my grief silent as I choked with it. I wanted to howl out loud in misery at the thought of what he had suffered. Inside, I did.

Much later it was so hard pretending to be sleeping as Thomas stood near the bed and gently trailed a finger through my hair, bending to kiss the very tip of my ear. I wanted to kiss him, to feel his arms tighten around me, the warmth of his body pressed against mine, to submerge myself in his love, have him submerge himself in me. But I didn't want there to be any pressure on him to make love to me. Now that I knew what he had suffered, I could understand that there were appalling memories to be exorcised before we could get back to anything like the relationship we had enjoyed before.

Eventually, I must have slept, waking to the morning in a panic. The simulated daylight in our underground world suggested to me that it was late and I had heard nothing from Lissy. I was alone in the bed, Thomas had clearly not slept there – no tangle of bedclothes to offer evidence of his nightly battles in hell. But I could hear noises from the living area.

"Hey! Look who's awake!" My darling man, already washed and dressed, came through into the sleeping area and sat down on the bed. I held my breath, looking at him… them. Thomas was holding Lissy, also washed and dressed, kissing her nose and cuddling her close to him. He was … smiling … excited. Thomas's smile, I had almost forgotten what that looked like. Don't spoil it, Kat, don't cry… I thought as I attempted to smile back.

"She spoke to me! Inside my mind! She said 'Dadde'! Quite distinctly. Lots of times. Last night *and* this morning!" He couldn't wait to tell me.

There was a living note in his voice that I hadn't heard for so long. I reached up and stroked his cheek. Lissy had achieved something I couldn't.

"She loves her Dadde, how could she not communicate with you?"

"But to speak, mind to mind, already!"

"She has us for parents, how could she not be special."

"Well, you at any rate …"

"Both of us. You're so loved, Thomas. I love you, Lissy loves you, Bess loves you. You're all that matters in our world, our universe, wherever we are within it."

I spoke directly to his mind as I'd begun to be afraid of doing and I felt the surge of his love in return.

"I love you too. Forgive me if I shut you out. I know you once said you wouldn't forgive me for that, but sometimes my mind can't reach yours, sometimes I'm trapped somewhere I don't want to be, but I do, always and forever, love you. Please, please don't ever think that I don't. I could never stop. Forgive me when I can't bridge the gap between us. I'm always fighting to get back to you, don't give up on me, on us. Please don't."

We hugged, the three of us, until Lissy decided she had done enough hugging and wanted to be fed, giving one of her cross little wails to remind us of her needs. I put her to my breast and Thomas sat with us, sharing the moment, his arm around my shoulder. For the first time since we had come back to the complex, we were behaving as if we were a family, and that brought with it a feeling of peace. But I didn't delude myself that we had done more than take a tiny, though significant, step. I took a deep breath.

"I know how busy you are and how important the work you're doing is, but as soon as you can leave the project for a while I really need to get away from here. This place still reeks of Anstey for me. It's dragging me down. I don't want him in my head." A cautious step two underway. I felt nervous.

"But I thought you were enjoying it here, with the teaching and the comforts of complex technology to make life easier with the baby … with Lissy." Thomas sounded bewildered and worried.

"This isn't the world I know and love; it never has been. Some of my time in the complex has been wonderful – the you and I meeting part of it, our hand-fasting in the sanctuary – but being with you is just as good wherever we are. Don't you feel that the outside world is so much more real and alive? This is an underworld, a subterranean rabbit warren with endless hateful memories."

I looked at Thomas, hoping my words were having an effect, but I had to be fair and acknowledge my debt to the infirmary while still allowing my pent-up feelings to tumble out. He had been right to bring me back for the birth. If only it wasn't now killing him.

"We needed to be here to help our baby into this world, and I'm truly grateful to everyone who aided us, but now that she's strong, I'm strong, I need to be away from here. There are too many people, all trying to keep their minds closed, one from another. And so many partial voices crowd in on my tired brain, all striving to keep me out of theirs. It's endless people, people I don't really know, and how I miss the sun and the sky … everything outside."

I hadn't had the time to plan a convincing argument, but this had the benefit of being heart-felt, however garbled. Even *I* hadn't known how much I needed to get away as well. Thomas bent his head and kissed my neck, his mouth lingering on one of my bluest swirls, until I could feel it right through me.

"You should have said before. I've only stayed because I thought it was best for you. I'll speak to the others, we already have a prototype, I'm sure they won't mind if I'm away for a while. What about your class?"

"I'll talk to Anne Gomfrey; I'm hoping she won't object to getting involved in the classroom. She could even move the class to the library. Anne often comes to me with her own ideas of what should be taught. She's a bit stricter than me, but at least I think she's made her peace with Megs and the other human girls – though she doesn't approve of Megs co-habiting with one of the men from here. They won't boycott Anne's classes, and she knows how I integrate the two groups so that the older ones don't feel uncomfortable learning the same things as the smallest ones."

I leaned my head against his chest, letting the comforting warmth of our closeness sweep through me. He cradled my face with his hands, looking at me as he hadn't in ages.

"Will you be alright if I go now and sort things out in the laboratory? I'm truly sorry, Kat, I never realised how tired and unhappy you were. I've been horribly selfish, too wrapped up in myself."

This time he kissed my eyelids, one by one, then tenderly stroked the tip of a finger down my cheek. I sighed, wishing he could stay and that we might prolong this time together. Soon, soon perhaps, but he looked so thin and tired and ill. It broke my heart.

"I'll be fine once I know we can leave. I realise that it's bound to take a few days to sort everything out. You head off to make the arrangements. Lissy's fast asleep now, I'll get ready and drop her off with Alice." I touched his hand, gently. "Go on, off you go." I kissed his cheek and shooed him in the direction of the door.

Thomas was still lingering. Some nameless worry in his face.

"I'm sorry, truly sorry. I know I let you down with picking Lissy up yesterday. It was thoughtless of me."

Thomas had turned from the door and his face made me certain he was begging forgiveness for more than just failing to collect his daughter. How could I fail to forgive him anything, knowing what I did?

"Don't fret, you more than made up for it when you did come home. I'll see you later, and we'll plan how and when we can leave to be a proper family again."

"*I love you.*"

"*Love you too ... forever.*"

As the door closed behind him my thoughts moved ahead to the glorious prospect of getting away from the complex and what I needed to do first. I wanted to dance. But if we were really leaving, I would have to ask Alice about contraception to take away with us, yet another thing that was unavailable outside this medically advanced (and emotionally bankrupt) complex. I wanted to be ready if Thomas ever felt like making love again. Though I could understand why he might not. True there were condoms made from sheep or pig intestines – designed for men's safety, no doubt, but I couldn't begin to imagine how much they might chafe a woman. Worse, there were herbs that might be brewed and drunk after the event. But these were chancy and unpleasant solutions. Joan had been a reliable fount of knowledge. However, if we ever made love again, Thomas and I, we would need something; I doubted Thomas could cope with another dangerous birth. I had said nothing to him about that of course. We – I mean I – hadn't reached such an advanced stage in my planning.

*

The laboratory was still the clean, functional, oddly welcoming space it had been since the day he had dreamed up the project. It had become a place of refuge for Thomas, away from the bleak thoughts that assailed him everywhere else, not least because working occupied his mind. On a normal day he tended to arrive early, stay late. Yesterday it had failed him though, sending him panicking outside to somewhere he could breathe properly and maybe escape forever from the nightmares that were slowly eating away the man he had once been.

Unusually he was the last in to work that morning. The day felt different and new. He had lingered in their room, his, Kat's and Lissy's. For the first time since her birth, he had stayed to watch Kat feed Lissy. He hadn't felt such tranquillity inside himself since they'd arrived back in the complex, rushing in the end when Kat's pains had come on early. Last night, Lissy had begun to thaw that aching coldness inside him. His child, his baby daughter, such a vulnerable living being and completely dependent on him … her tiny fingers curling around one of his. How could he ever have blamed her for Kat nearly dying? That had been his fault. If he could only cling to her and to Kat, he might get through this.

It was important not to get involved in anything work-related before he had told the others of his firm intention to quit. He was more than a little afraid that it would not be a popular decision, but he was determined not to be swayed from it.

"Stephen, Ralph, can we have a word?"

At first he remained standing, barely inside the door, unexpectedly anxious. These were the two he had to persuade. They were the ones most closely involved in the project with him. The trouble was that although it was a community project, because it was *his* idea, he had found himself in charge – albeit assisted by a small team from the home-world in more subsidiary roles. Thomas kept reminding himself that his own presence was no longer essential. Of the supporting technicians, both Ralph and Stephen were perfectly capable of organising and carrying out the work without him. He had to admit, however, that neither had seemed particularly keen to take over from him when he had hinted at it before. Taking a deep breath he moved over to his work bench and sat down on the stool there, waiting for them to leave what they were doing and approach.

Truthfully, he admitted to himself, Stephen was only working there very reluctantly. He had taken to life outside the complex and had enjoyed living in Kat's father's spare house. Thomas couldn't help but appreciate what it had meant for him to have to move back so that Alice could help Kat when Lissy was born. And then to stay on when Alice's skills were in such demand in the infirmary. It was Stephen who was always his most dependable, most trusted friend. The one who had helped him save Kat's life more than once – first in the sea and then getting the drugs she had needed to her. Thomas felt guilty about asking more of him. Alice too, she had saved each of them more than once. He shuddered when he thought of how many times death had threatened to snatch Kat from him. And himself, first fighting death, then flirting with it. How could I think of doing such a thing? he thought. Disgusted with himself, he couldn't help but think what a selfish bastard he was.

Since last evening, he had been worrying about Kat the whole time, angry with himself for not realising before how tired she was. Even when Lissy was sleeping, he had not gone to bed – sitting up all night, not wanting to risk waking Kat by crying out in the throes of some hideous dream. It depressed him to think how self-absorbed he could be. He should have done that before. Why hadn't he thought of it? But if only he could rest and sleep properly even once. It would allow her to rest too.

How difficult it was to break through the numbness and

emptiness, to reach out and connect with Kat again. They'd become so separate. How difficult it was not to continue to hide from her love and concern. When he had looked at her, *really* looked at her, that morning, she appeared so worn down, as if she'd cried over and over. His fault. He was immeasurably grateful that Alice had stopped him yesterday. Another moment or two, a tiny step – a ghost walked over his grave – how could he even have thought of doing that to Kat? He hadn't been in his right mind. The trouble was, how could he know that he wouldn't feel the same way as he had then in an hour, a day, a week? Thank God Kat wanted to get away from the complex. It gave him the right excuse, and he could be firm about leaving. Everyone was grateful to Kat, appreciating her amazing part in freeing them from Anstey. There would be no argument about him taking her away to recuperate.

He looked up and saw that Ralph and Stephen had come over and were waiting patiently for him. Thomas forced himself to surface from the treadmill of self-recriminatory thoughts to tell them of his decision. Under the work surface, where they couldn't be seen, his fingers were tightly crossed.

"I hope I'm not letting you down. Well, I guess that I know I am, but the truth is, I really need … I *have* to take Kat away from this fucking place. Can you manage without me? I want to go as soon as I possibly can; I need to do this for her. I have to."

Ralph looked concerned. "But isn't she better off here, with the baby …" He trailed off, and Thomas could have sworn that Stephen had glared at his work mate. He decided he must have imagined it. Stephen and Ralph got on really well, always had, it was one of the reasons he felt comfortable about suggesting they take joint charge.

"We'll be fine, you do whatever you need to," Stephen chipped in quickly and firmly, preventing Ralph from continuing. "There's absolutely no reason for you to worry about us. We're both happy with the final test results, any lingering doubts and problems have been well and truly laid to rest. There isn't anything else that needs your personal attention now that we know for sure how the weapon works on a living Domum-Orbis subject – though I still don't think you should have been the one we used to trial it on. And you don't need to worry, I do appreciate that we can't risk trying it out as a test on a human subject in case it does them some real damage. I promise we won't do that – but then, if we're being attacked by pirates, I don't think we'll care too much about their well-being, so tests are probably pointless. If it works on us it'll be bound to work on them."

There was a brief silence; Stephen glanced at Ralph, as if expecting support, before clearing his throat and continuing. "If you get the paperwork ready today, I can see no reason why we shouldn't start to organise the manufacture of field units and have them ready for initial training purposes by next week. Subject to the agreement of the committee, of course, but they'll be pleased, I'm sure. That's the Anstey and banished-enforcer threat dealt with, at least. The new security guards will be grateful to have them. Once that's completed, we can issue them to anyone who might have genuine need. Besides – and I know I'm repeating this, but that's because you just won't listen – I really don't think it's good for us to use the device on you anymore. These weapons may not kill, but they've certainly knocked you out more than a few times. It can't possibly be good for you."

"No problem, whatever you think is best for your wife." Thomas was relieved when Ralph finally gave Stephen a quick look and added his approval.

"Thank you both. I really appreciate it. I don't want to leave you in the lurch, but it's important to us, to Kat and me, and to the baby."

Feeling a look of pride spread over his face as he thought of Lissy, he had to share his sense of wonder with them.

"She *spoke* into my mind last night … our baby, Lissy, I mean … she said, '*Dadde*' and she's so tiny!"

They looked suitably impressed – grinning at each other (or, more probably, laughing at him… who knew). He had resolved to pretend to love the child for Kat's sake, and then… everything had changed when his own baby daughter, his Lissy, reached out to him, mind-to-mind. He thought again of that warm, innocent bundle in his arms, loving him, anchoring him, starting to melt the ice deep inside his body.

Stephen was saying something; he forced himself to pay attention.

"Have you decided where the three of you might go? Or, I suppose it will be four – I don't imagine Bess will want to be away from you for too long, however much she loves Eddie, and Kat's father too."

Good point – he shook his head. He hadn't planned anything beyond the fact of Kat needing to leave. It was typical of him lately, Stephen was the mature, practical one in the friendship, since… well, ever since he'd fallen in love with Kat, if he was being honest. Thinking as he spoke, he admitted: "Nothing's definite yet. I'm know I'm being impetuous, but I just wanted to clear it with you two. Make it real and happening. You're the ones who will be most affected anyway. I haven't thought a great deal about where Kat and I could go exactly. William, Cecily, and Edward may not be all that appreciative of us descending on them permanently. And there's always the worry of attracting attention from the authorities. That's a lot of households under one roof. Perhaps we won't go far. There's always William's other house, the one near here, though it's a bit derelict now."

"No Thomas! Think! You can't possibly go there. Kat would *hate* going back. Stop and think of everything that happened to her there." Stephen sounded horrified. "Look, why don't you talk to James and Robert? They returned from their other office last evening and are due to be around later on: they're looking for volunteers to take care of a merchant's house and warehouse in Barnstable. It's one the Thornes forfeited when their assets were seized. Go and see James as soon as he's back in the sanctuary at lunchtime. Ask Kat, I'm sure she would like that." The idea felt like a lifeline. More than he could have hoped for. He smiled, looking gratefully at Stephen.

"Is someone able to take over Kat's reading class? Your godson enjoys her lessons, and he's coming on so well with his reading." It was Stephen's turn to look the proud father as he spoke of his son Thom's precocious abilities. He was vaguely aware that Kat was achieving a great deal with all the young ones and felt sad to think that it was at such cost to her own health. At least she would be able to carry on teaching Bess and Lissy – well, perhaps not Lissy for a while. Though maybe… He thought with less satisfaction of the replacement Kat had suggested and frowned. That would take some 'selling' to the youngsters.

"Kat mentioned Anne G. I think Anne has probably mellowed since the battle and Anstey's defeat, though I'm not sure that's a general view. She can put people's backs up, but I think Megs put her straight. The young humans have surprised Anne. I hope that she's beginning to respect the variety of life that exists here in the community now Anstey and his council have gone." Thomas shook off the feeling that Anne didn't altogether like Kat or him. He wasn't sure why – after all, they'd helped her daughter Cecily, with Edward and her grandson, escape from Anstey. It wasn't their fault if Anne's family was reluctant to return.

Ralph looked as if he might be about to add something to the conversation, perhaps something about Anne, but Stephen chipped in again, saying quickly, "I'm sure Anne will be fine." Ralph subsided, looking faintly aggrieved. Thomas had the oddest feeling that Stephen had tried to prevent his co-worker from speaking. He hadn't realised how much Stephen was concerned with Kat's welfare. While he'd been neglectful of her. Anyway, Kat and Stephen had been good friends ever since they'd worked together to rescue him. It was perfectly natural for them to be close. But Thomas couldn't dwell on such things today. For once he was the one actually achieving something for his wife.

And such a vista of hope was swelling in his chest. Barnstable would be completely perfect. Thomas felt that he could breathe properly at last. The prospect both excited and soothed him. A peculiar combination.

"I'll talk to James, it would be ideal, the chance to be somewhere totally new. Together, just us – Kat and me." He tried to calm himself as he thought about it. "I've never been anywhere the Thornes have lived, I don't think Kat has either, but I gather Anstey had set them up in nice places." He grinned, allowing his feeling to get ahead of him. "I'll go along to the sanctuary at lunchtime and then let Kat know if it's alright – I don't want to build her hopes up if they've already found someone. Thank you both. I'm sorry to land this on you, but we *are* nearing the last stage of this programme, and you're both capable men." He smiled at them.

Stephen squeezed his shoulder in a sympathetic gesture. "Don't worry, Thomas, I know James would rather have you in charge in Barnstable than anyone else."

Barnstable. Where better? It wasn't here for a start. *Anywhere* not here would be good. Thomas sighed with relief. Stephen had sounded confident. Almost as if it was a done deal. And he could make sure that Kat didn't work too hard – there were even rumours that the Thornes had installed some unobtrusive Domum-Orbis technology in all their former properties. The complex might have, did have, evil memories, but not every device and idea that the refugees had brought through time and space was bad. Thomas admitted to himself that he always struggled to overcome a certain fastidiousness in his nature – a fastidiousness that found the lack of complex-style cleansing rooms in the outside world quite distressing. Privies that worked, didn't smell, and could recycle effluent struck him as a positive example of something good that advanced engineering could provide. A shower … like the one he and Kat … He was getting ahead of himself, that was asking too much. He sighed and attempted to return to the present. Think about what Kat needed, not his own desires. And there *was* a positive for her. More than one room in the house – he could sit up at night in a chair and read, it would allow Kat to sleep if his nightmares continued once they left the complex. He even allowed himself to harbour the faintest of hopes – that they would cease altogether.

Right. Enough. He managed to pull himself together and focus on the paperwork necessary for handing over control of the project. But the second they broke for lunch Thomas hurried toward the sanctuary. Now that Kat had spoken about it, he realised just how busy it was everywhere. He must have been moving about in a frozen bubble of his own not to notice. Thinking about it, he couldn't honestly say who he had seen or spoken to, apart from on work-related issues, for days, even weeks, past. Had he ignored them all, spoken to no-one? He did know that he had obsessively and determinedly kept his mind guarded at all times. Even in the evenings with Kat – reading, listening to music, being as absent as he could get away with. To protect her, as he had thought.

It was a relief to find that James and Robert were back, Thomas had worried that they may have been delayed. He experienced a frantic and overwhelming need to get everything sorted out now. Surprisingly both men actually seemed to be expecting him and welcomed him in, promising to join him as soon as they had finished writing up whatever legal document it was that they were engaged in working on.

This was the only place in the complex where Thomas felt quieted and peaceful when he wasn't working. Despite what had happened there, the blood that had been spilt. There was a small shrine in the main room, commemorating Henry's life. James said little about his dead twin, but Thomas guessed that no day went past without James thinking about him and missing him. It renewed Thomas's sense of horror at the thought of what he would have put Kat through without Alice's timely intervention the previous day. It didn't matter that he knew there were others who would take care of her better. Kat had chosen him. Always and always she was the one saying how much she loved him, and she'd done so much to prove it. He had to keep remembering and trusting in her…

Though God alone knew why she had chosen someone like him, he hoped it hadn't been just because of the need to escape from Anstey, or pity because of what she'd learned of his life in the mind-share. There were times when he worried about that, despite the way that she said she loved him, and was eager, more than eager, to share his bed. Yet it was also true that she hadn't known anyone else among the exiles or anyone else anywhere. Could she be capable of saying 'I love you' mind-to-mind if it wasn't completely true? Might she even believe it, without it being true, not having known another lover? But the fact remained. They were bonded, his life and his love belonged to her for as long as she wanted him. Surely, she *did* love him. Alice seemed to think so.

For now, he was determined to get Kat away from the complex as soon as he could. He must stop letting these depressing thoughts take hold. Do the practical stuff. Make a list, tick things off. As soon as James came over to where he was sitting, waiting, Thomas plunged straight into his request.

"Stephen mentioned that you were looking for someone to take care of the Thornes' former premises in Barnstable. I need to get Kat and Lissy away from here; it's not suiting Kat, or the baby, now that the dangers of the birth are all in the past. We would be happy to look after things and work with the human partner who is currently keeping things going. Would you like us to? Is it possible?"

Thomas shut up quickly, desperate not to sound too stupidly enthusiastic. Had he ever been as volatile as this, before everything that had happened? Veering from hope to despair to hope in a giddy cycle, without break. But the more he thought about it the more the Barnstable plan seemed to be the answer he was looking for. Surely James and Robert would say 'yes'. Kat would then be liberated from the memories this place evoked, and he would too. Perhaps free from the endless nightmares that were driving him into madness, to the edge of the clifftop. He couldn't look at James for the moment, afraid he might say no.

"Yes of course!" James's immediate agreement and positive smile broke into his thoughts and were balm to Thomas's anxious concern. "We should be incredibly grateful if you would be interested in helping out. Can't think of anyone better. In fact, Alice mentioned only yesterday evening how tired Kat was looking and how much she hoped you three would take a break from the bedlam generated by a complex such as this."

James looked at Robert, who had wandered over; the two smiled at each other. "We are always glad to get away to our rooms in Barnstable, aren't we, Robert? It ought to be the other way around, given the dangers we face there, but it isn't."

"Finding someone capable and reliable is quite urgent," Robert added. "The human partner is actually leaving, and it's one of those enterprises that could go downhill quite quickly. We're not looking to enrich ourselves in the same way as Anstey, but the complex has expenses that aren't fully met by the estate rents, especially now that we have new dependents to feed and clothe. The businesses help to fill that gap."

Thomas was quite surprised; he'd never really thought about the financing of their small community. His duties had always lain with the science and engineering concerns of their everyday living, keeping the complex working, but he couldn't see why he wouldn't pick up the necessary business skills as easily as he had most things in his life.

"The sooner you could be ready to leave, the better." James's voice suggested to Thomas that he was even more enthusiastic about the plan than Thomas himself, if such a thing were possible.

He felt his heart steady and hope begin to grow. For the first time since they had arrived back at the complex, Thomas could begin to see a way forward for him and Kat: a future arising to save them from the despair that had threatened to extinguish their life together and his life entirely.

By the time he left the sanctuary, he found that he had agreed to wind up his involvement with the weapons programme over the next two days and had promised that they would be ready to leave as soon as Kat had organised her classroom replacement. James and Robert both promised that they would ensure that he and Kat knew as much as possible about the new undertaking before they left, so that they could start work straight away.

He might not be able to make love to his wife, but Thomas began to feel that he was doing something positive for her. If he could organise things properly, they would at least be away from this place. Last night and this morning had been important. In his anxiety to hide his problems from Kat he had shut out their love and he couldn't do that to her. Not again. He would just have to make sure that none of his darker thoughts reached the surface and passed into her mind. Thank the Lord that Alice had reached him in time. He felt sick to think that she could, so easily, have been too late, that he could have consigned himself to oblivion and left his wife and children to cope alone without him.

James's other surprising offer – of someone to talk to – he was less certain about. He didn't know what Alice had said to James, nor what James knew of the details of his treatment by Anstey and those fuck-awful monsters of his. Thomas hugged his arms around himself – why would he ever want to say anything about that out loud? He couldn't take back Alice's knowledge of it – even that made him feel sick – but the idea of further sharing something that he felt somehow shamed him was more than he could bear at present. Yes, he did know, rationally, that it was bizarre to blame himself, but admitting that as a fact didn't change anything.

Yet he had felt able to talk to Megs and the others when he was brought back to the hellish place that they were all kept in. They had talked to him, the human girls, he had talked to them, even though he had blamed himself, his shameful, pathetic weakness, for failing to protect them. But he wouldn't talk to them now, determined never to put that awful time back in their memories, though Megs had tried to tell him how it had helped her, and the others, to 'have a rant about it' to someone in the infirmary. She was thoughtful, but he didn't really see a lot of her now, though he was glad she was happy with whoever it was she was with. Someone capable to protect her and keep her safe.

What had happened to the girls had shamed those who did it, not those it was done to. That simple fact Thomas was totally certain of, and hoped the humans were too, always fearing they might not be. While he suspected that the humans had a broader and more pragmatic view of what to expect from the world, he still didn't quite believe they would ever recover fully from the horror that was Anstey. It was a dark club to be a member of. He could recall his own grandiose ideas of 'escape or die' – what an innocent – that was the stuff of books. Instead it was what happened in between capture and death that was the worst. What had happened to *him* – an insidious voice inside him repeated over and over – how could it not shame and humiliate him? He should have found some way to have died first. It should not have been impossible. The fewer people who knew, the better.

Chapter 5

Barnstable was certainly different but we settled in well. It was just as busy as it was in the complex, but a different sort of busyness. All those people, crammed into a vibrant living town, but with minds that were not defensively tight against trespassers. Above us, no perpetual roof pressing down. Real daylight. On our first night away from the complex, we'd taken Lissy outside to look up at the sky, and I'd whispered to her, "Dadde was born far away in the stars." And sometimes after that, when we saw them above us, I felt her whisper of *"Dadde … stars"* inside my head.

At first, I felt a little guilty about mind-reading. Thomas too, he'd confessed it to me. I hadn't really registered the extent to which, all of my life, I had unconsciously listened in to everything that was happening around me. Was that nosiness or an unforgiveable incursion? Since being a child, I had always thought of it as interest in others, something different from the mind-probing my mother had prohibited so vehemently. Take my father. I never tried to penetrate his deepest thoughts, his plans and intentions. When I was younger, I would just whisk through that lightest surface skim of thoughts to check if he was happy on a particular day, if it would be good to try to get him to play or take me out for a ride. I barely knew I was doing it. Anyway, Barnstable was full of that kind of interest. And you always knew what people really thought of you. No possibility of a traitor like Richard here – at least not for those of us who were born with the blood of Domum-Orbis in our veins and shared the abilities it conferred.

All this seemed to be having a positive influence on Thomas's mind-set, however much he tried to avoid eavesdropping on the humans around us. Was it time to begin on the next stage of my plan? I waited for a quiet evening, a week or two into our new routine. Up until then, feigning sleep had delayed confronting the problem.

Sitting on the edge of our bed, a proper bed, I started to undress, slowly. Lissy was tucked up, fast asleep. It was just the two of us for the moment, and I was about to be naked – despite my worries about my post-childbirth body. Thank goodness for the warmth of the fire and the dim lighting. Watching him, watching me in the candlelight – just enough brightness from flame and fire to draw a shimmer from my markings – made me give a little shiver of desire, but also of apprehension. Rejection was a risk, and it would be hard to bear. I stood and moved close to him, drawing his tunic off, while his hands reached, involuntarily, for my skin, running his fingers lightly over me, then kissing me hungrily. How could I make our physical relationship unthreatening, without revealing my reasons?

I unfastened his breeches, trying to ignore the sudden tension I felt in him.

"Why don't we just look at each other and cuddle? Could you bear to do only that? I'm feeling less than desirable at present. I know I'm not that wonderful a sight." I noticed that I was holding my breath for his response and tried to sound more normal as I attempted a light-hearted tone. "Though perhaps I don't look quite as bad as the first time you saw me with all my sores and bruises."

"You look lovely, you always look lovely to me." I couldn't believe how choked up he sounded as he said it. His voice half broke on the words and he stripped off the rest of his clothes. Drawing me over to the bed with him he lay there willingly beside me, holding me close. His hands stroking over my skin.

"I can think of nothing better than lying here with my eyes open, seeing your beautiful body beside me."

Perhaps … I wished I could believe it. Thomas could be quite unrealistic when he was feeling so emotional and he knew that I feared our separateness above all else. Since he had realised just how much his problems had made him neglect me when we were back in the complex, he was prepared to do anything he could to ease the guilt he had confessed to me. Without admitting the source of his difficulties. I was sure he would at least humour me and try to make me feel less alone and unwanted. That part was easy, I could persuade him, without any difficulty, that I needed the reassurance of his touch and gaze to make things better – because it was true, I did.

We lay naked on top of the covers, eyes wide open, seeing the shape of each other despite the semi-darkness, feeling each other without going further than the softest of touches, whether hand, finger, or lip. It kept the two of us in the present moment whilst our minds, independently of our bodies, communicated the love we felt for each other in plain, simple words. Somehow, in the mind, there seemed to be no repetition of love that could ever grow stale. An interesting choice of words. I smiled and bent my head to kiss Thomas's chest. I was half-stealing from Master Shakespeare's *Anthony and Cleopatra*. Delusion free, I couldn't compare myself with her: age would definitely 'wither' me, probably it was doing so already, but would 'custom stale' my 'infinite variety' for Thomas? Who knew, perhaps Thomas's and my love might yet rival hers and Anthony's. Hopefully not the ending though. It was nice to have been able to bring books from the library with us and read words from plays that were only now being written and performed – so many words about love to think of and act upon as I tried my best to seduce my husband.

We stroked each other's swirls, tenderly, exciting the sensations we had once shared so easily. I could feel that Thomas was beginning to be fully aroused, his erection pressing hard against me, and I didn't want him to reach the point when a nightmare vision would darken his thoughts and plunge us back into our separate hells. Instead, I cuddled his naked body close, sliding down him and moving between his legs to gently take him in my mouth. I felt his hand tentatively stroking my hair, breathing unevenly, as I relentlessly kissed and licked, teasing his throbbing glans with my tongue before enveloping him in the wetness of my mouth and moving up and down the length of his, thankfully, firm shaft.

"Are you sure, Kat?" He managed to gasp, drawing in a shuddering breath. I thought for a moment he might stop me, but he gripped my head and then he was crying out, completely unable to draw back. And, in the end, thrusting deep inside my mouth, he released himself willingly, warm and salty, a taste of my Thomas inside me.

Kissing me achingly sweetly and whispering, "I love you, so much, Kat," it was only natural for him to reciprocate. His fingers traced tantalisingly down from the swirls, to part my labia, arousing me there with light but insistent touch and sliding one, then two fingers inside me. The relentless movement of his fingers, his lips on my swirls – the sensations were completely irresistible. In a haze of pleasure, my body arched and trembled as I lost control to a quivering tidal surge of physical feeling. Then we just held each other tightly, breathlessly, as overwhelmed as if he had achieved the penetration he feared to attempt. I felt sated and smug as we slipped under the coverlet together. The bad dreams were held at bay for another night … by me. And might be again. I could live with that. So, could he, judging by the satisfied smile on his face.

*

Thomas treasured the time that was now theirs. Time spent with his beautiful wife, his amazing daughters, and with Anstey firmly closed off from his everyday life, locked in a dark back room in his mind. He would never willingly return to live in the complex, no matter how much James tried to warn him that things were changing there. Not even when James suggested that more like-minded people were needed to stand for the council if it was not to sink back into the kind of place where someone like Anstey could take charge again. How could it possibly do that after all that had happened? James was exaggerating. He had to be.

Everyone that he personally knew was too relieved to be free of that old life to let it re-emerge. But Thomas did acknowledge that most of those closest to him were away from the complex now – apart from Alice, Stephen, and Thom. They had stayed to help him and Kat leave with easy consciences, but Alice had been pressured into remaining, and, of course, Stephen was with her. Perhaps he should talk to some of the others, gauge their opinions.

Of those he knew well, Cecily, together with her husband and son, intended to continue living with Kat's father in William's old house, the one Kat had grown up in. They were happy there, but it was a sore point with her mother, Anne Gomfrey. Anne must have exerted so much pressure over her daughter and her family in times past. She had even insisted that Edward took Cecily's name at hand-fasting rather than allowing his to be joined with hers. Cecily, having once broken free, was determined not to be within Anne's sphere of influence ever again and Anne bore a grudge. Nothing he could do or say would influence Cecily. That was definitely a non-starter.

Whereas Margery had always been a loner, so there was no family to influence her decision one way or the other. But the little girl he had grown up with now spent all her time in Barnstable, mostly dressed as male, and out with human friends – male – who called her Mathias. There was no pressure on her to return. Quite the reverse.

He thought about her with affection. There was a lot to admire in her brave determination to live her own life.

According to Margery it was perfectly safe to live as she did. She could see into the minds of her companions and they all believed her to be the young man she claimed she was. And it was fun – she laughed when she told him – she could do whatever she liked, and she did so enjoy fighting. He acknowledged, not without reluctance, that she was far better with a sword than he was. Despite the fact that he'd been the one who'd taught her, defying Anstey, when they were children. To be fair, he was getting better again himself: working out and shadow-fencing a lot now. Mainly because he liked the way Kat looked at him when he did. He'd let himself get too thin since that time. Now his muscles were getting more respectable.

And then there was James, perhaps the closest to him apart from Stephen. But for all his own warnings he spent more time in Barnstable than back at the complex. Perhaps that was because his human partner and lover was less comfortable in the complex than out here in the bustling, living world that Robert had known his whole life. No matter if you were born there or had lived most of your life there, the complex still had a deadening effect on life and love and laughter.

Thomas wondered if it was for similar reasons that Kat preferred to be in their new home. She had lived most of her life in this corner of Elizabethan England. Sacrificing much of the technology he had grown up with was a small price to pay for giving pleasure to the woman he loved, and for his own freedom from endless nightmares. Though he did still wish that the Thornes had found some way of creating an off-complex shower room. He had a repetitive and more than pleasant dream of sharing such a place with Kat, as they had just that once. What wasted opportunities while they'd been there, when he'd been unable.

The complex itself, despite Anstey's overthrow, always seemed such a place of gloom and foreboding (he wasn't quite sure why), locked permanently away from the true light of day. Maybe the lack of natural light … perhaps something else lacking in the environment, or was it simply all due to the memories? The last thought allowed a wisp of his darkest recollections to escape from that locked room in his mind, but he firmly secured the door on it again. What had happened was done and gone and could not be changed. His body had recovered, more or less. Kat didn't know his shame and humiliation. Why should remembering what had happened keep trying to creep back into his life? He had defeated such periods of frozen despair many times in his life. He was happy. He was with his family. Nothing should ever be allowed to jeopardize that again. Even so, he did feel guilty that he was perhaps evading some of the responsibility that it was his duty to shoulder. The pull – between Kat, Lissy, and Bess on the one hand and those who were his first family, together with the humans he'd sworn to protect, on the other – was occasionally unbearable.

But he didn't want to think of all that now, not today when he had plans. William was visiting, together with Joan from his estate, and was happy to look after the girls overnight. Kat had left milk for Lissy. Thomas was going to take Kat out. He wanted her to be with him – alone. So far nearly all their time together had been fraught with danger. The happiness that shone on and in him from their family life was different from anything arising from their relationship as a couple. There were still shadows over the two of them as lovers rather than parents. Life had bounced them into such an intense relationship – where was the courtship, the romance, the laughter? So, he was intent on taking Kat back to a place where, for a few brief hours, it had just been the two of them and their love. Thomas thought that maybe there he could be with Kat as fully as any man with his dearly loved wife. It wasn't that he didn't appreciate what she did for him, he did. He understood the probable why, too – her endless compassion for him. But it couldn't recreate that mind-blowing feeling, that complete and utter ecstasy, which had been theirs from the very first time they came together – until Anstey destroyed it all.

Thomas was definitely not planning to return with Kat to his old room in the compound. That might have been the first place he had ever made love to her, but with all that had happened since, the magic of that location was gone forever for him. Now he was heading for both a time and a place. A special place, the cave they had made love in when he had ridden after her and Kat had forgiven him for his stupid anger. A special time that was theirs alone, before William had found them and cast that shadow over their coupling. A time when Thomas could innocently make love to his wife without fearing the consequences. A time before her father had told him that if Thomas made Kat pregnant, delivering a child of his would be almost certain to kill her. This time he knew that even though they were away from the complex Alice had continued to supply Kat with something to prevent the outcome he had dreaded most of the time they had been together since that day.

It had rained a great deal, the fields were sodden, but the day he had chosen was bathed in sunshine, like his mood. They took two horses, but he led the second, with food, drink, and blankets for sitting out. They weren't in a hurry and Thomas wanted her cuddled up to him, like they'd been that previous time. He laughed, privately. No Elizabethan human would have been likely to understand his fascination with the outdoors, the landscape. But then no Elizabethan humans had been trapped underground for most of their lives. Trite but true – for him sunshine, birdsong, trees, flowers, living water as it cascaded over waterfalls all were alive and special. It was the complete panacea to pain and worry and the best thing of all was Kat's smile, her body cradled against his. Her words of love in his head were bliss, as was her excitement when he had said they would go somewhere alone together.

She was his girl. She loved him. It was a different kind of pleasure from that of seeing her with their children. She was the best mother, like his own had been for him, but she deserved to be young and carefree too. He thought, with some envy, of Alice and Stephen. He would have liked a courtship like theirs, guilt-free time to just enjoy being with Kat, the two of them alone, and the knowledge that she had chosen him specially, not that he was the only man from Domum-Orbis she had ever met, not that she had been forced into hand-fasting with him to save her life. That was the strongest reason for choosing to return to the cave. At the time, when they were first there, it had seemed a new beginning. It still felt like a landmark in their lives. Her forgiveness washing over him and making him sure of her love – she could so easily have walked away – and he had been briefly convinced that she wanted to be with him more than anything else in her life.

And then they were there, in the present, crossing the river and leading the horses into *that* clearing. He didn't rush her, however much he wanted to. They ate sitting on the blanket on the damp grass, talking about stories they had read, music they had heard, touching every so often, kissing, laughing, brushing crumbs off each other. The perfect dinner for two. Privacy.

Kat stood. "Outdoor cleansing room – I'll be back in a moment."

He tidied everything away, and, grinning, took the blanket into the cave. Which was fortunately empty – he hadn't thought to check. She came in behind him, taking him by surprise as she tapped his shoulder.

"Your turn."

He grabbed her tightly, kissing her, holding her close to him.

"*Ribs, Thomas!*" But she was laughing, he remembered her saying that before and he couldn't let her go.

"Oh hell!" Thomas laughed and groaned. "I have got to go outside, and I can't let go of you." He thought she was laughing too.

"Surely I don't have to come outside and hold it for you." Yes, she was laughing, practically convulsed with it.

He relaxed, kissed her fiercely again, then let her go while he dashed outside and found a convenient bush.

"All better?" she said, teasing him as he re-joined her.

"Not yet. It will be when I have you naked."

Thomas advanced on Kat, a hungriness for her consuming him as his hands removed every stitch of her clothing and he could touch her, at last, every inch of her skin just waiting for him to explore with fingers, lips, and tongue. His girl, his willing lover, his forever wife.

And her fingers were busy removing his clothing. Unlike previous occasions, his erection increased with want and need, rather than diminishing with fear and memory. He was completely dizzy with desire for her. In moments they were lying on the blanket. Ignoring residual dampness and the hard rock underneath. Skin against skin, swirl against swirl, he slid inside her, thrusting harder … wanting more … wanting them to be totally merged … wanting to watch. Feeling her gasp of pleasure, he moved inside her over and over, owned by her as she came around him, squeezing him tight, calling out his name. Thank heaven, he could not resist her even had he wanted to. With his final thrusts his semen gushed into her, beyond his control, as he cried out both aloud and inside her mind, "Kat! Oh Kat! I love you, you're mine forever. I'll never let you go."

And, somehow, she was crying with love for him, he was gently kissing away her tears, tasting their salt, and for those few seconds, minutes, it seemed to him that nothing could ever separate or hurt them again.

Unlike the previous time they were together in the cave, they didn't waste it dressing. Thomas reached out an arm, drawing his cloak over them both, and they slept. Their naked bodies wrapped around each other, careless of anyone finding them, though Thomas kept his sword near at hand.

The morning found them making love again — sweetly, slowly, tenderly. This time he was confident that he could stay erect, the knowledge allowing him to focus on arousing her, exploring her body, giving her pleasure before he allowed himself to experience his own. The sequence of their first night together. Thomas let the happiness that consumed him create a fortress around the part of his mind that encompassed just the two of them. He must allow nothing to connect dark old memories with the glorious feeling of moving inside her, the feel of her — warm and soft and wet around his aching fullness — the sensations as she tightened around him and he let go, releasing all that fullness inside her. No-one would ever do to her what they'd done to him. His promise to her. This was a miracle, their miracle, with no resemblance at all to what those fucking bastards had done to him. He had survived and she would *never* experience anything like that as long he was there to take care of her, it was over, and those memories could lie buried and forgotten.

He held her in his arms, wanting to stay there forever, so thankful that he had at last reclaimed her from the nightmares. What would it be like to open an ostium and remain forever inside it, stilling time into one exquisite and unending moment? He had read about the elite women from Domum-Orbis, and his heart knew that Kat was powerful enough.

Chapter 6

I stood outside our door to say goodbye to Stephen as he set off, Thom was in front of him on the saddle. It had been good to have him visit, though he seemed a little subdued. In fact, both of them did. Being so close to Alice had originally prevented me from fully appreciating Stephen as a person in his own right. His steadfast determination to help Thomas escape and all he had done for me as we prepared for our assault on Anstey had changed that. Our shared time had made me value him properly as the true friend that I felt he was. Also, he was Thomas's best friend – had always been there for him – he deserved my affection for that alone.

"Thomas was sorry not to see you off. He had to meet with our shippers early this morning, before they caught the tide. We were so glad that you were able to stay with us on your way through to my father's, though I'm sorry that Alice is too busy to visit at present. Tell her how much I miss her when you return to the complex."

Stephen frowned; he didn't look as if he'd smiled much recently. "It's difficult for her. There are others with medical skills, but not sufficient numbers of them at present and few with her empathic talents. She's busy training some of the younger ones who show an aptitude, but that's a long process. Sometimes I wish she would just tell the council to get on with things. They take advantage – some of her patients won't trust anyone else. They managed fine when she was away. It means she's missing out on Thom's childhood as well; she doesn't get to spend nearly enough time with him. And just now I'm nothing but a distraction. She doesn't want my company at present."

There was hurt in his voice, but his words sounded a little rehearsed. I wasn't sure he was telling me the whole story. I wondered whether he blamed me for their return to the complex.

"I feel guilty, if I hadn't needed her so much when Lissy was born …" I admitted hesitantly.

"Oh Kat, no, I'm sorry, I didn't mean to suggest that you were to blame. Alice was truly concerned for you herself and she knew Thomas was worried too. She would always do anything for Thomas, and now for you as well. We owe him everything. You can't imagine … Seeing you with Thomas and Lissy makes it all worthwhile. I was just griping about some of the other exiles, the demanding ones who have minor aches and pains and complain endlessly. Forget I said anything, it will all sort itself out."

Stephen bent down awkwardly from his saddle to give me a quick farewell kiss and allow me to bestow one on my husband's little godson. Thom wasn't interested in kisses. Well, not mine at least. He just snuggled nearer to his father – who was currently the only person of worth in Thom's small world. I wondered if Alice knew what she was forfeiting. And then my Thomas was there too, rushing up, just in time.

"I was afraid I'd miss you! You're too rare a visitor to allow you to leave without a proper farewell." Thomas was alongside smiling and reaching up to give Thom a hug. "Don't leave it such an age to come next time, and stay longer. I know you're anxious to get off on your journey now." Thomas's arm curved around my waist, hugging me possessively to him as we stood there, waving Stephen off.

An hour later, more or less, we were busy working in the office part of the house. Bess was reading, curled up by the window, and Lissy was alongside with her ABC book. I was wholly engrossed in my ledger when the peace was shattered. Bess had put her book down with an uncustomary bang, and then jumped to her feet, looking anxious. "It's Thom!" She hugged her arms around herself. "I think something is wrong – there's such a feeling of turmoil coming from him."

"But they're well on their journey. How can you possibly feel the child's emotions over such a distance?" Thomas was concerned but puzzled.

There was something faint, whispering in my mind. "I think I feel something too … but Stephen, not Thom. Almost, but not quite, his voice."

"Surely you don't hear Stephen's voice, you're not that close, not like you and I." Oddly, Thomas almost sounded jealous. He didn't seem to have grasped the seriousness of what Bess and I were saying.

"Don't be silly, of course I'm not close to him like I am to you. But my mind is sensitive to your friends, it's needed to be." I was hurt and cross – was I supposed to support his friends or not? But now was not the time.

"Oh – when I was imprisoned. I forget that you all had to work together when I was the bait in Anstey's trap." He still sounded morose and disinclined to take Bess seriously. Seeing Stephen had somehow rekindled his feelings of inadequacy. Why, I couldn't imagine. I had to remind him of the reason he'd needed rescuing.

"When you were imprisoned because you bravely gave yourself up to send me the drugs that saved my life."

But he still managed to get the last word in.

"When Stephen took them to you."

Bess gave an exasperated snort. "What does it matter who did what? Thom is frightened. Something has happened." She didn't usually speak to Thomas or to me in such a sharp way and I wasn't sure how Thomas would react. He wasn't the typical father of this day and age, but nevertheless…

I touched Thomas's arm. *"Bess isn't usually wrong about such things. Listen to her."*

"And you, what can you add? Can you really hear something? Stephen is behaving slightly strangely anyway. Didn't you notice?"

"A bit subdued, perhaps. I don't know him as well as you. You've been friends forever. But I do pick up odd things from our kind if the person isn't shielding. My mother did too; she told me."

I felt guilty speaking privately with Thomas when Bess was so anxious and was just about to include her in the conversation when there was a bang on the door. We all stopped breathing for a second.

Thomas leapt to his feet, now thoroughly unsettled and went to answer it, with me following closely. A grubby, ill-cared for child, possibly eight or nine years of age, stood there, wiping his nose on his sleeve.

"Who's Mister Alban?"

Thomas squatted down to the child's level. "Who wants to know?"

"I've a message – him sending it thought Mister Alban lived here."

"What's your message? I'm Mister Alban."

"He said you'd give me money."

Thomas drew a coin from his money purse and handed it over silently, together with a cloth for the child's nose, both were quickly pocketed, but otherwise ignored.

"The burned man says to tell you he's took a friend of yours. The friend with the kid. We was robbing your friend – we pull the old soldier trick, the ruffler and us – but when we took your man's clothes, we could see that he was a bit strange." The child tapped his neck, with a significant glance at Thomas. "Our ruffler, he reckons that you might pay a bit to get your friend back without him being reported. The ruffler says you'll understand the danger. Oh, and he says to tell you he's holding the little kid too."

The child's mind was something of a jumble, but it corroborated his words, by and large. I'd heard tell of rufflers, men who pretended to be discharged soldiers, definitely armed and dangerous. I was afraid at first that the 'burned man' might be one of the banished enforcers, which would skew the odds against us. Reading human minds made quite a difference. But no, I saw the image of a human vagabond in the boy's mind, one who'd had his ear burned through for some earlier misdemeanour.

"Where do we take the money? How much?" Thomas made eye contact with the child, perhaps he was able to read more of the situation. Such as where they were hiding. He was better with human minds than me.

"All the cash you got. No weapons. You just follow me. The burned man is staying hid with a spare horse a street away. He's the one who spied your friend leaving this morning."

Bess had crept out to the door and was listening to the boy's mind too. I heard her gasp and whisper, "Thom!" I didn't want her involved if there was likely to be trouble, however capable she was.

"Stay with Lissy, Bess. I'll go with father." Thomas turned to glare at me.

"No Kat, stay put, no need for us both to go."

"Don't be crazy, Thomas. You don't know how many of them there are, and the child said no weapons."

"I have a stun weapon in my purse. I'll put it on my hand while I'm riding. They won't have a clue what it is."

"I'm coming. You'll have two weapons then, the one you designed and my less well-behaved mind. Afterwards you'll need both of us: we'll have to take care of Thom as well as Stephen."

While this argument was going on silently and the child was focused on Thomas, I pushed Bess gently back into the office – I could tell she wanted to come too – before carefully unlocking the money drawer and removing a bag of coins. Hopefully it would be sufficient. I slid a small dagger into my sleeve, making sure Bess saw me. She knew what I would try to do with it. She'd seen me before.

"Please Bess, look after Lissy. She's frightened too. Don't worry, I will go with father to rescue Thom. He'll be alright. We all will be." I whispered silently in her head. With relief, I saw her take hold of Lissy's hand and persuade her back to the window seat. She wasn't happy, but I knew she would do as I'd asked. I could hear Lissy's voice too, but Bess was quick to reassure her, telling her we had to go out, but would be back soon.

I returned to the doorway and spoke to the boy before Thomas had a chance to say anything more. "I'm bringing money. All we have. Show us the way to the horse, we'll share one."

The child looked disconcerted as I glared at him and started to protest. "Two of you? The burned man said nothing about two."

"I'm a woman, I don't count," I said matter-of-factly with my fingers crossed and attempting to influence the child's thoughts.

Thomas sighed. *"Little does he know – try not to kill anyone if it isn't absolutely necessary. It might complicate things and I really want to try the stun weapon on a human."*

"Promise. I love you." I kept my thoughts light, flippant. There was absolutely no reason for Thomas to worry about me.

We followed the boy to the edge of town, where a man was waiting in a back way with his own horse and Stephen's. I flinched as I saw the man's ear – probably not long done, it looked red and angry, like the man himself. From his thoughts, slightly more coherent than the boy's, we gathered that there were three of them, plus the child, involved. It was sobering to see Stephen through the burned man's eyes – naked and trussed up – even worse to see Thom crying and another man laughing and threatening our godson with a dagger.

We didn't allow our feelings to show. Or tried not to. As I suspected, the burned man had no qualms about my presence. He was confident that I would impede Thomas rather than bring any extra danger to his friends. It was Thomas he addressed.

"If I'm not back within the hour with you and a bag of money, your strange friend will be hauled in front of the law. The ruffler'll kill the youngster and say we came upon the father sacrificing his kid in some wicked ritual." The man obviously enjoyed our expressions of horror and embellished his account. "P'raps we came upon your friend dancing naked around the body. Your friend'll hang for sure."

Thomas shuddered and mounted the horse, hoisting me up in front of him. "*On second thoughts, feel free to kill any of these savages. Do you have a knife hidden?*"

"*Oh, yes. They'll be no match for the two of us,*" I whispered smugly in Thomas's head.

"*Dear God save us, now he's thinking of what they might do to you. I'll kill him if you don't!*"

"*I know, he's not very imaginative, let's get this done.*"

The burned man swung the child up behind him – evidently, they were together: possibly another complication – and we were off along the road, with our reins firmly held in our captor's hands and his pistol trained on us. We didn't have to go all that far. I wondered why it had taken so long for the ransom demand to reach us. As soon as we reached the first patch of really dense woodland, the burned man led us off the road. Then I heard it. Thom's little voice screaming in my head, Stephen's frantic calls for help. I looked up at Thomas, seeing him register the contact too. He was already surreptitiously donning the stun weapon, masked from the burned man by my body.

"Our priority must be Thom. He's gagged, hysterical, no wonder his mind is open to us."

"I'm trying to reach him, reassure him and Stephen."

"You can hear Stephen too?"

"Can't you?"

"Yes, but we've been friends for a lifetime."

"He's in so much terror at what they might do to Thom, I think every exile within a hundred miles must hear him. His mind is open to anyone who might help. You know Bess sensed Thom."

Where were they? They sounded so close now. And then, through a gap in the trees, we saw them.

Thom's small figure was gagged and bound and one of the men – wearing Stephen's clothes – was standing with a foot negligently placed on the child's chest. Stephen was trussed up, naked, watching in horror. A second man was lounging against a large oak, to which their horses were tethered. The second man was dressed in a soldier's uniform … the ruffler. The burned man leapt down from his mount and the boy nimbly slithered off the horse on his own.

Thomas hugged me close and we remained on horseback.

"I'll try to stun the one with his foot on Thom. Cover me and be ready."

The man with his foot on Thom suddenly jerked and clutched his head, before collapsing on the ground. Fortunately, not on top of Thom. The rest of the group were taken by surprise, failing to realise that we were in anyway involved. Acting instinctively, they rushed toward the fallen man. While they were in turmoil, we dismounted, and Thomas hurried to release Stephen. I balanced the knife from my sleeve on the palm of my hand, feeling power and anger rising in me. But I was getting used to it. I could hold back if I wasn't needed.

"Look out, it's them!" The child was quicker to spot what was happening and shout a warning. Our captor swung round, looking only at my knife. Thomas stunned him, before turning back to try to release Stephen. The soldier raced toward me. With silent apology to Thomas I let the knife find its destination in the man's throat. Completely lethal, as always, I groaned … all or nothing. The child, with presence of mind, grabbed the knife out of the ruffler's throat and flew at me, but Thomas stunned him before he could stab me. I took hold of the knife and tried not to look at Stephen, who had rushed to Thom.

I was glad to see that the stunned child was breathing and I made him as comfortable as I could. When I looked around Thomas had dragged the other stunned man away from Thom and was removing his – well Stephen's – clothing. Tossing the garments to Stephen, who was hugging his son to him and whispering "Thank you" into both (I think) our minds, Thomas noticed me as I turned to look pointedly the other way.

"*You can look, he has his breeches on,*" my husband actually sounded amused.

"*I'm sorry about the other one.*"

"*It couldn't be helped, and he deserved it. Though I struggle with being judge and jury.*"

"*Well you weren't. It was me, if anyone, and I wouldn't have done anything if he hadn't threatened me first.*"

Stephen joined us, trying to fasten his breeches and cuddle Thom at the same time.

"Thank you both. I'm an idiot. It was the soldier, he seemed to be an ordinary sort of man, chatting, riding alongside, telling me about how he was back from fighting. I wasn't really paying attention and didn't bother to read his mind, there seemed no need. Then, when we were passing this woodland, he just grabbed my reins and dragged us off the road. His two mates and the boy were waiting, and they had my weapons before I could even think about what they were doing. Then, of course, they grabbed Thom and I dared not resist. I hope you don't mind that I told them to come to you, that you'd pay a ransom. The threat was so horrific, and I knew they wouldn't be expecting Kat and your stun weapon, Thomas."

He hugged Thom even closer.

"What shall we do with them? How long before they come around?" I wanted to concentrate on the practical, deal with the shock later.

Thomas had no idea. "An exile takes around ten minutes or so. We didn't dare try it on humans."

"No, Heaven forbid we should have done such a thing," Stephen said with more than a touch of sarcasm. "We know how long an exile is unconscious, because you're the only one we tried it on. You were always too worried about the well-being of the humans. Now we can't take a chance on waiting too long. We need to wipe their minds of us; perhaps we could replace their recent thoughts with the idea of a falling out among thieves. They won't be too keen to speak to the authorities if they think they are the ones who committed the murder. Can we make them have some responsible feelings toward their youngster? Or is that too much manipulation."

"I'll take Thom and head back for the road while you two sort it out. I don't know how you used to wipe human minds in your enforcer days. Only that you did it to save lives." I looked proudly at Thomas – why would he *never* take credit for all the good things he did? "I only hope that losing the chief actor in the 'soldier' charade puts them off attacking anyone else."

"I don't think that the others were so keen on killing. It was the dead one that thought of threatening Thom. He got very excited when he saw my markings and came up with a way to make some easy extra money."

Thom was crying again, but held my hand obediently and willingly as I held it out to him. I was forcefully struck by how different he was to the happy youngster I had taught and known. More than just the horror and fright of this episode. We walked with two of the horses away from the clearing toward the roadway, Thom kept looking back, unwilling to be too far away from his father. I reassured him as best I could.

"Dadde won't be a moment. He and Uncle Thomas have to deal with those nasty men and make sure they don't hurt anyone else." The child said nothing.

When Stephen and Thomas joined us, they reported a totally satisfactory outcome, although they had needed to wait until the men were regaining consciousness to implant the ideas.

I was sure Stephen would want to come back to our house with the little one, so I wasted no time in asking.

"Come back with us, stay another night or so 'til you are both recovered from your ordeal. Can we get word to Alice?"

"That's kind of you, Kat, but I'm anxious to get on our way. I can't wait to be at your father's place again, to catch up with Edward and the family. I've missed our life there. Thom needs to see what the world is like away from the complex, he's getting close to forgetting."

"You won't stay away from us for so long this time, with Alice unable to get away from the infirmary, will you?"

Although Stephen replied in the negative, he didn't fully look me in the eyes as he said it. It seemed odd. Thinking back to earlier, I wondered if he was afraid that I might again be thinking he was blaming me for his wife's continued need to be back at the complex.

Thomas was unusually quiet too, but added that Stephen and Thom would be very welcome to stay longer with us. Stephen shook his head firmly, while thanking him.

Stephen mounted and Thomas handed Thom up to him, giving the boy a little hug. Stephen hesitated and then asked quietly, "Please don't mention this to Alice. I don't want her to think that Thom isn't safe away with me. I don't want to worry her unnecessarily."

"We won't say anything if you don't want us to. Not that we're likely to see her for a while anyway. But you should tell her, surely. It's likely to be something that could affect Thom at some point. If she doesn't know it'll be harder for her to handle it."

"No. It's up to me to sort out and I won't worry her." Stephen was decisive, shutting down Thomas's concerns, and he didn't seem to want to linger or discuss the matter.

"Thank you both."

His thanks seemed final, surprisingly lukewarm. He waited only to see us safely mounted too, before he waved in farewell, and headed on his journey. Thom, still tearful, waved forlornly from around his father as they disappeared where the road dipped away to the left and out of sight.

"Well, what did you make of that?" I was puzzled and more than a little concerned.

"I think Stephen felt shamed by what happened, how helpless he was. You seeing him... I can understand that."

"Men!"

"Please understand us. We've been brought up as if it was our job to be brave, our responsibility to protect our women and children and hide from ourselves the fact that our women are so much stronger than we are. On Domum-Orbis the top women were, presumably still are, an elite class. Anstey, when he chose this time and place, set his mind on reversing the situation. Your mother defied his attempts but wasn't strong enough in the end. I think that's why everything in the complex was arranged as it was while he was in charge – the clothing, lack of riding and fighting instruction for the women. Anstey tried to make us conform to his idea of Elizabethan norms, and it rubbed off on us children, turned it into a compulsion that we struggle with."

I snuggled closer to Thomas. "I do understand, at least I think I do. And I'm sorry I killed the one man; I know it doesn't help when I do things like that. I'll try to learn how to use the stun weapons. They were brilliant. You did so well. I'm just afraid that I won't be able to use them, like I couldn't use the other lethal ones."

"I'm not sure you're not patronising me – you defend yourself so easily. A mind-stun device doesn't come close. It wasn't your fault – the man, I mean. I already said that. Forget about it. I just want you to understand that Stephen feels it too. He knows how exceptional Alice is, and how her empathy helps her in her work in the infirmary. Lots of the exiles can do what Stephen does – that's not to say he isn't a valued member of the community – but hardly anyone can do what Alice does as well as she does it." Thomas grinned at me, trying to lighten the mood and looking a bit self-satisfied. "Besides, I don't think I would have wanted to stick around if things had been reversed and Alice had seen me trussed up and naked and had to ride out to rescue me."

I kissed Thomas. "You're such an understanding man. Stephen is lucky to have you as a friend." He held me closer, stroking back my hair and kissing my neck, with a struggle, above the ruff line.

"Come on, sweetness. Let's get back and tell Bess and Lissy all is well." He laughed. "Cuddle up to me and we'll try to project re-assuring thoughts to them both. I hadn't realised how advanced Bess's empathy is getting nor how wide a net you can spread to catch unwary thoughts."

"Not 'unwary.' Only thoughts from freely opened minds. There's a difference. I don't ever intrude unasked. But I'll forgive the insult as long as I can take up your offer of a cuddle. Just be careful what you say. I've never forgotten how angry you were that time in your room, when I tried to trespass in *your* mind, nor have I ever done such a thing since."

Thomas said nothing, but hugged me. The usual form of his apology.

Chapter 7

Walking along the back alley on his way to call on Robert, Thomas noticed a cloaked figure lurking in a doorway within sight of the house. With an unpleasant jolt he was sure he recognised Thorne and thoughts of his parents flooded back. Along with the good part of William's gift of memory came the bad part: the sight of Thorne riding along the beach, ready to lead his parents to their deaths at the hands of Anstey's interrogators. Pretending not to have seen the man, he made sure his path led him to pass right alongside his target. Before Thorne had a chance to react, he had him by the throat and backed hard against the wall. There was no-one around to see what was happening.

"What the fuck are you doing here?" he demanded, as Thorne struggled ineffectually. When the bastard saw that Thomas already had his dagger in hand, he stilled quickly enough and stood looking sullen, glaring defiantly, at his attacker.

"We're not banned from Barnstable. You and that whore of yours, you murdered our son and stole our home, but you can't stop us from living where we please, and we choose to live here."

Fury surged through Thomas.

"Stay away from my wife. And don't fucking call her a 'whore.' You and your son betrayed everyone, murdered my parents, tried to kill us. And you raped my wife's mother – don't think I don't know all there is to know about you. Fucking venal scum. You deserved everything you got. And Richard did too."

"You were the one that murdered your p—" Thorne didn't get to finish. Thomas's fist, with the hilt of the dagger in it, was faster. If he hadn't been holding Thorne so tightly, the man would have fallen. As it was, Thorne's nose was left bleeding, probably broken. With his face an inch from Thorne's he could easily have slit the man's throat – if his hand had not been shaking quite so much. Better not to. Breathe. Try to control the anger. It would be wrong to kill someone who offered no resistance. Even scum like Thorne.

"*You* murdered my parents when you betrayed them to Anstey's interrogators. Their souls were long gone before I gave mercy to their remains. Don't you *ever* say that I killed them. And don't come near my home and my family if you want to remain alive. Stay away, or I will kill you, you and your wife both."

He dropped his hold and Thorne slid down the wall with his hands covering his face, whimpering coward that he was. Thomas stood away from him and sheathed his dagger.

"Get going, now." Thorne crept away and he made himself stay still, resisting every urge to draw his sword and run the man through.

It took him a while to calm his feelings, leaning up against the wall until his heart rate recovered. Thank God there was still no-one around; he shouldn't have done that, why had he lost control?

Almost immediately, he made the decision not to upset Kat by giving her a full account of the encounter when he reached home later. Perhaps it would be better not to give too much detail to Robert either. This afternoon's meeting was purely business; by the time he and Robert were back at the house for a shared meal, he would have calmed down completely. He would just say, really casually, that Thorne had been seen around. Remembering her mother, Kat might not think that it had been a good idea to threaten the man. She would say better to kill than to threaten. As long as he warned her that Thorne had been lurking. Thorne wouldn't dare return anyway; the man was a devious coward. But he had been stupid. What was new?

*

Bess and I were shopping while my father stayed at home with Lissy. He enjoyed spending time with both of his grandchildren and they each helped him, in their different ways, to live without my mother. Thomas was meeting with Robert and Margery and would be bringing one or both of them back to our home for the midday meal.

Our routines were well settled after nearly two years in our new home. Visiting the cave with Thomas last year had helped a lot. It wasn't always quite that amazingly good, and there were still occasional nightmares, but it was near enough for me and for Thomas.

There had been that recent glitch with rescuing Stephen, but my killing of the would-be robber and murderer hadn't made Thomas draw back from me. And our sex life continued, uninterrupted. If I thought about the incident, I even felt guilty for not feeling more guilty. But to be perfectly honest and truthful the only thing that would make me regret such a killing would be if it was accidental and unprovoked or if it damaged my relationship with my husband. As far as the whole episode went, all I hoped was that Stephen and Thom were safely back with Alice, and that she could soon spare the time to visit us herself. There was no way I could bring myself to arrange for us to go back to the complex, which would be necessary if I was to visit her … and I missed her.

Bess was in a bouncing mood on our shopping trip, more like a child at that moment (we suspected she was around twelve or thirteen years, but, like most young people, she veered between child and adult on a daily basis). I would have had to have been careful, if not for the rain, to ensure that she kept out of bright sunlight – with her ruff carefully hiding the markings which were strengthening and beginning to offer compelling evidence of her mixed human/Domum-Orbis heritage. I wondered if we would ever learn which of the enforcers, living or dead, had impregnated her human mother. I guessed, post-Anstey, that no-one would particularly care. Few of the enforcers were or had been worthy of being claimed as a father and Bess seemed blithely unconcerned, though I wasn't altogether sure I really knew the fullest extent of her thoughts and feelings. Sometimes, like today, she was a child, sometimes she wasn't. She had suffered a very adult trauma in her young life, one that should never have happened to anyone, let alone a child. It had left her a very private person. For the moment it was good enough to know that she loved, trusted, worshipped Thomas. He was more than sufficient father for her, and he, in turn, adored his two girls equally – the one of his heart and the other of his flesh and, at long last, his heart too.

Food was not plentiful in the market. I could hear the grumbles, the sullenness in minds that were learning to tighten their belts more than a little. It was the rain, the relentless crop-destroying rain. If we didn't have fish – we would all have gills before long – who knew what our diets would consist of. I was thankful that we were near enough to the sea for the fish to be transported safely. We were also fortunate to be given some of the synthesized protein from the complex. (I had never imagined using the word 'fortunate' in the same breath as 'synthesized protein' but food shortages created new perspectives on acceptable nourishment.) Any visitors from the complex, collecting our earnings, brought some with them, knowing the problems outside. Adding a vinegar, juniper seed and salt mix to it made it taste a little like real stored meat and meant that we were not taking food out of the mouths of the local population who had nothing else. We had begun to feel ourselves to be a genuine part of the community: we felt their joys and ills acutely, and the guilt that came with being in a more fortunate position, hiding a secret they couldn't know. I tried to repress a worrying thought: I could easily imagine the catastrophic way in which the complex could be overrun if its existence were to become known. We had decided to rescue those humans we had harmed, the ones who had encountered our population in Anstey's day. On the odd occasion we offered sanctuary to someone in sore need. But more than that we couldn't achieve, and an acute awareness of the unrelieved suffering around us sometimes felt oppressive. I still regretted we had done nothing for the robber's boy. His age wouldn't protect him if he was caught.

Anyway, guilt aside, Bess and I had enough in the basket to feed our visitors when combined with the store cupboard at home. We were soaked through, cold and shivering. As we walked back down the street, a preacher on the corner was warning the crowds that the rain was a visitation on the sinful people living there. A latter-day Noah? I wondered if he could be right; certainly, a lot of people were listening avidly to his words. But I was equally certain that I disagreed with his definitions of sin. Anstey and his guards were the personification of sin to me. Not the whores, the strumpets the preacher was ranting against, women who would starve without the income their 'sins' brought in (though I guessed that, for the majority of them, most of it went to the men who hired them out). Nor could I see the sin in such kind and loving men as our friends Robert and James, the so-called 'sodomites' being castigated by a joyless, loveless 'man of God.'

I wondered, with a grim smile, what the preacher would have made of the things I had done to try to heal Thomas's heart and body sufficiently for our loving closeness to return. And what I did now to prevent another pregnancy. It had helped knowing what had caused Thomas's nightmares and the baby steps I had taken to give him peace of mind without ever revealing that I knew what Anstey and his men, in their drug-fuelled depravity, had done to his body.

We, all of us, Thomas's family and friends, tried to remind him of the times he had saved us from some ill or other, but I was the one who held the key because of his fears for me. His regret at his own helplessness when Anstey and the worst of the guards had held him prisoner and he'd been unable to get free to warn me still lurked in his mind. Thomas had such tangled thoughts, even now that he was able to make love to me. Why couldn't he just be happy that all the worst things he'd feared for me hadn't come about? Why did he dwell on what could have happened rather than what did happen? He knew that my mind was powerful. Why not just accept the fact that, with the help of our friends, I had managed to overcome Anstey's cruel plans for me? After all, I wouldn't have been alive without the drugs Thomas had managed to obtain and he would never have been captured if he had not given his freedom to ensure Stephen was able to get away from the enforcers and bring me what I needed.

Bess held tightly to my hand as we splashed through the puddles on our way back, cloaks soaking. Her mood had changed and all at once she was the 'adult' child, if ever there was one, concerned to know what I might be thinking. She knew when I was lost in thoughts and plans, never demanding my attention for herself, yet always loving discussing the stories she'd read with me. Thomas and I were by now convinced that she was at least partly empathic, like Alice. A child who understood the need, sometimes, to be a silent companion.

Back in the house Joan took Bess off to get dry, leaving me to change out of my soaking garments and warm myself by the fire she had lit for me in the bedroom. She was so good to me – my former maid and now my friend – travelling with my father to Barnstable for a short visit and to help me with the children while I worked in the business alongside Thomas. Fortunately, a cook also came in daily. Cooking was another skill I was less than perfect at. Thomas preferred me to work alongside him or kindly pretended he did.

Anstey had set the Thornes up as cloth merchants and we were continuing their trade. That wasn't all good news, but while the war with Spain had adversely affected our income, we were still producing a small profit from our sales to friendlier parts of the globe, including Iyreland and the New World. To be fair to the Thornes, they had set the business up well. Not that I ever felt the slightest inclination to be fair to the Thornes, after what they'd done. Dead Thornes would be good Thornes. I liked the thought of dead Thornes. For ourselves, we had been fortunate in shipping and had lost no cargoes to the pirates … so far. Others had not been so lucky.

Thomas was home not long after me. Rushing into the room to hug and kiss me, he let me know Robert had arrived and that the meal would soon be prepared. It was nice to have different guests — exiles, humans, and those, like Bess and me, who were a part of both worlds — regularly gathering around a meal table.

"I tried to persuade Joan to join us. But she says she's already eaten with Lissy. Margery couldn't come, she has a meeting, though she said she would call in this evening, or perhaps tomorrow. Robert has something he wants to discuss, and he's hoping your father and I might be able to help."

"Sounds intriguing. Do you know what it's about?"

I had the feeling Thomas didn't want to say.

"I have an idea. But I'll let him explain for himself."

There was something else he was reluctant to share with me as well. He hesitated for a moment and looked anxiously at me. Then he sighed and holding me firmly admitted: "I don't want to worry you, but you should be on your guard. I saw Thorne today. He scuttled away when he realised that I'd spotted him. It seemed to me that he was watching the house. Margery has promised she will keep an eye open. That's one of the reasons she might come over later."

A shadow crept over my soul and I shuddered, hoping it was just chance, though I hadn't thought that the Thornes would want to remain in the area. We were just beginning to feel permanently settled and breaking free from the bad memories. I was angry to think that they might turn up again and threaten our new-found peace and stability. Thorne had got off lightly with forfeiture of his property and I hoped he had no plans to try to take it back from us. He'd drugged and raped my mother. Pretending that Anstey had compelled him to do it had eased his punishment, but I was certain that wasn't true. Everything he had done had simply been for gain, I was sure of it. He should be languishing in some cell, or dead, not walking the streets of Barnstable as a free man.

Also, I wasn't sure if Thomas was telling me the whole story. Marriage had allowed me to develop something of a sixth sense when it came to things Thomas didn't want to share with me. Not saying that he was lying, exactly, just that there was more to it than he had admitted.

He kissed me again, longer and slower. "Don't worry, I won't let them hurt us, I promise. I won't let you down this time."

I felt the tears prick my eyes, but managed to say, in as unemotional voice as I could manage. "You never let me down, ever."

"Oh, but I do sweetness, I never mean to, but I do it all the time."

Thomas held me close as he said the words in my head, then, abruptly, he whirled me around and let me go.

"Come, wife, our guest is waiting. Your father is keeping him entertained, but the food is ready." His voice was teasing, but he always had to have the last word if that word was something disparaging about himself. He grabbed my hand, and we hurried to join the others before I could say anything further.

*

Later in the afternoon, when we were all replete, Robert came to the point of his visit. He took a swallow of wine, as if he wasn't quite sure if he should be voicing his request.

"I won't pretend that this isn't something that I'm asking for myself … for James and for me. But it affects others too. Ever since there started to be some mingling of humans and exiles, this was something that was bound to come up at some point. A mix of the two species wanting to be together. I know you, William, and your Elizabeth, were content to be married in a human church, but some of us can't go down that route, could never," he closed his eyes and I saw him quail at the thought of what would happen to James and to him if they were ever exposed as lovers. "And some, like Megs and Anthony, would prefer the more intimate experience of hand-fasting rather than a human marriage."

My father looked at Robert and nodded agreement.

"As a human, I understand how you all feel. Elizabeth and I were incredibly close, but, even then, I always envied that she knew what I was thinking directly, and I never knew her thoughts in the same way. There was always a part of her that was never totally shared, never wholly mine."

I had never thought about my parents' relationship in that way. It was a curious feeling and explained the hint of an imbalance that I had always sensed between them. Even on that final journey, when the assassin had come after us, she was still keeping secrets from him. Always for what she considered to be his own good. But I couldn't help thinking that Thomas did that to me too. Hand-fasting didn't solve everything. True, though, it was harder for him, because of my access to his mind, but, even with that, there was a lot that could be guarded and kept hidden outside formal mind-sharing. With a jolt I remembered our lost baby – it was me as well as Thomas. I had kept knowledge of my pregnancy from him. I was as bad as he was. It was no wonder that the mind-sharing part of the hand-fast was so greatly revered – otherwise we were a secretive lot.

Robert twisted his hands together, uncharacteristically awkward for the moment. "Thank you, William, I really appreciate your understanding."

He turned to Thomas, "James thought … I mean, we know, that William let you share his mind … Is there any way at all we might achieve a proper handfasting, with the mind-sharing too?"

Thomas and my father looked at each other. It was obvious they were remembering that moment in the cave, and how much it had meant for Thomas to see his parents, brought to life in my father's mind, that one last time.

"Sharing a willing human mind is not a problem. I didn't hurt you, did I William?"

"No, not at all, I was scarcely aware of you, only a compulsion to reach back to that specific time and day in my mind. I couldn't have hidden anything from you. You channelled my mind in some way."

"No drugs were needed," Thomas said slowly. "The problem is the other way around, I have no idea if *that's* possible. Does James have any idea what formula the chemists use to produce the sanctuary drugs?"

"It's not really James's area, so I don't think so. The laboratories have always supplied them to him, already created. It's an incredibly ancient Domum-Orbis formula, they seem to have had tailored drugs for anything and everything, that's all he and I know."

"I suppose it's theoretically possible. It's the action of the drug that opens the Domum-Orbis mind and makes it impossible for the subject to shut down and hide their thoughts or show the mind-sharer anything but the absolute truth." Thomas was thoughtful, interested, sipping his wine with his eyes half-closed, immersed in the problem.

The conversation was leading somewhere I didn't want it to go. I shrank back from it. Any moment now Thomas would feel impelled to offer to return to the complex and help to analyse the drug, assess how it might be adjusted to enable the humans to share our minds. I did know how wonderful it would be if they could experience what Thomas and I had shared. But no, please no, I didn't want Thomas returning to that place, ever. He was so much better than he had been. He deserved to be better. The nightmares were more and more rare, how could anyone ask him to return to hell?

I had closed my ears as the thoughts ran riot in my head, but when I reluctantly re-focused on the room I heard words I dreaded:

"If Kat could manage without me for a few days, William and I could ride back with you in the early morning and have a look at the formulation as soon as we get there. At least we would be able to see how it works and possibly make some recommendations. I gather some preliminary work is going on already with the willing co-operation of some of the human and Domum-Orbis couples on site, and William can talk us all through his own experience as well."

Oh no, please no. Don't do it. I couldn't say the words, either aloud or in his mind. How could I stop him from being Thomas? Always so eager to help his friends. Desperate to be useful to them – to make a difference. I knew that he was often filled with guilt because he placed his need for me above the needs of all of those that he had sworn to take care of. He was looking over at me, concern on his face.

"You will be back by Monday, won't you?" I managed to say.

"I promise, Kat," Thomas held my gaze anxiously. "It would be so good if we could help."

"Yes, of course, I'm happy you can assist." Such a lie. "Just hurry home though, Lissy and Bess don't like to be without you for long. And you did say the Thornes were about."

"*And I shall miss you.*" I couldn't help adding in his mind.

Robert had always been a good friend; he had risked his life for Thomas and me when we'd needed him, but I truly believed I hated him at that moment. Hopefully I gave nothing away in my face. I couldn't help but be conscious of all he had done to help my father and mother as well – long before he had even met James. I was relieved when he left, promising to return early the next day. All his talk was of the complex and his concerns about the way things were going there. Thomas was listening and worrying. He said little but I could see it in his face.

Later that evening, I hid my fears and sadly helped Thomas pack up a few things so that he could be away at first light. In bed we nestled together, but neither of us had the heart for more. I knew that if I really begged him, Thomas wouldn't go – but he wouldn't know why I was doing it. He would suspect that I was being selfish and he would forgive me anyway. God protect him. His own welfare was always his very last thought. Any conflict in his mind was always between the different groups whose well-being he had taken to heart and vowed to protect.

At the last minute, Bess, who rarely asked for anything, agitated to go along as well. I have to confess that it was after I had hinted to her – quietly, mind-to-mind, she always kept open to me – that her father would be so much better with her company. Bess always picked up hints without requiring long explanations and she, beyond all, was aware of what he had suffered in the complex. She had been there to comfort him when I had not.

The party grew larger. Although Bess was probably nearly thirteen, Joan bravely offered to ride with her, despite knowing that they would be riding hard and without a break. They should both be fine, and, never having suffered there, Joan was always intrigued by a visit to the complex. I don't think that Thomas was altogether comfortable at the thought that it would leave Lissy and me entirely alone, but Bess had always had to share Thomas with her sister, and I lied – perhaps not altogether a lie – telling him it would be a treat for her to have him to herself. I was ashamed at how willing I was to use our daughters when it came to protecting Thomas. Did that make me a bad mother? Perhaps not, since his well-being was so central to their happiness too. But it did make me understand Thomas a little better. When the welfare of those you loved could be in competition, how did you choose?

Thomas hugged me tightly, apologetically, and I clung to the warm strength of his body against me. Not quite so thin now.

"I'm sorry Kat. I hate to be away from you and Lissy, but this will mean such a lot to Robert and James, and to any other mixed couples who want to share what we've been lucky enough to experience. You know how much better I am. I'm strong enough, you've done that for me, I'll survive a night or two in the complex, no problem."

He looked as if he guessed how unhappy I was but misunderstood the reason.

"*You* won't have to go to the complex, I promise. Margery will be here later as she didn't make it last evening – I'm sure she'd stay over if you would rather not be alone. Insist that she does."

I was trapped by my own subterfuge. Thomas thought we'd come here for me. He had no idea that it had all been part of a plot to get *him* free of the complex. Trying hard not to cry, I hugged him close, reluctant to let go.

"Lissy and I will be fine, there's no need for Margery to stay, unless she wants to. I'm not such a fragile flower. Come back safely, come back by Monday. Don't leave us here by ourselves for too long."

"It's only a few days, I'll be thinking of you all the time I'm away. I won't let you down, you have my word. Do as I ask, please: persuade Margery to keep you company, don't forget. You may think you don't need her, but I'll feel much better if she's here with you – it won't matter to her, she could easily stay over until I'm back. Make sure that you ask her."

I flung my arms round him again and we clung together in our desperately fragile little universe before he kissed my hair and gently disengaged my hold.

"Quicker I go, quicker I'm back." He grabbed my hand. "Come with me to say goodbye to Lissy. I'll be home by evening on Monday – you won't even miss me."

My father was equally reluctant to leave me and his granddaughter but added to Thomas's assurances that they would be back quickly. Like Thomas he tried to persuade me that I must have Margery to stay over, but I didn't want to – so I said nothing and made no promises. Margery had her own life, and this was all making me feel like some incompetent dependent with no resources of my own. Why did everyone forget that I was the powerful one of this partnership? All I wanted was for Thomas not to be damaged by having to return to the scene of his torture. I hugged my father.

"Take care of Thomas," I whispered in his ear.

Chapter 8

They accomplished the ride in reasonable time, with a brief overnight stop on the way, despite the relentless rain and the surface water turning the dirt to thick mud on the most-frequented routes. Keeping to the rockier by-ways helped, but they were all soaked through by the time they reached the complex.

Thomas tried to keep his thoughts away from the courtyard as they dismounted in the stable block and handed care of the horses over to one of the human workers who had stayed on as stable-hands after Anstey's departure. He had always appreciated the men remaining – even though he knew that it had much to do with the fact that the wages were good. They shared the hiding of the secret willingly rather than keeping quiet from fear as they had before. But they still knew their jobs would be gone, and their minds wiped, if they ever betrayed their employers. He could always sense that in their thoughts. In their shoes, and given a choice, he would not have stayed, not for all the money in the world. Even today, despite having the others around him, he was aghast at the wave of misery that washed through him. He felt as if he was struggling to breathe properly. He could almost see the men, hear their laughter. So much for thinking that such feelings were safely locked away in the past. Looking over at Bess, he hoped she was not affected too. Should he have let her come with him? But she and William were chatting and laughing over something. She loved her 'grandfather.' And she was so much braver and more resilient than he was.

Trying to focus on the friends around him and the present moment, it was a relief to see James hurrying out from the manor entrance to greet them. But he was taken aback to notice that his friend looked surprised. Or was it just that he was expecting only Thomas and William? No, it wasn't just that. Thomas heard Robert explaining, as he rushed to hug James.

"Thomas and William offered to come back with me to see if they can help us with the mind-sharing problem."

Puzzling … it sounded as if James hadn't wanted Robert to ask for his help. For a moment he couldn't think why. He'd assumed that the request was from both of them. Wondering if Alice had persuaded James not to try to bring him back, he remembered that James had once offered to talk to him about his ordeal. He wasn't sure how he felt about the idea of Alice and James discussing him and his problems. Behind his back. Why would he want to share his feelings with anyone, except that once with Alice?

That must be it; James knew way, way too much about him thanks to Alice. He frowned; he didn't like the thought that James wouldn't have turned to him so easily as Robert had done. He saw James looking back guiltily. Then Alice was there, following James out, and she was clearly less than pleased to see them.

"They're only staying overnight and tomorrow," Robert said quickly. He seemed anxious as he looked at his lover, who had moved away from him as soon as Alice arrived on the scene. She frowned at Robert, it was almost a glare, and turned to look directly at him.

"I'm surprised you've left Kat and Lissy on their own." Alice sounded cross as she noted who was in the party.

Hiding his guilt as the comment hit home, he strove to justify himself.

"It's only a few days. It's not as if I'm moving back in here. Margery is hoping to call in each evening and I've told Kat to ask her to stay. I'll be home with them before they even miss me, I've promised. The sooner I can analyse the mind-sharing drug, the sooner we might have some answer to these issues with extending the hand-fasting ceremony."

"I know it's important, but even so … Did you know there's been some experimental interaction between humans and exiles already? Not always with good results." Alice didn't expand on that rather terse comment and for some reason he didn't want to probe. "But I'm still concerned with Kat's welfare," she looked him in the eyes, "and yours."

He avoided her pointed gaze. "Let's get inside, it's wet and we're tired and hungry. We're here now, let's get this done and then we can leave for home by tomorrow afternoon at the latest."

They hurried down into the complex. An icy feeling constricted his chest, there was no escaping from it, but he resolved to be away from there by the morrow. Perhaps if he worked through the night and ate as he worked, he could try to leave before midday.

Outside, the weather had showed no sign of improving, and he was beginning to worry that the road home might become impassable. Facing the fact that he regretted rushing impulsively into this visit, he was still torn, as always, by the conflicting desire to help his old friends. There had to be at least some point, some value to his existence for the others who had stuck by him through everything, and he was truthfully eager for those in mixed pairings to experience something so life-changing as the hand-fasting ceremony. But there was another side to the coin. He didn't want anything he did for them to be at Kat's expense. He'd made that mistake before, almost disastrously; it had nearly cost him his marriage. But the others he cared for, both human and from his home-world, they all deserved the happiness that bonding could bring. It had begun to seem to him that love and family were the only things worth living for. It would be so good for others to know that such mixed partnerships could make sense of their exile and draw their two worlds together. But in his deepest thoughts he yearned to be gone from this place. "Oh Kat, I wish… how I wish I could be home with you right now."

Alice was at his elbow, dragging him into the here and now and distracting him from his depressing reflections. She was insisting that he should work in the infirmary, and seemed disturbed by his abstraction, his lack of response. He agreed to avoid her keeping on about it – not really caring one way or the other where he ended up working. It seemed as good a plan as any. The laboratory there was by far the best equipped for the kind of analysis he had planned and she offered to get him something to wear so that she could ensure his clothes were cleaned and dried in the laundry for him before the next day.

"I'll fetch you something to eat in a while. Let me get your family sorted out first. Nobody else seems to do anything in this place if isn't in their job description. I'm sure James will see to Robert. Would you like me to arrange a room for you?"

The thought of sleeping in the complex was completely repugnant to him. He felt sick at the thought.

"Thanks Alice, but no to the room. I'm getting worried about the weather – I've never seen anything so heavy and persistent as this rain and the rivers are too swollen to hold much more. I'm inclined to work through the night as soon as James brings me the drug to analyse. It would be better to set off for home earlier in the day tomorrow, even if I have to return for some of the results in a week or so. So no, I won't need a room; I don't intend to waste time sleeping."

"You need to sleep; you've ridden all day without a break. You'll be doing the same on the way back."

He felt annoyed. How dare she scold him when she knew how it was for him?

"Do you imagine I *ever* sleep here? Unless you count hours of fucking nightmares." He rounded on her bitterly for a moment and immediately regretted it. Aghast that he could have spoken like that to Alice of all people, he didn't miss her slight recoil from him and her tone, as she answered, was cold.

"I'll leave you to get settled in."

"No, please don't go, I'm sorry Alice. I didn't mean to snap at you. I apologise for swearing. This place brings out the very worst in me. You didn't deserve any of that. I know you're only trying to help."

To his relief, Alice straight way put her arms round him, hugging him. "I'm not offended, I promise, I know how bad it is. Robert shouldn't have brought you back though. James is angry with him too."

He made himself respond and hug her back, but he could feel that the baleful effect of the complex had already made him withdraw from the warmth of friendly contact. Practical help would be useful though.

"Is Stephen free at all? I wouldn't say no to some help."

They were good at working together, and Thomas was keen to see how Stephen and Thom were faring after their unfortunate encounter. Keeping his promise, he couldn't ask Alice. As far as the work went, he was optimistic that Stephen would be keen to be involved, but Alice frowned. She looked upset ... unlike Alice.

"No, he's still away. The project he was working on finished; there was no need for him to come back. You remember he and Thom went back to our outside home – didn't he come to stay with you on the way? Well he hasn't returned – he's had enough of being here, and I can't get away at present. Perhaps I'll follow him in a while."

Alice's tone didn't invite query. Thomas looked at her in surprise, but kept his mouth shut, holding back from asking the questions such a bald statement demanded. It was unlike anything he'd ever heard Alice say about her family before. And the tone … he decided she must be missing her husband and changed the subject.

"I'll use the infirmary shower then, if I may, and get ready to work as soon as James brings the drug over."

It felt good to be warm and dry at least. He idly wondered if he could invent a shower that would work in the outside world. It was getting to be something of a fixation for him. He smiled, thinking again of him and Kat in the shower, the first she'd ever experienced, and their lovemaking under the gushing hot water. There were some happy memories associated with the complex. He shivered pleasurably at the thought. Why couldn't he dream of those? But he knew he wouldn't. If he could only avoid sleeping, Thomas was sure he'd survive such a short visit without any problem.

James came in while he was getting dressed and sat down.

"Here, I've brought you the drug to work on. I see Alice has given you dry things. That rain is something!"

"I've everything I need now; I'm intending to work through the night and get away as early as possible tomorrow."

"I'm sorry you were dragged back here; Robert had no right to ask you. Not after …"

"Don't feel badly, don't, on any account, be angry with Robert either. I volunteered, I truly did. I want to do what I can for you, and for Megs and her boy. Have you talked with William?"

"Yes, he's already been really helpful. He wants to do whatever he can for us too. Some of the other humans here, mainly your young women, have already been working with willing exiles over the last couple of months."

James stopped and looked at him with something approaching awe and envy. "I wish Robert had known Henry. It would be such a gift, the chance to get back before the moment of his death. It's all I see of Henry now, in my mind. What William did for you, back in the cave, that must have been such an experience."

He was quiet for a moment, thinking back to that cathartic instant of certainty which William's memory had freely given him. The final proof that his parents hadn't betrayed him, that they really had always meant to come back, that they hadn't just said it because they'd been captured.

"One of the most important of my life," he said, quietly, as he put the phial of drug that James had brought for him down carefully. "Important for you and the others too. Our parents, they did always mean to return. It helps to know that ... to finally see Anstey's lies for what they were."

He became brisk once more. "Now, let me get on with my work. I want to be done and back with Kat. Oh, and promise you'll forgive Robert. He loves you, don't punish him for that. No-one deserves to be punished for that."

James stood up, ready to leave, but looking anxious. "It isn't only the drug. Robert also wanted you to see first-hand how things are changing here. The newly elected council. I don't want you to destroy yourself by coming back, but your absence, Margery's absence, William's absence ... Cecily and Edward – who always kept Anne's traditionalism in check – they won't come back either. Even Stephen is gone for the moment. I'm afraid there may be something wrong between him and Alice, though I can't imagine how that could be, not those two."

Thomas looked at him in consternation. "But I can't do anything.

I can't bring Kat back here. And I would lose my reason, such as it is, entirely. I can't even sleep here." He shuddered in utter panic at the thought.

"I know, I know, I'm sorry, I'm not asking. I would never … all I wondered was whether you had any ideas. Perhaps you might be able to persuade some of the others to base themselves here. Cecily and Edward maybe? If you talked to them. I think it's Edward who's determined not to return. Although Cecily doesn't have a good relationship with Anne." James sat down again and looked pleadingly at him.

"You really wouldn't believe how many of Anstey's old friends have places on the council now. Even his former secretary – you remember that pompous, fucking toad. There was never any direct evidence against them, Anstey's 'yes' men. They weren't involved in his excesses, only in the letter of law as it was expressed in the contracts and Domum-Orbis traditions. I'm so afraid that if Anstey should turn out to have survived, he might manage to return to the complex. If that were to happen, he would find that there are those – more than a few – who would support him, despite the judgements against him. And then we would have the banished enforcers pardoned and returning, the fucking bastards that nearly killed you. It would all have been a waste of lives and time. Henry would have died in vain, John too, your own wife's mother."

Thomas closed his eyes tightly. Thinking about returning. He couldn't do it to Kat, and he feared it would destroy him altogether – at some point the cliffs would beckon to him and he would not have the strength to resist. But there was duty too – always, *always* at war with his love.

"I'll talk to Kat, see if we can persuade some of the others to spread a new message, understand the effect of their absence."

"Be very careful – if anything were to happen, I would find it hard to forgive Robert for dragging you back here. You're a hero to many, but he knows there are those who whisper against you and Kat. You did know that Edith and Hugh returned a year or so ago, didn't you? Around the time you left, or just before. She hasn't changed. Even after everything you went through there are voices who say that you and Kat led a rebellion just so you could get to fuck her. They say, albeit in whispers, that what happened to you and to the humans was exaggerated. Gossip is powerful. It's only a few covert voices, but they come from people who are gaining positions of actual power. I've never understood the war on our home world before now. These days I'm beginning to see, horribly clearly, how it could have happened."

Chapter 9

Halfway through the morning Thomas was near to completion. He tried to stay fully focussed, despite James's words echoing in his head. One more result to get in. In preparation he changed back into his outside clothing, thankfully dry, and started to gather his things together while he was waiting. The ache of being away from Kat made him decide to go on ahead of the others, even though it would mean travelling overnight, and might disappoint Bess. At least the rest of the family could then travel together at a more leisurely pace. Bess and Joan, even William, had looked tired when they arrived – maybe they could stay an extra day or two, even a week, wait for the weather to improve.

Alice raced into the room.

"Quick Thomas! – the library, I need to show you something, right now."

Scared by her frantic demeanour, he didn't ask questions, leaving everything, and following her in a breakneck dash for the library. They weren't even halfway there when a wailing siren filled the air, something Thomas couldn't remember hearing in his entire life.

"Floods!" Alice managed to gasp out. "Run! The doors are shutting down. You won't get out to get back to Kat unless we can reach the library exit in time."

"Why not the main exit?" he queried breathlessly as they pelted down the corridors.

"Impossible, everyone's surging in that way. I don't know what Anne does with the hidden exit, but no-one else knows that way out – I can only think she must close it herself to keep the secret."

The library seemed deserted as they entered, then he saw Anne standing by an open panel at the far end of the room.

"Wait, wait! Anne! Thomas has to get out, to get back to Kat." Alice was yelling as she ran.

"Too late, he'll just have to wait until the all clear is given."

"He can't, he has to get to her now. I've been reading future accounts of this – look the book is still out on the table where I left it. Barnstable is hit as badly as the valley below us. Kat and Lissy are in the house alone and half the town will be virtually washed away."

Thomas listened in horror as they hurtled toward Anne.

"Let me out, Anne! For the love of God! I have to get to my family."

Anne remained stony. Thomas was reminded of two things in that split second. His six-year-old self encountering her implacable insistence that it was his duty, and no-one else's, to end his parents' lives and that niggling suspicion that she didn't like Kat, at all, however much she pretended to get on with her.

"I'm sorry Thomas, it's my duty. It's always been against the law of the complex to leave any manual flood door open when the automatic doors seal. As soon as the siren goes, *no-one* is allowed to leave, no exceptions, and the flood doors remain closed until the danger has passed. Kat and your daughter will have to take their chances; perhaps you shouldn't have left them." Her face looked somehow smug.

He watched in disbelief as he saw Anne give another twist to the hydraulic wheel that she was operating and felt a white-hot rage shoot through him. He didn't give a fuck what she said or what the consequences might be. His dagger was out and at her throat before he was even aware of what he intended.

Dragging Anne forcibly away from the wheel, he yelled to Alice to open the flood door again.

"Open it, or I'll cut Anne's throat and do it myself."

He knew Alice would willingly have done it without the threat, but Thomas hoped she could guess that he was protecting her position – making sure Anne didn't believe her to be his accomplice. Not that he thought he could have brought himself to murder Anne, however distraught he was. But there was no need – Alice was already racing to work on reversing the wheel.

The minutes were ticking past and the door was agonizingly slow to re-open. He was afraid someone would reach them and overpower him. Never in his life had he hit a woman, but he hit Anne at that moment. As she fell to the floor, he grabbed the handle from Alice.

"I'll do it, I'm stronger."

The feeling of slow motion persisted, but finally, creaking and groaning, the door re-opened.

"Go!" Alice urged. "I'll get help with closing this, not that there's any rush here, and see to Anne."

He was gone in seconds, racing up the steps, running into the manor. It was deserted. He registered thankfully that everyone must already have descended into the underground chambers through the main doors. No-one to stop him or chase after him for what he had done to Anne. For once he had no time spare to worry about crossing the courtyard. He was in the stables before he even noticed where he was, and in another few minutes, he was saddling up, possibly the fastest a horse had ever been saddled in the history of the complex. It did occur to him, as he rode out, that the cliff-top exits would have been fine left open. It was only a precaution anywhere other than at sea-level. At any point where the complex opened out into the manor there was no risk at all – something Anne could easily have worked out for herself. And no-one but Anne and the few who had used it as an escape route, just that once, even knew the exit was there.

On the cliff-top he stopped for one horrified moment. The village below, everything, was gone. The valley was all raging water. Uprooted trees, bits of building, boulders were being flung into the air as if they were mere twigs and stones – trapped between the spate and the surge from the sea. Such total and utterly unbelievable devastation. In an ironic twist the afternoon sun was shining weakly and the rain had stopped. Thomas trembled at the ferocity of such a force of nature – it was far too late to save the lives and livelihood of anyone who had been caught down there when sea and river had come together with such force.

He didn't stop to watch any longer. Sick with fear, he rode like a man possessed. Constantly forced to change routes, his horse stumbling as darkness fell, Thomas was close to despair as impassable areas of flooding continually blocked his way. At night it was difficult to distinguish between water and track. He avoided the lower routes, knowing he had to approach Barnstable from the far side of the main river, guessing his only chance of doing so would be well above the town. But it all increased journey time. At first his luck held, starting down from higher ground on the Bedyford side he was at least on the town side of the surging, murderous river. Then, at first light, he was above what should be the town.

"Oh God, no, please … is this the town? it can't be." His heart plummeted, Barnstable was indistinguishable from the sea, just acre upon acre of water. Even from this distance in the miserable, wet grey dawn he could see that there was no bridge anymore – or else it was somewhere submerged – and all manner of massive debris, feverishly fast, was being swept out into the estuary and beyond. Thank God he hadn't come from that direction.

For the final part of the ride Thomas slowed down. The adrenaline had run its course now that he could see that the flood had beaten him to it and his horse was exhausted – he couldn't imagine how many extra miles they had travelled, all without rest; instead he was frantically trying to map the Barnstable he knew onto the featureless body of sea and river that confronted him. The watery sunshine, which was now trying to break through, exposed the soul-destroying scene. Being so much closer, he could see the tops of some of the buildings, especially churches, poking above the surface of the flood. There were people clinging to the odd rooftop on an occasional building that somehow had remained standing. Faint wails of human despair mixed with the inhuman roar of water. When his panic subsided enough for him to focus, he could see people with boats, staying in areas where the flood was shallower and slower moving, attempting rescues. He resolved to steal one, but as he approached, he was aware of a camaraderie among the humans that it would have been wrong to disrupt. A desire felt by many to help each other. There was such shock in so many minds – a wall of water had come in from the sea meeting the surge of the swollen river with catastrophic results. So many people searching in hope and fear for lost loved ones. While Thomas had no doubt that there were plenty who would only act selfishly, or take some advantage of the disaster, he was equally certain that there were countless others who would assist anyone in danger. How could he steal a boat from those who were on a similar mission to his own?

He was ready to leave his horse untethered, not wishing to leave the beast trapped if the waters rose further, when he spotted a man struggling to draw his boat out of the water with a woman and baby still inside. The man's face was familiar – a neighbour perhaps?

"Do you need help? And a horse?"

"Please friend. I know you, don't I? The Albans. Have you brought your wife and child out safely yet? How come you don't need the horse?"

Thomas risked the tether for the time it would take to help with the boat and went to aid the man, whose name he was struggling to recall. Kat was so much better at that, but he listened to the man's thoughts for some clue. Ah, he was Philip; Thomas saw the name in the wife's head. It was more informal than his address should have been, but now was not the time to worry about such things.

"Philip, isn't it? I'll swap you the mare for your boat. I daren't leave her tied up in case the water rises further and she's trapped. I was away from home. I have to find Katharine and our Lissy; a boat seems the only way."

"That suits me fine. I had the boat off some other man anyway. We're all doing what we can for each other. You're from Boutport Street, near the Inn, aren't you? If so, you need to head for the crooked steeple – that's still standing. But hurry, the water's running incredibly fast, I've never seen anything like it, and your street's very near the river. Nothing can withstand that current – and when it meets the incoming sea it's like a boiling cauldron."

"Where I've come from, further along the coast, everything is totally destroyed – no dwellings left standing. I rode for here like fury. I'm hoping she got out in time, but I have to check."

Philip looked at him with sympathy and Thomas quickly helped him aid the woman and baby from the boat.

"The horse is tired," he confessed. "I rode her cruelly hard, but if you take it slowly, she should be some help. Better than being on foot, at any rate."

"We're heading for Ilfraycombe, so no rush, it's a long, long way round to stay above the flooding, the horse will be a great help. I heard talk that upper Ilfraycombe's stayed pretty dry despite the devastation everywhere else, that's why we're headed in that direction – I hope you find your family safely, perhaps we'll see you there."

"I hope so too. Safe journey to you."

The woman carrying the baby was grateful for the horse, he could sense it from her mind. At least he'd been able to help someone.

He dared not allow himself to fear he was too late. But he had read the man's immediate thoughts and knew Philip was certain there was virtually no chance of him finding Kat and Lissy alive if they had stayed put. Where else could he start to look though? Hopefully Kat had possessed sufficient sense to leave as soon as the water started to rise. Of course, she would be bound to have done so; Kat was anything but stupid. Desperately trying to read any mind that came near him, he hoped to see some picture or mention of them in someone else's thoughts. But nothing.

Waving his thanks to Philip, Thomas had already pushed the boat back out and leapt in before the man had untethered the mare and lifted his wife and baby onto its back.

Chapter 10

It was absolutely no use worrying about Thomas but knowing that I didn't stop me. I tried to tell myself that he would only have one night in the complex if all went well, and he had promised, faithfully, that he would be back by Monday, which wouldn't leave him very long there at all. Most of his time would be spent travelling, and he would have Bess and my father and Joan for company. I felt guilty but pleased that I had encouraged the three to go with him – without him being aware of my influence. Bess had wanted to go with Thomas. She had confided to me, just the once, that any nightmares she suffered were filled with only one man – the man we two had failed to kill. Any dreams she had were forward-looking dreams of vengeance; imagining the man dying in some horrible manner. The worse the better. Much more like me! Such images had diminished over time and were unaffected by place. Bess cared as much about protecting Thomas as I did – I had not needed to coerce her, nor would I have done so. She had understood that I was not afraid of being on my own with Lissy, but that I needed Thomas to think I was, giving him that all important excuse to return swiftly.

Margery turned up the first evening they were away, as promised, and I was happy for the visit, though assuring her that there was absolutely no need for her to worry about me. It didn't take long for me to become aware that she was immensely excited about something.

"I've talked with Robert and James. They understand, I really believe they do. I'm hoping you and Thomas will too. I'm risking everything and joining an expedition against the pirates on Lundye! The Earl of Nottingham has given authority to the Mayor and Alderman here to send ships out to capture pirates and I've volunteered. I've told them I'm Mathias. They believe me, *I* almost believe me! Even with James and Robert I try to stay in character nowadays. It frees me to do the things I want to do. Would you, could you, call me Mathias from now on?"

It took me a moment to adjust. I was conscious of not having seen much of my friend recently – too wrapped up in Thomas and in the baby. Such life-changing decisions, and I, as always, was too preoccupied with my own worries and concerns.

"I'm sorry to be slow, of course I remember that was your intention, but I've been so immersed in my own problems. It's best if you don't ask us, just do it, you don't need our permission. Be yourself, be free. We love you whatever you decide. Tell us what you want us to say or do and I … we'll stick to that. It's your life. Just be careful though, it's hard enough keeping our other-world markings secret, without having more to hide. Especially so on board a boat I imagine. I'm not brave like you, and I never stop worrying about James and Robert too. Perhaps it's because I've lived longer out in this world and seen first-hand that punishments for anything deviating from Church practice are savage. You know James and Robert could be hanged for loving each other? I don't know what they would do to you if you were discovered."

"But it's the best chance I have to fight and that's what I want to do more than anything. I don't care about mere surviving; I want to make a difference. I want to *live*, for however short a time. The markings aren't a problem, my friends think they're tattoos! You must know that I suspect Anstey is still alive and hiding out with the pirates – if we engage with them with local help, we might find out for certain and put an end to the man. How Thomas didn't vote death for the fucking savages who abused those human girls I'll never know. They beat him up pretty badly too, didn't they? I saw him, briefly, when we found you three. He looked like death. If I have a chance to kill Anstey I won't hesitate. I'd rather die doing something than sit at home stagnating as I grow old. Men have all the best fun."

Did she know I had failed everyone at the end? I wasn't sure whether her declaration was a criticism of me. Did I just sit at home? But then I never had the courage or the skill, only a stupid mind I couldn't fully control. But, if you knew Thomas … why would you be surprised at his stubborn stand against putting anyone to death, despite the anger he suffered from? I tried to make Mathias understand.

"You know Thomas. You've known him longer than me. Anstey would always have been the one voting for death, regardless of circumstances, so Thomas would – will – always be the one voting against it." I was guarded, noticing that there was no mention of the sexual abuse Thomas himself had suffered. I kept quiet about that aspect of Thomas's unbelievably heroic determination to avoid revenge killing.

"I was glad he put a sword through the enforcer who allowed John to die and was attacking me!"

"Oh, something like that would always be different in Thomas's eyes. A fair fight. He might even join you in your new venture. Suffice to say he has a horror of cold-blooded judicial penalties. After seeing his parents' minds destroyed, after having to end their half-lives himself … Anstey always pretended he was justified in destroying anyone he hated. He always invoked some law or other."

"My parents suffered the same fate as Thomas's, but Anstey didn't bother to make me watch. And I never understood, then or now –

even though I was only the same age as Thomas at the time – why Anne made him do the final deed. She's so much of an old-school traditionalist."

"Was it not custom? Thomas seemed to think so, and it was mentioned in his parents' last letter."

"From what I've read of our Domum-Orbis in Auriga, I think that the custom was dying out by the time we fled. Even with the rule-book mentality that dominated there. By the time of the war, I'm sure that decisions such as that one would have been made by medical people and carried out in an infirmary. I was given permission to have a final meeting with my mother, and she never asked it of me – or even mentioned it. Anstey or one of his men did the final deed. The grief was bad enough. Asking me to finish her wasn't something I could ever imagine her doing to me – she would *never* have made me responsible in the way Thomas was. More likely with Thomas's parents it was because Anne was granted full access to the Albans before their interrogation and influenced what was said by them. Only Anstey could have given her that access, and we both know how much he would have enjoyed imagining Thomas, with his incredible moral code, suffering over *that* for the rest of his days. I imagine it's what Thomas does, doesn't he?"

I had to agree, beginning to form a much more negative opinion of Anne Gomfrey. Anger even. However, this was not something to be discussed with Thomas. I tried to picture his reaction, whether he would feel better or worse if he thought he had been coerced into the act that perpetually haunted him and had caused him so much pain.

Fortunately, I hadn't yet obeyed Thomas and asked Mathias to stay over, as she – he – then continued on, still enthusing over the chance to attack the pirates.

"About tomorrow, will you be alright if I don't come? There's a meeting to do with our plans to put an end to the Lundye vermin. I promised to be there. We're meeting away from the town, the manor house higher up towards the moors, so that no-one can get wind of our intentions before we're ready to put them into execution. It will make it difficult for me to get back to call in. I think they're expecting us to stay over – a good test, ahead of being on a boat or ship, or whatever it is we end up on. I wish I could grow a cock to piss with, it's always a problem making sure I'm alone. Some of the other men tease about it. I joke and say it's such a small one I'm embarrassed to show it."

I laughed, I couldn't help it, it was so Margery … I mean Mathias. She … he really didn't care what others thought, only caring about things that inhibited the carrying out of any daring plans he might dream of. I decided to go with Mathias and 'he' even in my thoughts. I knew it was what he was asking, and it lowered the risk that I might be the one to give him away. And I knew it filled some deeper need that had always been there for him. I must tell Thomas how important it was; it might be more difficult for him – the loss of a sister and the gaining of another brother – I thought of their early closeness. Thomas would worry. When didn't he?

"Don't worry, I'm completely fine," I reassured Mathias. "He'll be back on Monday. You know how Thomas wraps us up in cotton wool, Lissy and me. I just wanted him to have an excuse to return quickly. I don't think it's good for him being at the complex. It has such a depressing effect on him. But please be careful of yourself. We'd both be devastated if something were to happen to you. You're so much braver than I am. Too brave sometimes."

We were subdued for the rest of the evening, sharing a welcome goblet of wine (well-watered for me, as I had gotten used to drinking it that way when I was feeding Lissy – hard to believe our baby girl was now an advanced three and ate at the family meal table). Then we were reminiscing. Mathias and I, for all the world like two old people, sitting recalling the momentous day when we had ridden into the complex and cheated Anstey and the Thornes of their prey.

A corner had been turned, however. It was now Mathias and not Margery that I bade goodbye to once we were at the door and in sight of the street. Hugging him as I would have hugged her, I was glad I hadn't made him feel guilty about staying away the next day. It was just lucky he'd spoken first. I hoped he would be alright and avoid discovery.

"See if you can do what I failed to manage. Make sure Anstey is dead. And, if you get the chance, get the one that was closest to him and always with him. We need him gone too – for what he did to our Bess. But stay safe yourself and come back to tell us, Thomas, Bess, and me, that they're finally gone."

"I will. Don't forget to lock up at night. Remember the Thornes are about – Thomas did tell you, didn't he?"

I nodded and waved as I turned back from the door, but not before noticing how determined the rain was still and hoping Thomas and Bess were warm and dry somewhere. Perhaps I shouldn't have persuaded Bess to go. But I knew Thomas would do everything to keep her safe, as would my father, and Joan.

Returning from Church on the Sunday, talk amongst our neighbours was all of the rain and the height of the river. It was level with the banks, brimming over in places, no craft could get under the arches of the bridge. Our boots and lower clothing were wet through by the time we reached home, just from the water lying in the streets with nowhere to run off to. Lissy wanted to jump in puddles, holding my hand, and not be carried. Sensing the very real concern in the open minds all around me I began to worry whether we should be preparing to leave. Our house was not in a good position, though it was sturdy and tall. Surely, we could last out any flooding in an upstairs room. I wished I'd paid more attention to books about Barnstable in the Library's Future Earth collection.

I tried to make a game of it with Lissy, not to make her afraid. She helped me light a fire and we dried our boots in front of it. Suggesting we might have to go on an expedition, like Dadde, I let her help me pack a small easily portable bag with essentials, and some food and drink. My mare was stabled nearby (luckily, I had recently – regretfully – sold my pony and bought a sturdier mare for me to share with Lissy) it would only take moments to leave. There was a sign fairly low down on the wall opposite, something to do with the shop there. I resolved we would go if the water in the street reached it and wrote a note for Thomas, telling him of my intentions. All I could do was suggest some landmarks on higher ground where we might meet up if the worst came to the worst.

By early evening the mark had been reached. The wind was howling, the rain worse, if such a thing were possible. Besides, there was an exceptionally high tide due. I had heard that from more than one mind.

We were nearly at the door and free when it smashed open and two figures pushed their way in. I was taken completely by surprise, with Lissy in my arms and the bag strapped on my back. Before I could even register that it was the Thornes, Mistress Thorne had snatched Lissy out of my arms and Mister Thorne had a flintlock pistol primed and pointed at her.

"Back upstairs. We're waiting for your husband. As soon as he arrives you both have some papers to sign. Re-assigning the business back to us. That's if you want your dear little daughter to survive. Please notice neither of us carries a dagger, or anything else you might turn against us like you did when you murdered our son."

I dared do nothing that might endanger Lissy's life. She was crying out aloud but calling for me inside my mind. All I could do was speak to her as soothingly as my heart-stopping panic allowed – without letting them realise how advanced she was and that I could communicate easily and silently with her.

"Don't hurt her! I'll sign anything you wish for. Let me do it straight away and let us leave before the floods get worse. You know there's a really high tide's due in. Please, she's only a child, I'll do anything you want … we need to get away now."

"I want both of you here. The floods won't reach this level." Thorne looked at his wife and my child. "Perhaps we'll keep her." He indicated Lissy with a careless flick of the weapon in his hands. "You did deprive us of our child after all. But that's only if we don't kill her, which we will, if you or your husband attempt anything reckless."

Mistress Thorne said nothing but kept a tight grip on my daughter. Her mind was tight shut against me, I couldn't tell what she was thinking and dared do nothing. His mind felt deranged, like Anstey's, a jumble of hate and ferocity leaking out. He would risk all our lives in the flood before he would give way. I was certain of it. It was going to be a long night, and I couldn't afford to let my guard down … keep talking to Lissy, keep listening for Thomas, though the following afternoon was the earliest I thought he could possibly be with us.

Chapter 11

It was an uncomfortable wait in the dark, particularly listening to the storm raging, and being miserably aware that the flood water must be steadily rising. I was glad that I'd forgotten to bank the fire in our rush to leave; it had burnt low, just glowing embers left, but it gave us a little light. Thorne wouldn't let any of us move away from our seats to check on the actual level. I saw with some satisfaction that Lissy had wet her captor's skirts, but such satisfactions were small when I knew how hungry my little girl was, and how much it had upset her to do it. She prided herself on using the chamber pot. I was dying to piss as well. In the end, I did too and made a joke of our situation, sharing it silently with Lissy, and was rewarded with a small, very shocked smile.

As a grey dawn light began to make some sense of the room, I still found myself unable to see how far the floods had risen in the night since Thorne kept me in a chair well away from a window. He was fearful I might see Thomas arriving and warn him. I both longed for Thomas to arrive, afraid the floods would prevent him, and feared that he would. Perhaps the talk of signing documents was a pretence and Thorne simply intended to kill Thomas when he reached us … Thomas and then Lissy and me. I listened, intently, for any sound of him.

Downstairs, an immense crash shook the whole building. I heard it with terror, guessing it was the force of the high tide, the one everyone was so frightened of, rushing in from the sea. Thorne's wife rose with Lissy still held firmly and went out to look down to the hallway. She returned, looking worried.

"Perhaps we should try to leave," she murmured to her husband. "I can't see much in the dark, but it looks as if a surge of tidal water has smashed through the back and front doors. It's right the way up the stairs. Can we get on the roof here and call for help?"

"No! Go back and sit down. I'm not passing up this chance to get our own property back and punish two murderers. We'll be fine. This is a tall building; the water and any debris will just pass underneath us."

Mistress Thorne didn't look convinced but sat down again. Lissy was crying softly, hiccupping sobs. The flood had already moved so fast that I didn't need to see it, it was up to my ankles now the door to the landing had been opened. I had to do something; we would be washed away before Thomas was likely to get here. Earlier Thorne had gone out onto the landing; I think he'd gone to piss down the stairs. The flood water made any civilised means of relieving oneself impossible. While Thorne was occupied in this manner, he had handed the weapon to his wife, and she hadn't retained such an unwavering aim on Lissy. Our little girl was beginning to show early signs of mind power – her ability to speak inside our heads, Thomas's and mine, was beyond precocious. Maybe she and I, working together. Next time Thorne went out might be our only opportunity. I managed to speak reassuringly and silently to Lissy.

"Good girl, don't let the nasty lady know you're talking to me. Mamma might want you to do something in a while. Be ready for me."

"I'm hungry. Where's Dadde, I want Dadde."

Not quite the response I'd hoped for. But she was only three and at least she was listening and talking.

"Dadde will be here before long and, as soon as we've got rid of the horrid man and woman, we can get food from our bag. Think about helping Mamma push that thing the man's holding away if the man goes out again or if Dadde gets home. We'll have to make sure the nasty man and his wife don't shoot Dadde."

"I hate them! I'll help keep Dadde safe."

Consequently, I thought I was as ready as it was possible to be in such a precarious situation. As it happened events took every one of us by complete surprise. But I was the one alert and waiting.

Thorne was by the window, thankfully with his back to it. His wife was looking with some distaste at Lissy, who had wet her again and, this time, was smiling a self-satisfied smile – sensing my approval. I was surreptitiously checking out the flintlock pistol which seemed to be wavering in Thorne's hand. It looked as if he might be falling asleep. Then there was another massive crash, the whole house shaking with the impact, as the surging water slammed a boat into the window, sending it smashing through the glazing the house was blessed with, demolishing the window frame and cannoning into Thorne – dislodging the weapon from his grasp.

"Now Lissy, the weapon to me."

I focused my mind on the weapon, felt hers join me as she wriggled out of Thorne's wife's arms and onto the floor as it flew to my hands. I held it awkwardly, but with sufficient menace to prevent Thorne making a move on me. At that very second, joy! it was him. Thomas had been lying in the bottom of the boat, prepared for the impact and, avoiding the shattered window and its frame, he leapt out of the boat and flew at Thorne's throat. I felt the urge to shoot Thorne, but it would have been too difficult to avoid Thomas. Besides, Thomas was younger than Thorne, and seemed to be getting the better of it. Mistress Thorne looked as if she would have liked to have taken a hand, but she didn't dare while I had the pistol in mine. I made sure to place myself between her and Lissy, who had crawled through the water to me and was raising herself, hanging on to my dress.

"Dadde's home. He will punish the naughty people. And I wee'ed on her, I'm going to tell him I did!" Her voice in my mind was full of satisfaction.

"Kat, get in the boat with Lissy and keep down low." As he spoke Thomas punched Thorne with such force that the man fell to the floor, seemingly unconscious, and Thomas was able to take the pistol from my shaking hands.

"I'm taking my family in the boat," Thomas addressed Mistress Thorne. "I recommend you climb out onto the roof: I'm sure one of the rescuers will pick you up. There isn't sufficient room in our boat, and quite a few people are waiting to be rescued from rooftops. You won't be alone. I will help you up there if I can lodge the boat on this sill for long enough."

Thorne chose that moment to regain consciousness, if not his wits.

"No! Keep your hands off her. We have no need of anything you can do."

"Fine, suit yourselves. Stay here and hope the water doesn't rise over your heads." Thomas looked at me, and I nodded.

"They *both* threatened us. They *both* threatened to kill Lissy! Let them fend for themselves. It was their free choice to come here and stop us from leaving." I was angry and shaking.

Then Thomas's voice was in my head, calming me.

"I can't promise we'll get away. But we'll all be together. I love you forever, Kat, Lissy."

I bundled Lissy in my cloak, wrapping her for protection against the sharp debris from the shattered window, and put her into the boat together with the pack we had prepared so much earlier. I followed her, gingerly. Thomas, keeping tight hold of the gunwale, gave a fierce shove and another, finally dislodging us and frantically throwing himself into the boat as it broke free and hurtled into the current, bumping hard against the walls of the house as it tried to smash its way past. The last we saw of the Thornes they were sitting up to their waists in the water that had gushed in through the now empty window space and apparently shouting at each other. Their mouths were opening, but I couldn't hear what was said with all the pandemonium around us. I hoped they would drown. I was nothing like my husband. He owned all the forgiveness and kindness in our family. I was the savage.

There were oars in the boat, but it was difficult to do more than try to stave off larger pieces of wreckage – bits of people's furniture, timber from houses, massive branches of trees. Once we saw a cradle, miraculously floating the right way up, Lissy and I reached out our minds for it, but when it came alongside it was empty. I hoped that the baby was already safe somewhere. Thomas was now attempting to use the oars to try to edge us out of the fiercest current and toward shallower water, though it sometimes put us in the path of buildings that were less deeply engulfed in the flood water. He had to remain focused on pushing us away from everything that impeded our passage.

At first, I didn't want to break into his concentration, remaining on guard for anything I might need to divert with my mind. There was no doubt in my head that with the three of us in danger Lissy and I would continue to be able to summon sufficient power to do anything needful – she had picked up on doing this incredibly quickly and together, curiously, we were so much more potent. But the force abated as we drew nearer to the edges of the torrent, and eventually Thomas was able to use the oars properly. I judged it safe by then to sit on the rowers' bench, with Lissy tucked into my arms. Unbelievably she had fallen asleep. I hoped that I hadn't left her too drained by asking her to join with me in helping us escape.

Thomas was smiling across at me, relief on his face as the task became easier. I smiled back, deciding I liked watching him row. He might be slim, but he had muscles where it counted. What a strange moment to start feeling so aroused by my own husband.

"Thank God you came for us, you were sooner than I'd dared hope. I thought we would be drowned long before you reached home."

"It's a long story. I'll tell you about it when we're out of this filthy water and back on dry land. But Kat, sweetness, I was so frightened for you both."

"Tell me now, we're safely out of the worst of this." There was an anxious note in Thomas's voice which made me feel the need to press him. He continued, reluctantly.

"There are bad floods in the valley by the complex, and Alice found a future book that showed it was the same here. I was petrified I'd be too late … when I saw this sea of water … I was frantic. All I could hope for was that you were already away, but I had to check. Thank God that I did – I never dreamed the Thornes would be keeping you prisoner in the house." Thomas looked haunted, but then he caught my eye, and half smiled, as he confessed. "Hitting the man was very satisfying."

"I was glad you did," I said, with a savage smile, answering his. "I told you, he threatened Lissy, they both did. They were going to kill her if we didn't do as they demanded and keep her in Richard's place if we did." I smiled again, this time with pleasure. "I don't think Mistress Thorne enjoyed that bit. Lissy was on her knee and wet her, twice, in the night. That was so good. But *you* saved us, it was like a miracle, we were so frightened and I couldn't do anything while he had the pistol trained on our baby girl."

Thomas was smiling a real smile again. "I said I wouldn't let you down. I promised to be there for you, and, this time, I was."

"I love you."

"Love you too."

Bad floods near the complex, I fully registered Thomas's earlier words and began to worry again.

"Bess, my father, Joan – are they all safe?"

"Oh yes. They couldn't be safer; they're tucked up warm and dry in the complex. Sirens I'd never heard in my life started blaring, and automatic doors were closing." He stopped smiling, there was a grim look on his face as he added. "Kat, I had to do something bad to get out and back to you. I rather think they won't let me get away with it. It's a very different regime in charge since the latest elections to council."

I felt an uncomfortable lurch in the beat of my heart. I had no idea what he meant, but a chill of fear ran though my chest.

"Thomas, what on earth happened? Surely no-one would have stopped you leaving."

"I had no idea, but it's apparently an inflexible rule of the complex. Once the flood warning sounds and the doors start to close no-one is allowed to leave. Alice came to fetch me; she had the brilliant thought of running for the library and the secret exit. But by the time we got there Anne was already closing its manual flood door. I begged her to stop, to let me get out first. I pleaded with her, explained that you and Lissy were alone, that you would need us. She was implacable: she kept saying it was the law." He stopped, obviously unwilling to continue, and focussed on the rowing. I willed him to go on, and after long moments, he swallowed hard and continued quietly.

"So … I did the only thing I could think of … I threatened her with my dagger while Alice tried to open the door again. Alice wasn't strong enough to do it alone. In the end I knocked Anne out and did it myself. I *think* I made it seem as if Alice was forced to do my bidding to protect Anne from my threat. Anne was unconscious when Alice actually helped me with the door. I don't think she will be in any trouble. But me …"

"Oh, Thomas, no. How could Anne do that to you, to us?"

"I couldn't believe it either. But it was like the time when she said I must be the one to kill my parents. Everything about the original contracts and Domum-Orbis traditional laws is ingrained in her thinking. And I didn't have time to argue with her. I had to get back to you. I wish I'd never left, never gone back there. I should have foreseen that all the rain would become dangerous at some point. I should never have left you two alone, knowing the Thornes were about. It was incredibly stupid of me. Such a misjudgement. Forgive me. I was so eager to help the others have the same kind of joy we share, but I never meant to endanger us, our family, by doing it."

"Well, we won't ever go back. They won't have a chance to do anything to you if we stay away."

I tried to say it firmly and decidedly, something not to be argued with, but Thomas was silent, steering us into shallow water and jumping out as the boat ran up onto mud at the very edge of the flood.

He managed to beach the boat, despite my weight and Lissy's, and avoided answering me. I tried to smile at him as I handed Lissy out and clambered after her.

"This would seem familiar if I hadn't been unconscious last time. You're always rescuing me from drowning. How did you get hold of the boat?"

"I swapped my horse for it. With Philip – you know Philip, a few streets away from us, the one with a young wife and baby. He said Upper Ilfraycombe's pretty dry – he's heading there."

Thomas must be a wizard. No sooner had he spoken than Philip rode up, leading Thomas's horse and with his wife and baby on another.

"There are so many loose horses everywhere. The stable hands must have let them all free when the flooding started to get really bad. I've put my wife on one, and I thought I'd bring yours back, though I didn't dare imagine you'd get your family out safely."

Thomas embraced him. "Thank you, good friend."

Philip looked embarrassed. "One good turn … Here, I'll help you get the boat up well above the flood water so that someone else can use it. Then I'll be off. See you in Ilfraycombe, maybe at the inn just above the harbour. Shall I take a room for you?"

"Please, we'd appreciate it, that would be very helpful. The town will be filled with refugees. I'll give you money for a room and a meal as well. We'll sit here briefly, until these two" – he indicated me and Lissy – "have recovered a little, and then we'll be after you."

My legs would hardly support me, but I moved to a dry spot under a tree, holding a still sleeping Lissy. As Philip moved off, and Thomas brought the horse over, I looked up at him, holding his gaze.

"Thank you for coming to save us – despite the cost." I hoped he knew I'd be in his arms if I wasn't holding the little one.

"I cut it rather fine." He grinned at me and I could feel his sense of triumph. "But you needed me, and there I was. For once."

"As you always are. That's twice you've saved me from drowning, apart from everything else."

He looped the horse's reins over a branch of the tree and sat next to me, putting his arm around my shoulder and kissing my cheek. I nestled against him. "I don't know what happened to my horse. I hope they set her free from the stables."

"I'm sure they did. We'll find her in the end." He stroked my hair slightly abstractedly and, after taking a deep breath, he said, "I don't care what happens now. I couldn't leave you alone and in danger." He closed his eyes, before adding, softly, "I told myself I wouldn't, but

I think on reflection that I actually *would* have killed Anne to get to you. Your life, and Lissy's, mean more to me than anything. The price for saving you could never be too high, no matter what it might be."

I had the worst sinking feeling inside; I was certain that he wouldn't try to evade whatever punishment the council dreamed up for him. There had to be something I could say or do to prevent him from giving himself up to them. My mind was blank.

"Here, hold Lissy, we'll head for the inn, get dry and eat before we talk about this. It's not right for you to be punished. It should be Anne."

Thomas took Lissy and laid her down gently without disturbing her sleep. He said nothing but helped me onto the horse and picked Lissy up, passing her to me. He swung himself up behind us, holding me close against him, kissing my neck, brushing his lips against my cheek, my hair.

"Oh Kat, I love you so much."

"I love you too, Thomas. Please, please protect yourself for me. When you endanger yourself, it endangers me. I can't exist without you. Think of that before you do anything rash."

"I promise to take care, but I have to do the right thing. You must understand that I can't betray who I am. I wouldn't be the man you fell in love with if I were to run away from this. I'm sure they won't do anything too dreadful. Oh! please don't, I know you're crying, please don't break my heart."

"I'm sorry, I know I'm making this worse for you. Take no notice of me. I can't pretend that my heart doesn't hurt at the thought of anything terrible happening to you. I'm desperate to keep you safe; I want the same for you as you want for me. But it doesn't mean that I don't understand what this means to you. Even while not agreeing with you, I know you must do whatever you need to. I just wish I could be sure that they'll understand why you had to do it — everything in the complex seems to come down to the letter of the law without mercy or compassion. Especially with those who are in charge now. But I'll always be here

for you whatever happens."

We were both exhausted, yet that night in the inn, with Lissy tucked up asleep in the truckle bed in a curtained alcove, Thomas determinedly and silently undressed me completely and went willingly naked to bed himself. Warm under the covers, we explored every inch of each other's bodies, tracing the swirls which were hidden from view in the dark. Skin touching skin – stroking, kissing, tongues exploring. When the moment came Thomas was as desperate to be inside me as I was for him to be there. This had none of the light-heartedness of our encounters in the cave and since. I didn't know whether his hungry need for me had been aroused by the fear of losing me, by the fear we would soon be separated or by the triumph that he had succeeded in saving me and Lissy. I was scared it was the fear that we would soon be separated. But I didn't enquire too deeply, feeling him hard and full inside me, exulting as he crushed me ever closer, thrusting again and again until I surrendered to the physically overwhelming pulse that spiralled through me at the exact same moment that he came inside me, flooding me with his semen – both of us keeping our frantic pleasure as quiet as it was possible to do under such circumstances. I thought, belatedly, about the fact that my contraception had run out. It wasn't something I wanted to mention to him, as we held desperately to each other. Time enough when we knew what was in store for us in the immediate future.

Chapter 12

They came for Thomas. Almost before we were properly settled into Ilfraycombe – we had been there a scant few weeks and I had no idea how they could have known where we were so quickly. Two reformed enforcers, or complex guards as they now styled themselves, arrived. I wondered if either of them had been amongst those who had done those things to Thomas. He gave no indication. Anstey might not have been the only one to make-believe in a brown cloak in order to escape justice. Only the ones with burnt fingers had been easily identifiable, and that was because they had been Anstey's chosen men using Anstey's weaponry, not because of proof of abusing the girls or Thomas. I felt such a mix of fury and fear. It choked my throat, but I managed to scream at them. Fruitlessly. Then I wished I hadn't. They just stood there waiting for him and Thomas looked resigned, quiet, acquiescent … broken. As if he was closing down some part of himself. He kissed me softly, apologetically, without passion.

"Please sweetness, calm yourself. I have to go with them. I broke the laws of the complex and I have to be held to account. If everyone considers themselves above our laws, the charter will come to nothing, and we have to maintain our own justice system. The alternative would be accepting the outside rule of law as it stands in this time and place – with all that would mean for James and Robert, for Mathias. We can't leave ourselves with nothing to live by. They will understand, I'm sure. Perhaps there'll be a reprimand, a fine, or I might be banished for a while, as if I would care about that."

I was desperate enough to want to shake him, hit him, *kill them*. I just knew that something beginning like this would not end well for him. But I did none of it. I went and packed for the three of us and dared the guards to prevent me going with them. They made me ride separately from Thomas, with Lissy in front of me, and tied Thomas's hands behind him. That final humiliation stoked the anger inside me to fever pitch – it was as if he hadn't willingly agreed to accompany them. They seemed to be intent on shaming him. Perhaps, too, they were afraid of me – rumours of what I could do had spread – they may have thought that making sure I had my hands full with our child would hamper me. As if that would have stopped my mind from finding something to cause them injury. If I did nothing it was simply that I couldn't go against Thomas's wishes. Their safety was entirely in his bound hands.

It was a short journey over the cliffs. The whole way I could see him riding ahead of me. He didn't turn, but I felt his mind reaching out to me.

"I'm truly sorry to make you suffer this. I've gone over and over it in my mind and I can't think what I could have done differently."

"We'll make this alright. You of all people have given so much. How dare they treat you like this."

"Hush, little one. It will all come right in the end. It's not as if they intend to put me to death. We'll get through this and I can face anything if you are there waiting for me. I should be unselfish and tell you that you should move on, find someone who doesn't always mess things up, but I can't, I need you too much."

"Survive this, Thomas. I love you forever, there could never be anyone else. How could you even begin to imagine there might be? Don't make me angry with

you for suggesting such a thing."

*

The trial was the travesty I had always feared and secretly expected. I was horrified at the extent to which the desire for peace and quiet – surely an understandable desire, one which had made us long for a happy family life, far away from the trauma we had suffered – had opened the way to politically active elite-worker groups and administrators who were flooding the new committee with a resurgence of strictly traditional ideas. It struck me how much more the views of the new council were in line with old Domum-Orbis, with its inflexible fixation on law and contracts, and how much further away they were from a compassionate understanding that could encompass all beings, including the humans. Obviously, those who were increasingly in charge had read nothing of equity in the future-Earth library and were hellbent on re-imposing the old rules, ignoring the fact that these had led to our home-world's disintegration into violent factions, and, eventually, all-out war. With all the excuses I could come up with, I was gloomily conscious that *we* had let it happen here. Those of us who hadn't stood for office, those of us who hadn't bothered to vote, those like Thomas and me who had imagined we could live our lives in the outside world without taking an active part in the fledgling life of this community to which we were inexorably tied.

Afterwards it was difficult to talk about the trial without crying. And I seemed to do that endlessly. Thomas … alone, brave, honourable. Thomas's friends … disempowered, speaking to morals the council no longer possessed, hopelessly trying to justify actions that anyone with heart or soul would have regarded as self-evidently appropriate. Thomas's accusers … shades of Anstey, jealous, rigid, uncaring, vengeful against someone so much better than they. Yes, a total, complete travesty.

That last day, I had spoken for him, told of the Thornes and their

121

attack, how he had saved me. Reminded them of all he had done, of the stun weapon he had developed for them, of everything that shone light on how much better than them he was.

It was a complete waste of breath.

Chapter 13

Council Records: Post Anstey (Earth year 1601)

Notes (for information) on the formation of the eight-person 1601-2 Council which is currently adjudicating on all Complex matters and will do so until the last day of that time period. The 1601-2 Council was democratically elected under the new charter by all members of the complex, each member of the community having one vote to cast. For the first time there was no statutory requirement for all parts of the population to be represented, requiring only that each person elected received sufficient votes to come in the first eight of all those standing. Not all complex members exercised their right to cast a vote. The 1601 election was the first one in which no humans, Domum-Orbis/human hybrids, or anyone with lower-grade skill sets were chosen to serve on the council, none of their representatives having received the requisite number of votes.

Members of the 1601-2 Council duly elected (alphabetical order) (the abbreviation ADO represents a full-blooded former resident, or the full-blooded descendent of such a resident, of the Domum-Orbis in Auriga): R. Archer (ADO) Imported-equipment expert; A. Gomfrey (ADO) Library and computer technician (council leader);

M. Heron (ADO) Infirmary technician; J. Lowth (ADO) Computing analyst; J. Notfeld (ADO) Notary and lawyer; G. Obson (ADO) Administrator; G. Stockton (ADO) Administrator (council secretary); T. Ufford (ADO) Administrator.

Here follows the record of the first judicial action carried out under the auspices of the above Council.

<u>In the matter of Thomas Alban</u>

Alban is charged with:

1. putting the complex, and the lives of everyone in it, at risk by preventing the closure of a manual flood door;
2. threatening the life of a council member in the course of her lawful duties;
3. assaulting the same council member.

Judged guilty on overwhelming evidence. Pleas for mitigation received and considered. Sentenced to four months solitary incarceration in the complex cells followed by a period of a further six months banishment. In view of previous services to the community there shall be no forfeiture of property.

James Notfeld wishes to have his dissent to the majority verdict, and complaint regarding the severity of the sentence imposed, placed on record.

The charges being considered against Alice Derricott (for aiding the accused) and Katharine Wrenn-Alban (for attempting to incite her husband to resist arrest and harassing officers of the complex) are to be suspended but held over on condition that they both leave the complex and do not return within the ten months of Alban's overall sentence.

It is noted that protests at Alban's sentence have been received from a substantial number of his supporters – none of the protesters hold office in the complex, other than Notfeld, whose objection is noted above, and therefore have no weight in this matter.

It is further noted that additional protests have been received as a result of Alice Derricott and Katharine Wrenn-Alban being evicted from the complex without receiving the opportunity to say farewell to their husbands and families. This is similarly judged to be irrelevant to the proceedings.

Reserved Additional Confidential Papers (Not for general release, only to be made accessible to the inner council.)

Edith Hawkins approached the council prior to the trial and gave sworn evidence that Wrenn-Alban is the former director's daughter, and that Wrenn-Alban and Alban colluded in the murder of Richard Thorne to hide their own plan to take over the complex. There is compelling evidence that the first statement is incorrect, given that the human William Wrenn has confirmed paternity and there are genetic resemblances – for example eye colour. There is little evidence for the second claim, so it cannot be proceeded with, but it does give some warning that Alban may be a material threat to the new council and should not be tolerated.

The man has considerable support among the worker grades, modernising elites, and the resident human population, so direct action, beyond the period of imprisonment imposed, is considered to be unwise. However, Alban is believed to be mentally unstable and was probably too readily believed with regard to his claims of harsh treatment by Anstey. His close friend Alice Derricott may well have exaggerated his injuries and those of the humans who were supposed to have been abused by the former guards.

It is recommended that the council explore ways in which Alban may be placed in continuously stressful circumstances during his incarceration with the aim that he might suffer a complete mental breakdown and thus reveal his inherent instability of mind and unsuitability as a leader. It may then be possible to impose total isolation and confine him indefinitely (for his own good).

A close watch should be placed on his supporters, who will doubtless forget him eventually. However, it may be necessary to abort the plan should there be a dangerous level of outside interest in his treatment – he should not appear to the complex population in the guise of a martyr. Exclusion of Wrenn-Alban and Derricott from the complex should assist in the stated aim of council and prevent excessive outside interest in Alban's well-being until it is too late.

Signed by the Secretary, on behalf of the inner council:

G. Stockton

Counter-signed by the leader of the council:

A. Gomfrey

*

So that was how it was; Alice and I were forcibly ejected and retreated to Ilfraycombe. Alice went without Stephen and Thom. Her husband and son had returned to the complex for the trial but had not left there with us – I didn't understand why, nor why they had been apart from Alice for so long in the first place. Me, I went with Lissy but without Thomas or Bess. Bess had bravely volunteered to stay near to her father because I was forbidden to. My father remained there as well. It tortured me to think of Thomas, alone in a cell, locked up, unable to leave the scene of his nightmares. Why had the sentence insisted on solitary confinement? Did that mean he couldn't have visitors? Thomas had never dreamt they would be that harsh – at least, that was what he'd said. I *hated* Anne Gomfrey. Agonized by not even being able to speak with him when I was forced to leave, I just hoped someone would have been able to explain to him that I had been escorted out of the complex. I needed him to understand that it was not that I couldn't bear to talk to him after all that had happened.

Chapter 14

They didn't waste energy on daylight-quality lighting in the last tunnel, the one which branched off just before the beach exit. It was only necessary to have some perpetual dim lighting there for the previously unoccupied damp, subterranean cell it contained. In the new, post-Anstey era there was a permanent camouflaged guard's post just inside the main tunnel. At some point the council had agreed that it was preferable to have one guard at the entrance to the caves – preventing anyone entering – instead of having the cliff-top contingent of Anstey's day. The guards all specialised in non-lethal mind-wiping in an emergency. Thomas had done some work on that himself, before he and Kat had left for Barnstable. But the result was an almost total lack of discernible day and night behind the guard post (which had its own internal lighting), other than clues from the faintest extra daylight glimmer where the outermost cave curved around to the cove. The cell itself was in perpetual half-light. He had barely been aware of the continued existence of such a prison and would have vehemently opposed its inhumanity had he kept up to date with life in the community.

At first, he marked the wall every time the guard changed. He could feel, if not clearly see, the scratches. From what he gathered by listening to them talk, the guards did six-hourly shifts without a break. They seemed to go just beyond the outer cave to piss. He could hear, but not see them. From listening to their conversations as they switched over, he gathered that they brought their own food and drink down with them. His own daily meal – what looked like a half ration of the inevitable plain synthesized protein and greens, with recycled water – was delivered once a day. That was part way into what he reckoned to be a 24-hour cycle, but without any true sense of day or night. There was a lidless privy and a basin, all in the same room, a viewing panel in the door that could be opened at any time by one of the guards, so there was no guarantee of privacy, whatever he was doing. No change of clothing was offered. The sense of being transported back to his imprisonment by Anstey dragged him down from the first moment the door was locked behind him.

He tried to convince himself that he didn't really need to know passing time, but Thomas wanted to make sure they let him out when he was due to be freed. He didn't trust them not to forget about him entirely and he had to confess it frightened him. There was nothing to distract him from his fears. Nothing to read, no-one to talk to, just endless time stretching ahead. The council's hatred and distrust of his residual influence had permeated everything at the trial. His heart beat wildly every time he thought about it. It was almost as if Anstey was back.

Being deprived of a sense of regularly passing time was disorientating and contributed to the alarming sense of a mental breakdown which he felt might be terrifyingly imminent and was powerless to prevent. It was only four months, he told himself. But every time he closed his eyes and tried to get comfortable enough to sleep on the hard chair or coverless bed shelf the spectre of Anstey and his men and what they did to him was there to wake him screaming – to the amusement of some of those who guarded his door and peered in on him. When they'd said imprisonment, he had naively imagined having access to books, a proper cleansing room, adequate food rations. Why he'd imagined that he would receive such humane treatment he had no idea. Which went to prove how stupid he was, he thought miserably.

For the first two weeks or so the guards were members of the new elite, seemingly regarding it as their duty to keep him isolated. Then, gradually, the council seemed content to forget about him and lapsed back to using anyone, which, shades of his previous incarceration, included his old friends George and John. George, full of concern and sympathy, immediately promised to smuggle Bess and William down to talk to him. It was timely, Thomas already feared he was going to lose his senses in the hostile silence that surrounded him.

When the door opened and he saw them there, he nearly cried. Then he worried about the smell, the privy, the fact that the sink hadn't had water for a few days and he knew that unwashed and with no fresh clothing he stank too.

"Bess! You shouldn't be here, darling; this is a horrible place, and Dadde's too smelly to give you a proper hug. Is your Mamma here too?"

Bess ignored his words and rushed to fling her arms around him, tears running down her face. William stood back, looking embarrassed and awkward.

"Sorry to see you in such an awful place, Thomas. Bess and I are going to stick around to try to make sure that you're treated properly. They've banished Kat and Alice; made them leave the second your trial was finished. It was wholly unjust – first they threatened to charge them with some trumped-up offences and then said they were to be banished without trial. I'm so furious, I could spit. But there's nothing I can do. Alice has gone with Kat and Lissy back to Ilfraycombe, Stephen and Thom stayed here."

With a rush of relief, he at last understood why he had not seen Kat. Up until then he had been afraid that she was angry with him for letting this happen, tormenting himself with imagining she despised him for giving in to this punishment that was separating them so cruelly. If she were there now, he would have admitted to her that his determination to stand trial seemed plain stupidity in retrospect, rather than a properly justifiable moral stance. But how could he have even dreamed they would treat him like this?

Against his will, he found himself saying, "You mustn't stay long, it's foul in here and you must be careful to leave before one of the other guards arrives to check. George will let you come back when he can." Swallowing hard, he couldn't believe he was saying it, he fucking dreaded them going, but couldn't bear for them to see him like this. Bess was still crying. "You must go to Kat and Lissy, give them my love and say I'm fine, just missing them so much. It helps to know I can see you sometimes, even if it's a short visit."

"Love you, Dadde. We'll be back, every time we can. We can bring you something nice to eat, or anything else you need. George has promised."

"You're not alone now. We'll be back as often as George can arrange it – it'll depend on his and John's shifts. Can we bring you something, anything? We won't leave you until we're sure you're alright. James and Robert want to see you too."

"No, no, I'm fine, this place is a bit primitive, but I'm sure people put up with much worse. Now I know I can see you sometimes, I'll feel much better. And if you can get word to Kat. Tell her how sorry I am about all this."

One last hug from his tearful daughter, and they were leaving. Already. George was hovering anxiously in the unlocked doorway. It hurt to think of being apart from his family, knowing it was his own naivety that had placed him there. So many regrets, but the one thing he could not regret was doing what he had in the library. He had got out and he had saved his family. He kept comforting himself, over and over, with the thought that they were alive because of him. The

joy on their faces, Kat's and Lissy's, when he'd leapt out of the boat —
just for that he knew he would do it all again and more.

At least William and Bess were able to promise they would visit
Kat and Lissy as soon as they could. They didn't want to leave him
alone and friendless there, he could tell it was as difficult for them as
it had been for him to see them go. But knowing George and John, at
the very least, were looking out for him again, he was sure that they
would feel it safe to risk taking time out to contact Alice and Kat. He
was glad that the two women were together, but aghast that they
both were suffering because of him. Such a petty, vengeful thing to
accuse them too. And then to sentence them to banishment without
trial and prevent them even saying goodbye to loved ones. The
committee seemed to be determined that he should be deprived of
close friends and family. He wondered at Stephen's absence. Perhaps
his friend blamed him for the break-up of his family, though Thomas
wondered why Stephen didn't simply leave the complex and go to
Alice. Had he been in Stephen's place, he was sure that he would
have gone straight to Kat.

James and Robert came down to see him at the end of the third
week, bringing clean clothing and a promise that someone would fix
the water supply to the sink. William had spoken to them. Both were
raging at the injustice of having needed to actually apply for
permission to visit him. They doubted that they would have
succeeded without James being on the council and insisting that he
was Thomas's legal representative. They hadn't thought of taking
advantage of unofficial help but swore they would from then on.

"Forgive me, this is all my fault, if only I could turn back time."
Robert could barely speak and Thomas saw plainly how anguished
the man was. And it was true that his request had started the chain of
events which had ended with this cruel punishment. But this was all
down to the unforeseen floods and to Anne and her committee …
no-one could possibly have predicted such a devastating result to

such an innocent plea for help.

"It was all in vain, anyway," James told him gloomily. "The new council, as soon as it became aware of what we were planning, issued a decree forbidding mixed-race hand-fasting. It's 'against' Domum-Orbis traditions … apparently. They may not be as cruel as Anstey, but they sure as hell are more fucking reactionary."

So, all for nothing, that left a bitter taste. Even if James and Robert, Megs and Anthony could find a way of mind-sharing, their unions would never be sanctioned within the council's interpretation of traditional law.

"Hey, it's not your fault, you … we were trying to do the right thing. We will do it one day. This committee has to face election. Surely there are still some here who aren't of like mind? People who might fight to get the ban lifted?"

"Yes but look what coming here's done to you!" Robert looked at him. "That *is* my fault. I should never, never have asked you."

Unexpectedly Thomas found himself in the position of having to comfort both of his friends, trying to persuade them that he was fine. But already he knew that the cold, the damp, the periods of isolation, and, most of all, his inability to sleep, were combining to drag him down, both mentally and physically, and he could tell from the way they looked at him that James and Robert could see it too. Despite the time-lapse he had never really recovered his full physical strength. There were parts of him that had not healed as well as those in the infirmary had hoped. He kept that from everyone.

It was important to reassure Robert; he didn't want him to feel in any way to blame. How could Robert possibly have known what would be unleashed by his simple and reasonable request? If it was anyone's fault it was his own. He could have said no, he should have said no, he should *never* have left Kat and Lissy alone and unprotected like that.

"Look, you mustn't worry about me, it's not long, I'll be fine. I just want to get a letter to Kat. Is there any way you could check if she's alright for money? I have no idea how much of the goods and premises we were in are salvageable after the floods. She'll need something, even if she is staying with Alice."

"We'll sort that out, you don't need to ask such things. I'm sure that Alice will take care of Kat for now."

All he wanted of the two men now was for them to get a letter to Kat. To find some personal means of letting his wife and daughter know how much he loved and missed them – how sorry he was to have brought this on them. Robert promised to bring him writing materials. However, they warned him that it might be a while before they could get such a note away to her, since they were convinced that they were both being watched. Perhaps William and Bess could take it more easily?

Thomas's note was short, wet and smudged, written in semi darkness, but it said all he wanted it to.

Dearest Kat,

I'm so very sorry that I didn't listen to you, that I came back here. Can you ever forgive me? You're a lot wiser than me; you knew it was the wrong thing to do, but I was foolishly determined that I was doing what was best. I despair of what the complex has become, and in such a short a time from that moment when we thought all would be well. We will make it through this, I love you so much and we will soon be safe together again.

Please tell Lissy how much I love her too and kiss her for me.

James and Robert are taking care of salvaging what's left of the Barnstable premises. There's nothing for you to worry about. They'll get money to you to tide you over.

Please be safe for me. I won't survive if anything should happen to you.

Your own loving husband,

Thomas

His thoughts were harsh, and he didn't only blame himself. The one thing he was sure of was that he wanted no further part in the community. When he left this prison that would be the end of it. What of the complex, their community, their charter? What did he care for them anymore? The power structure was already sinking back to what it had been before. Cold and heartless. At present it was true that they were not harming the human population, but from what William and Bess told him he could see that the humans were gradually being edged out, mixed relationships discouraged and a new era of isolationism was beginning.

Domum-Orbis lifespans were longer than those of the humans but they weren't immortal. He couldn't understand why they didn't see that eventually they would all die out – some full-blood babies were being born, but not many. To be full-blood created a genetic problem in such a small pool of potential and many of the full Domum-Orbis exiles were closely inter-related. Without a new infusion of families from the home-world, an impossibility, the complex would moulder into dust in the longer term – unless the species was allowed to intermarry with humans. Why should he, and a scant few others, be the only ones to care?

*

At the end of the fourth week William and Bess came back with an oral message from Kat. George let them into the cell and Bess sat on Thomas's knee and whispered it to him.

"Mother says she loves you. Now that she knows where you are, she says she will come over the cliffs and try to be somewhere near you for a while each day, or perhaps at night. She says to listen out for her with your mind, and it may be that she can reach you. Joan and Alice are at the inn in Ilfraycombe to look after Lissy when they're needed. Mother promises that she won't take any risks, but she can't bear to be without speaking to you for all the time that stretches ahead. She says it is breaking her heart to be away from you.

She sends you this," and Bess kissed his cheek.

He hugged the child, feeling her tears wet against his face.

"Was your mother crying too?"

"Yes, it's part of the message. We love you, both of us, and Lissy does too, she's missing you badly, she doesn't smile at all. She misses me as well, but they're both glad I can be with you. Aunt Alice is very sad and sends her love. She hasn't seen Uncle Stephen or Thom. I think something is wrong between them, but I don't know what. I don't think Aunt Alice wants me to know."

Then Bess and William had to leave, before the guard changed. The feeling of loneliness as George touched the pad that shut the door behind them was at least, this time, alleviated by the words Kat had sent, and the knowledge that she would be trying to reach him. Was it selfish of him to want her there? He was fearful that she would put herself in danger because of the foolish and naive decision he had made.

Chapter 15

Alice and I were like lost souls that first week alone in Ilfraycombe. My Joan was with us too, missing being with John at home, but glad to be able to help and to spend time with Lissy, whom she adored.

I couldn't understand why Stephen and Thom hadn't come with Alice, nor why Alice seemed to have brought sufficient easily portable supplies and the money to start an Apothecary's shop. She was already actively looking for suitable premises and had agreed an income levy for the complex before all the troubles. At first, she was reluctant to tell me what was wrong, though I sensed that she badly needed to talk to someone. She seemed very unlike the Alice I thought I knew.

One evening, after Lissy was tucked up and Joan had retired for the night, Alice and I shared a few goblets of wine snuggled on chairs by the fire. In the late half-light of the dying fire she finally reached the point of feeling able to share her story. At first, she couldn't look at me, staring instead into the embers and obviously struggling to contain her emotions.

"Did you know Stephen and I were hand-fasted when we were only eighteen?" She began abruptly and I couldn't imagine where such an opening would lead. I was also surprised; it seemed young for such a commitment.

"We bonded – our markings drew us together and we could neither of us envisage there ever being anyone else for either of us. Nor would there have been if it wasn't for Anstey."

Shocked by the implication, I sat forward, reaching for Alice's hands and held them. The action seemed better than making any comment.

"Because we were so young, neither of us had much to learn about each other in the mind-sharing. We had both suffered the loss of our parents, Anstey's treatment of us all – our experiences were so similar. Sometimes I wonder if the ceremony should be repeated periodically, renewing our vows and sharing more of our later lives with each other. But it isn't, so what happened when Robert and Megs started questioning the possibility of mind-sharing between humans and us – it was a total shock to me."

Alice took a sip of wine; I couldn't fail to notice that her hand was shaking.

"One of the girls working with Megs, ironically another Alice, or Allie I think they call her, was part of the same group of vagrants that Bess came from. She knew Bess's mother, who had joined up with them, fleeing something or someone, prior to Bess's birth. The mother died when Bess was one or two years old and Allie and some other girls looked after her from then on."

I began to worry about where this was going; I imagined it had to have something to do with Bess's mixed heritage – her unknown father's identity. Adding that to the talk of Stephen and I began to have a cold feeling of anxiety for Alice. I squeezed her hand, but again felt unable to say anything worthwhile to her.

"He admitted it to me himself, I will say that for him."

Her voice was hardly more than a whisper. "They were all experimenting with cross-species mind-sharing, all the human girls and Robert and James of course – Stephen drew Allie as a partner. As soon as he saw Bess's mother in Allie's mind, he knew who she was. He tried to hide his reaction, but he guessed that everyone there realised something significant had happened. To be fair he came straight to me."

I think my face must have registered the shock I felt. Alice stopped and looked at me anxiously.

"I know this must be disturbing for you, with your close relationship, yours and Thomas's, with the child."

"Go on, Alice. We've always known Bess had a home-world father – Thomas and I have been prepared for a moment such as this since the beginning."

Alice looked away, closing her eyes for the moment. I couldn't believe this was my best friend – confident, loving, empathic Alice. She who saved people, always thought of others first, and never needed saving herself. When she continued with her story, it was as if she was away in some other time and place. Looking into the distance and re-living the nightmare of discovery.

"Stephen had excuses, plenty of those, but it was the fact that he had kept it hidden from me that hurt most. How could he keep such a secret when we were bonded? He must have realised it was a possibility when the whole question of Bess's parentage emerged. It was Anstey at the bottom of it of course. He took Stephen out with a crowd of the enforcers, to tempt him, when he was just nineteen – we had only been hand-fasted for a year. Anstey goaded him; said he was tied to my apron strings – you know Anstey's opinion of women. He had paid for a young girl to be brought to Stephen in a room at the local brothel-house. It took Stephen by surprise."

Alice stopped and took another swallow of wine. From her face I could see that she was angry as well as upset.

"Well Stephen fucked her, and Anstey gave her money. He told

Stephen to check on her and terminate any pregnancy that might arise. If it was only that once, and he'd told me straight away, I think I could have born that. I would have understood that he was just sucking up to Anstey to keep us safe. But it wasn't once. He really liked the girl, she flirted with him and flattered him, he said he felt like one of the men. I don't know how many times he actually fucked her. He was deliberately vague."

Alice's face was uncharacteristically harsh, and I'd never heard her speak like that before.

"Then the one day, when he went to the village to see her, she was gone, and no-one could say where. One of the other girls told him she was pregnant but wanted to keep the baby. She'd heard rumours of what happened to anyone falling for a child by one of Anstey's guards. Stephen said nothing, he didn't try to read their minds to find her – he knew he couldn't actively kill his own child – so he didn't tell Anstey. Anstey had forgotten all about it. And Stephen chose not to tell me either. Part of his mind has always been closed to me without my even knowing it. He swears he never did such a thing again. But to think of him … fucking her, and then coming home to fuck me. Both unprotected. How could he do it? He must have known there was a likelihood that he had a living child somewhere, but he never made any effort to find the mother or *his* baby. His *first* baby."

I hugged her then as she cried. Alice was always so strong, so happy; it hurt unbearably to see her distraught like this. Such a betrayal.

"What have you said to Stephen now? Does he want to come here to be with you?" She stiffened, and her expression hardened again.

"I told him straight away that I needed time on my own, that I didn't want to be with him for a while. He took Thom to our house near your father's – I was immersed in work – they only came back when he heard about the trial. If it weren't for the circumstances of our banishment, I might have brought Thom with me here, but I don't want our child to suffer because of our problems. It seemed easier for Thom to believe that the separation now is only because of the law – he adores his father – I don't want to this to taint their relationship. Will you … should we … tell Bess?"

Before I answered, I thought, hard. Despite my more confident words earlier, I suspected that this would hurt Thomas. He had come to regard Bess as wholly his own. There was a difference between some anonymous enforcer and his own best friend. Bess deserved to know, but not yet.

"Eventually we must, but not now, not while Thomas is imprisoned and I'm so frightened for him. Perhaps when we're all together again and this particular nightmare is over."

"You're right. I'm sorry to have burdened you with it. I just had to tell someone; it's poisoning me. I thought we had such a perfect life …"

"You're so kind, so good, my best friend. I wouldn't be alive if not for you," I was sobbing with her. "I wish this hadn't happened to you of all people. How could he do it to you?"

"I don't know what to do. I still love him so much, it would kill me to leave him, but when he tried to hold me, to kiss me, after telling me the truth. Oh Kat – I couldn't bear him to even touch me! What kind of life will we have if I feel like that? How can it ever be right again? But what will that do to Thom?"

I held her close. What advice was I capable of offering? She had always been the strong one. We drank some more. We both needed a temporary oblivion and wine was the best that offered.

Oddly it was the next day that my father came to visit, accompanied by Bess and Thom. Alice gathered Thom in her arms, hugging him tightly, and then said, in as bright a voice as she could manage, "I'll take Thom down to see the boats in the harbour, give you some private family time."

My father and Bess clearly had no idea of the situation between Alice and Stephen, they just smiled at Alice and her son, and Alice was gone before anything more could be said. I wondered if it hurt her to look at Bess just at present. If that was why she'd avoided visiting us. It wasn't Bess's fault, but I could see something I'd never noticed before: there was just the faintest look of Stephen about our dearly loved adopted child.

As soon as the door closed behind Alice, my father turned to me anxiously.

"I'm sorry not to have been before. Are you alright here with Alice and Joan? Bess and I were worried about Thomas, we didn't dare leave him alone in their clutches, but James and Robert are looking out for him at present and we have news now, a note from him."

How many times can a heart break? Mine did again as I read it, at the thought of him, all alone, writing it for me – apologising, worrying about me, when he was the one suffering. Bess rushed to hug me, seeing me cry.

"Do they let you see him?" I asked her. She nodded. I kissed her, cheeks still wet with tears, "Give him my love, Lissy's too. Kiss him for me." Bess nodded again and hugged me even closer.

"Where is he?" I asked my father.

The expression on his face was furious; I don't think I'd ever seen him so angry.

"They've got him in that last stinking hole in the rock that they pretend is a cell, barely lit, shut in all the time, with just a lidless privy and basin, all in the same room. It's only a short distance back from the main cave, but within sight of the guard they have stationed there. There's a viewing panel in the door, so they can look in on him any time of the night or day. You can imagine how upsetting that is for someone like Thomas. It's almost like Anstey's day, except that George and John, thank the Good Lord for them, do what he can for him when they're on duty. How can the others do that to him? I wish Thomas wasn't so … good! And *so* forgiving, *so* uncomplaining. It brings out the worst in the wrong kinds of people. He's too much for them to live up to, so they try to bring him down, to destroy him instead."

That was quite a speech for my father.

"Then I'm going to try to talk to him."

"How? What do you mean? You can't risk getting caught."

"Don't worry." Bess rested her hand on my father's arm as he looked at me in alarm. "I know what she means." Bess turned to me. "You're going to walk somewhere near the caves, aren't you? Somewhere your mind voices might carry. I think you could do it. I think you should try. Aunt Alice and Joan will stay here with Lissy, I'm sure."

And so, at the beginning of Thomas's second month of imprisonment, I found myself heading out from Ilfraycombe in the late afternoon following my father's visit.

Chapter 16

I'd forgotten how high the cliffs were. If it hadn't been for the thought of speaking to Thomas, I think I would have been too scared to try the crumbling path down into the cove. I had convinced my father that I would be able to achieve contact while still on the top of the cliffs, but I knew that wasn't nearly close enough. The deadening effect of the lined tunnels. I was determined he wouldn't feel he should deter me or tell Thomas I was doing something stupid and dangerous. Two or three times I slipped, hampered by my skirts. The last time I only just managed to grab hold of a clump of scrubby bush, scratching my hands, but regaining my footing. Thankfully that prevented me from falling the rest of the way. By the time I was sitting on a boulder at the bottom it was almost dark and I didn't dare let myself wonder how I might climb back up again later. Hoping my horse would still be tethered at the top if I survived, I promised myself that I would try to acquire male clothing for the next time. I could begin to see the attraction for Mathias.

The waves were crashing on the rocks noisily, with the tide in as far as it would be likely to go. Fortunately, it was well short of my position. I tried to calm my mind – and heart – and began to reach out to him.

"Thomas! Thomas, it's me. Please hear me, darling, I'm desperate for your voice."

"Kat! Can that really be you?"

His voice sounded ecstatic in my head, then worried.

"I knew you would come. But promise me you're not in any danger where you are."

I crossed my fingers.

"Of course not, how could I be in danger? I'm just out for a ride and a stroll and a chat with my darling husband! What about you though, my father is incredibly angry at the way they're keeping you."

"William is good to me. He does his best to get me extra food and makes sure he and Bess are able to visit when one of the kinder guards is on duty … you remember my friends George and John. They volunteer."

"I'm grateful to them all over again. Oh Thomas, I can't believe they could be so cruel to you, after everything. I love you so much, I miss you."

"It's not quite as bad as before." I actually felt him shudder – how strange when we weren't anywhere near each other – and repressed one of my own. If I could feel his … *"At least I know you're safe, that there's no-one plotting to hurt you as well. Once I'm free we'll go far away from here, take our chances, live solely in the human world. I'm through with this place."*

I hoped he wouldn't regret saying that. I thought of us making love in the aftermath of the flood and the fact that I was late with my bleed. Time enough to deal with that worry later.

"They don't deserve you. We'll just be our own small family. Though Alice might need us. She's in Ilfraycombe alone – some quarrel with Stephen. Have you seen him?"

I was happy that I was giving nothing away, but Thomas needed to be on his guard if he saw Stephen.

There was silence for a moment.

"Stephen hasn't been to see me, although I know from James that he and

Thom are still here. I thought at first that he was angry with me and had left with Alice. I could see that he might feel that I caused her to be banished. But I know that you and she left together, while he stayed put."

Thomas sounded hurt. I wasn't surprised – Stephen was always Thomas's best and closest friend. I guessed that Stephen might be too ashamed to admit what he'd done. Especially to the man he always looked up to. That meant I was angry with Stephen twice over. Now he'd hurt Alice *and* Thomas.

"I don't believe it has anything to do with you. It's something that concerns the two of them. Something he kept from her. He probably thinks you'd take her part – you and Alice always have that rapport. Perhaps he's ashamed of whatever it is and can't admit it to his hero."

Thomas snorted, or at least that's what it sounded like. *"Hero! Not a role I'm fitted for. Fool, more like."*

I was concerned to change the subject. We were skating closer but I couldn't tell him the whole truth. However, I couldn't tell an out-and-out lie either.

"Stop it, Thomas, I won't have anyone running down my darling husband. I love you. You're the best man in the whole world. Believe it!"

I pictured him with a resigned grin on his face.

"I think you're prejudiced. But I'm glad you are. It means so much that you're here for me. I wish I could touch you, just wait 'til I can fold you in my arms again. I'm imagining it right now."

"Me too. I can feel you – I'm hugging me and it feels as if it's you."

"I'd better be careful! Don't want the guard thinking I'm pleasuring myself in here! Oh Kat!" He seemed to hold his breath. *"I love you so much."*

"We'll make up for it when we're together again. I'm counting the weeks, the days, the hours. But I'll come here every day until then. You won't be alone; you can count on me. I love you forever."

"My sweetness, my darling little Kat, thank you for sticking with your stupid

husband." He went quiet for a moment and I could feel his anger with himself before he turned our talk away from his sense of guilt. "*How is Lissy? I'm missing her too. Bess said she was sad at being without me.*"

"*Oh Thomas, she does miss you, all the time. Perhaps I could send her back with Joan, next time Bess and my father visit? Then they could bring her down to you and it would be company for Bess too.*"

"*I'm not sure I want Lissy to see me like this. I'm disgustingly filthy, the water supply to the basin often doesn't work for days on end, and the cell stinks. I stink. I'm ashamed of what I must look like too — not that there's any mirror in here for me to check. I'm afraid I might frighten her.*"

"*That wouldn't matter to her, if it meant she could see you, talk to you. Couldn't George or John bring you some extra hot water to wash in? I'm sure if you explained.*"

"*Any water of any kind would be good! I'll ask them, but they do a lot already, and it's a risk if any of the current council or the newest elected guards were to find out.*"

"*That's what I'll do then. I'll send you Lissy. Let me know when you're ready and tell my father what we have in mind. Are you getting enough to eat, you don't want to go all thin on me again? Perhaps I can send something nice for you. Lissy will be pleased if she can bring something special for her Dadde.*"

"*You're so thoughtful; I don't deserve you. They're keeping me short of rations, not that there's anything appetising to eat anyway. A treat, something with taste. An apple? I'm looking forward to it already.*"

In the end we talked the whole night, and I didn't have to worry about scaling the path in the dark. At first light I began the slow precarious climb, trying not to look down. My heart felt lighter, and I focussed on the plants that clung there, a miniature world of tufts, insects, seed pods, the odd remaining flower. They clung on — I would too.

The fates were in my favour. My horse was there still, idly cropping, and my ride back to the inn was uneventful. Letting my horse amble along, I was able to revel quietly in thoughts of Thomas, hugging all those words of love into my heart.

*

The tall well-built man, standing in the shadows, had watched her all the way there and back from a safe distance. He was relieved that he hadn't needed to show himself; he wasn't sure if she would believe that he was only concerned with protecting her.

*

"Hello Thomas."

Thomas looked up, startled, he had been thinking, half dreaming, of Kat. He had barely registered the cell door opening.

"Stephen!"

"You look fucking awful; why did you let them do this to you? Why didn't you just bugger off instead of letting them bring you back here, to this?"

"You seriously imagine I don't wish that I had? Every single moment of every single day. To be fair I never expected them to treat me this badly. Anyway, you don't look so fucking great yourself. What made you brave the stench to come down here and see me after all this time?" He tried but found that he couldn't conceal the hurt in his voice. Two months without sight or sound of the man who was supposed to be his best friend.

Stephen flinched and crouched down alongside.

"I'm sorry, I'm really sorry, I'm a coward and I've just made everything worse. I need you to understand … I did something appalling, unforgivable. I've hurt Alice, let you down, and I've been too ashamed to face you."

It clearly wasn't just words. Stephen's face was grey, his clothing hung loose on him. It didn't look as if he'd eaten or slept in a long time.

147

"Tell me."

"I don't know if I can. It isn't only my tale to tell. It affects your family too."

"Just get on with it. You're making me imagine all kinds of terrible things, and I do *not* want to do that."

Stephen was shaking and he couldn't think what such a close friend could possibly have done that would have involved Thomas's loved ones. Except for something unthinkable. He'd wondered, once, aware Stephen admired her, but he trusted Kat.

"Alice has left me, and I deserve it. Can anything be more terrible than that. She's only let Thom stay with me for the period of her banishment. She's setting up an Apothecary's shop in Ilfraycombe. When she's ready she'll take him too."

Stephen's voice broke and he covered his face in his hands.

"What can I do! How can I live without them?"

"Tell. Me. Now." He was done with any idea of excusing Stephen before he knew what had happened. "I'm stuck in this fucking filthy cell and you tell me you've hurt my family and done something appalling. For the love of God, will you tell me what you've fucking done." He found he was shouting.

Stephen seemed to pull himself together, realising he was making things infinitely worse.

"I'm Bess's biological father."

He couldn't believe his ears. Whilst he'd had no idea what he'd expected Stephen to say, it certainly wasn't that.

"You'd better start at the beginning. Are you expecting us to give her up? You know she's like our ... she *is* our own child."

"No, no, not unless it's something she wants, and I doubt she would ever exchange someone like you for a pathetic idiot like me.

She doesn't even have to know. I just need to confess to you how badly I fucked up."

The story came out of Stephen in dribs and drabs but, having made up his mind to admit everything, he didn't try to hide his culpability, to pretend it was anything other than it was.

"I don't remember a time when you were such good friends with Anstey and his men. That must have been long before they made us enforcers."

"It was when you kept getting beaten and put in solitary for weeks on end. Another of Anstey's periodic all-out attempts to break you. Coward that I am, I wondered if there was another way of dealing with the man. Alice and I were newly hand-fasted, and I wanted to give her more, have money instead of food and clothing tokens, position. I was jealous too. Alice always seemed to admire you more than me, even though she said it was me she loved. As if I was a second-best sort of man, just joined with her because of our mindless swirl-bonding. The other one, Bess's mother, she made a lot of me, down there in the village. She made me feel I was someone special. How shallow I was. Probably Anstey paid the girl to act it out, and I was afraid to dig too deep into her mind. I needed to believe her. In the end, when she ran off pregnant, I realised how wrong I was, but the damage had been done, and I was too afraid of how Alice would react to try to put things right. I was afraid as well that Anstey would make me kill the baby if I traced its mother. I wasn't so far gone as to be able to do that, and I never imagined the truth would come out."

Stephen was sobbing. Thomas awkwardly put a hand on his shoulder, embarrassed.

"What can I do? I've lost the only people I've ever really loved. My wife and my son."

He hugged him, wearily.

"Be patient. Give Alice time to forgive you. Thom links you two together, she won't hurt him to hurt you. She'll come around."

"But do *you* forgive me? It's always mattered to you that none of us turned out like Anstey."

He sighed. With all that had happened since, he could scarcely remember how hard he'd tried to make them all keep faith with the ideals of their dead parents. What point had there been to any of it? Besides, Stephen had done so much for him and Kat. He mustn't ever forget that.

Trying to sound convincing, he said, quietly, "What's to forgive? You were young, Anstey played you. Someone had to be Bess's father. It's Alice you betrayed, not me. And you've been such a good friend to me since. The best."

"I wish I'd come to you before. It feels like I've betrayed you twice. I should have come in the beginning."

Yes, Stephen should have, that was what friends were for. He sighed again. He was afraid that however much he did ache, sadly, for Stephen, for Alice, for Bess's poor lost mother, he didn't have room inside himself to care, with any depth, about any of them at the moment. All that could penetrate the numbness and despair was his overwhelming love for Kat. His contact with her was the only thing keeping him sane. Surely fate would be kind to them now. Eight weeks to go, and he could speak to her every single day of those weeks, she'd promised, and then they would be together, in each other's arms.

He would never do such a thing to Kat, he was sure. Why would you risk hurting the person you loved, were bonded with, for the dubious pleasure of a bought and paid for fuck? Stephen needed to make peace with Alice and his own conscience. Thomas wasn't sure he fully understood his best friend anymore.

Chapter 17

Adam sat eating his lunch on the quayside. He was, as always, trying to remain inconspicuous, but the effort was particularly intense today – partly because it was sunny and his neck-gear was somewhat threadbare, leaving him in danger of revealing his skin markings, partly because he was surreptitiously watching the two women walking and talking further down the quay. The two women, he knew them both, though he couldn't ever quite put a name to the white-haired one. She was the one from the infirmary, the one who'd patched him up and had voted for him not to be put to death. The other one, the one he had been watching over at a safe distance for weeks, she *had* voted for him to die. Kat … Katharine, as Anstey had always called her. Now *she* had voted to end him. But he didn't blame her, it was her husband they'd done all that evil stuff to. If Thomas had been his loved one, he'd have voted death too. And here she was, unprotected. They had imprisoned Thomas, madness, in some appalling travesty of their twisted justice system. So now he was looking out for her because Thomas couldn't.

Sometimes Adam wondered how he'd got involved in all the trouble associated with being an enforcer. But it had made him feel good: Anstey trusting him, his mates around him, plenty of money. He had always skipped out of the drunken bouts with the younger girls, any of the girls in fact – no need – there were always humans who were more to his particular taste. They were cheerful, fun, and very accommodating for the right amount of money. Human minds were pathetically easy to read. In Adam's view there was nothing amusing or clever about forcing frightened, unwilling captives to have sex, just for the power trip. It was easy to find a willing and convivial partner – laugh, have a drink, share a bed.

Somehow, he had never put the two things together – the sex stuff and serving Anstey. Just because he wasn't interested in Anstey's brand of sex, that didn't necessarily mean he had to reject the whole deal, turn down the money and the camaraderie. After all, some of the men in the complex were technicians, some were labourers, he, himself, was a trained fighter. It was what he did, and he was proud of it – amongst the tallest and strongest of them – obeying Anstey without question, keeping himself to himself the rest of the time. So what if it was his job to kill occasionally? He only did it if it was essential. A necessary evil to keep the complex safe and hidden. For humans to be in the know would be dangerous. Far better to kill the odd one or two who blundered across them. After all, humans were not really an advanced species. It wasn't like killing one of their own.

But it was *that* which had been the problem in the end. Doing things to one of their own. To his everlasting shame, he hadn't quit straight way, when he first knew what he was expected to do. But toward the end of that last evening, the one that changed his view of it all, he had known he couldn't go on as he was.

How many of them had there been with Anstey, six? seven? Perhaps more. He could only see clearly his own part in it (and wished he couldn't). This time Anstey had required them to attend – not like with the girls, where it was just a case of 'if they took your fancy.' Adam shuddered, remembering.

Even when it was being done, the poor sod had tried not to

scream, and the more he didn't scream, the more Anstey, crazed as any of them, was determined that he should. Even Anstey seemed to have forgotten that they were supposed to be keeping the man alive, ready to lure his wife to ride in so she could get caught too. Somehow the blood and the lust, and the nips from Anstey's obligatory flasks of God-knew-what drugs, had maddened them until they were out of their minds with bestiality. And Adam couldn't say he hadn't been one of them.

But there had been that one silent, separate moment, right at the end, when he was suddenly, shamefully, totally in his right mind, detached from all around, looking down at Thomas Alban. First thinking he was dead, lying there naked, covered in blood and filth, blood still seeping from him. Then knowing he wasn't, seeing a tear, one single tear, drawing a flesh-coloured line down that dirty, ravaged face, and somehow knowing that the tear was not for the man himself, but shed in despair for his girl, his wife, who was going to come riding in to suffer the same fate.

Of course, Adam had backtracked from that shocking moment. Yes, it might be true that he'd 'failed' to fasten the man's shackles when he'd carried him back to the storehouse where he was being kept, and, yes, he'd carried him rather than dragged him, to the amusement of some of the others. But he'd still used that tired excuse of keeping Thomas alive on Anstey's orders. And, despite that earlier moment of complete clarity – the moment he had known with utter certainty how irredeemably wrong it all was – when the time had come for Thomas's wife to join them, he'd still been there, ranged with Anstey, still with that killing device on his fingers. He liked to think he'd never have used it – but he wouldn't ever know, and he'd paid a hard price for wearing it.

His gaze shifted downward at the thought of what she'd done to them – all those devices blasted to pieces – and he looked at the burnt, useless fingers that were almost welded together on his right hand. Good job he could still heft barrels, and was pretty good with his left, or he wouldn't have been able to hire out his labour, and thus survive. Conceivably, his thoughts could have been filled with revenge, but Adam knew he had deserved everything … and more.

Alongside that vision of Thomas Alban's tortured body, a vision that would haunt Adam for eternity, came the equally clear picture of that same man, quiet, gaunt, helped temporarily from the infirmary to give evidence and vote for the sentence, saying, softly but firmly, into the expectant hush of the council chamber: "*Not* death."

There had been a hubbub of noise. No-one but Alban's friends and family, who had half-smiled in resignation, could believe it. But there it was. Thomas Alban, a shadow, a wraith, with everyone unsure whether the poor man would even survive, could not bring himself to have someone such as Adam put to death. Not after everything Adam, with the others, had done to him. Alban would not even evade the question: he could have given someone a proxy vote and refused to emerge from his sick bed. Christ, he couldn't even walk unaided.

Thomas Alban was the best person Adam had ever met. And so, *he*, personally, was going to keep an eye on those pirates who were shadowing the women now that they were alone. He didn't know if he would be able to stop them on his own, but he intended to at least follow them and wait for an opportunity to re-pay some small part of the debt he owed to Kat's husband.

The pirates took him by surprise with their speed in the end. One, like a cat, pounced and grabbed the infirmary woman, one must have been down in a boat, just out of sight, below the quay. One charged up behind Thomas's Kat, throwing a sack over her head – that meant someone had warned them about her power – and shoved her off the side, so that she fell awkwardly, presumably into the waiting boat. They had pushed off and were moving into the channel even as he was belatedly making a run forward.

"Fuck!" Adam knew there was little use in following in plain sight. It was clear they were bound for Lundye. That was the rat's nest, where else would pirates head for? If he could steal or borrow a boat, once the others were well out to sea, he might make a covert landing during the night. Something else was bothering him too … Anstey. Could the bastard still be alive? Everything about the pirates' actions suggested that someone had been in the know about Kat. Adam was sure that if he could land unseen he would be able to judge the situation better — now all he needed was a local fisherman with a boat — he didn't mind swimming ashore when he was near enough, and stealing another to get the women away.

*

Anstey simply could not believe his good fortune. The pirates had gone out for Alice on his say so. He knew she had sufficient skill to sort out the sick bastard, who was disturbing all their sleep with his screaming and yelling (why they didn't just cut his throat Anstey couldn't imagine), but he hadn't thought she would be with Kat. The regular word that came back from the pirates' spies along the coast was pathetic really, but they had spotted that Alice (the pirates had named her 'the white-haired witch' when he'd described her and mentioned her powers … which showed how superstitious the creatures were) was in Ilfraycombe. No-one had thought to mention the small, red-brown, curly one with her. Now, here she was (such a good job he'd warned them all about her a while back). And, to crown it all, there was also word that Thomas Alban had survived, though he was currently imprisoned in the complex. Why on Earth was that? What could that pathetic idiot have done? No matter, it meant that he could still make the man suffer that final blow, make him suffer, impotently, the final destruction of his wife at Anstey's own hands. He found himself shaking with desire at the thought. That would teach Thomas to defy him, to stand against him. Thomas would understand, by the end, that he could *never* defeat Anstey, could *never* baulk him of his chosen prey. Kat would be completely and utterly violated and broken – as she so richly deserved. Sins of the mother visited on the daughter. Plus, Thomas would know that he had failed her, would see her suffer until her reason was gone and only then would Thomas be allowed to die. Then it would happen – Thomas Alban would be fucking destroyed, finally acknowledging defeat, and he, Anstey, would be there to see it. There wouldn't be any of his not crying then. God knew it had taken him long enough to drill that lesson into a defiant six-year-old. That was the key to peace of mind. For Thomas to know what Kat had suffered before death, to know he could never have saved her, to acknowledge himself incapable of defeating Anstey. Forced to admit he was a weak, hopeless failure, who couldn't even protect the woman he loved.

In the meantime, Alice was with the pirates. They seemed in awe of her. He was sure it wouldn't be too difficult to get them to let her go. Having Kat was enough. Alice could carry a message back to Thomas, some foretaste of the horror to come that would bring him charging, futilely, to the rescue as soon as he was freed. And, thus, it would begin again – only this time the final ending would be perfect.

Chapter 18

Thomas was worried, and there was no-one to help him. It had been much more than a week, he was sure, though he feared he was losing track of time. Kat had still not come back to him as she had promised. Their last conversation had played over and over in his mind, but there was nothing, nothing at all to indicate she would not be there the next day, as she been all the days previously – keeping him sane with her love and her company. She had promised, he heard her voice as it had been in his head … *"I love you Thomas, I'll be here tomorrow as usual."* She might be hurt. Surely Alice would have managed to get word to him if that was the case. Locked up as he was, he couldn't find out anything for himself. William, seeing how much more cheerful he had been when Kat could reach him every single day, had taken the children, admittedly at Thomas's own insistence, to visit with Cecily and Edward's young Eddie for a couple of days. He knew how much seeing him like this was taking a toll on them both. Lissy was too young, Kat should never have sent her, and there were too many reminders for Bess of that earlier imprisonment. Stephen had taken Thom with them too, trying to help him miss his mother less. Everyone was cheered at the thought Thomas would soon be out of there, only six more weeks, or maybe it was seven. It was right for William and Stephen to leave him there, no doubt they, like him, were concerned that seeing him was depressing the children. But now, how could he find out what had happened to Kat? Someone in the last day or so had even stopped George and John being on guard rota. It was clearly deliberate, he heard the guards talking, but he didn't know who was behind it.

Time dragged on. It might be 'only' five or six more weeks, but it didn't feel like 'only' if *you* were the one there, you were the one sitting in endless near darkness, humiliated and filthy, forced to piss and shit in potential view of the guards, shaking in the damp and cold and so afraid the smell of you would disgust your own children – if they ever returned – if anyone ever returned.

His Bess seemed to be getting on well with Stephen, he thought morosely, though she didn't know Stephen was her real father. Stephen had been bringing her down to see him before they went away, rather than William, who had brought Lissy. Both the children cried, however much he tried to be cheerful for them. They had eyes.

But it had all been alright as long as Kat, who couldn't see or smell him, thank God, came at night, every night, to tell him how much she loved him. Now he was living, entirely alone, in a God-forsaken silence. More than a week? Not her choice, he was absolutely sure. Something had happened and he had no-one to check for him. It was such bad timing; even James or Robert, who might have gone to Ilfraycombe for him, were involved in something or other urgent that was happening in Barnstable. Or perhaps the committee was preventing them from coming. Or maybe they just couldn't stand being near him, his fucking, stinking body.

Margery (no, Mathias, Kat had said, he must remember) was too bound up with the militia, or whoever they were, as they continued to plan their attack on the pirates – he hadn't come at all. Good. The fewer people who saw him, the better. But he needed to see someone, to get someone to go check on Kat. If anything had happened to her while she was all alone – alone because he'd been too stupid and proud to realise what they would do to him if he gave himself up – then *nothing* Alice could say would drag him back from a clifftop edge.

The cell door creaked open, and he thought for one glorious second that they might have let Kat back into the complex. Perhaps she had been arranging to reach him in person.

It wasn't Kat, it was Edith Hawkins standing there next to the guard. He couldn't remember the last time he'd seen her, but even in the half-light he could see that she looked as vengeful as ever.

"I see they've got you in the right place at last." Her voice sounded muffled; she held a cloth over her nose. "Dear God, how you stink. I'm surprised you're still alive. You don't imagine they're going to let you go, though, do you? The council are concerned at the way you and your half-human whore stoke up trouble – I've warned them about you and her – and you walked right into our hands. You and she killed Richard Thorne, you and she were responsible for the death of *my* Henry. I hear John Dinley died too in that ill-conceived escape bid, when you persuaded us all to renege on our contracts so that you could get her to yourself and shove your cock inside her. And now you've got a brat to show for it as well." She contemplated him and he imagined the malice in her eyes, even though he couldn't really see them.

"There's a few of us ready to make sure that you never see daylight, or her again. All that fuss you made, pretending Anstey and his men had been unkind to you and the human whores. You're such a liar. I hope it takes you a long, long while to die in here. I'll come every month or so to see how you're faring."

Darkness swept over him, drowning him as if he was swamped by the tide. The rushing in his ears drowned out her voice. He couldn't breathe or think, he was losing hold of his mind, control of his senses. He tried to fight back, to hold on, but what was the point? He'd never be free, never see Kat again, never even sleep, to dream of her. Despair and exhaustion broke him.

The cliff was unreachable, but unnecessary. He couldn't eat any more, anyway. The food had been choking him again since she was gone. He couldn't swallow properly. Why drink? Leant against the wall, facing away from the door, he didn't bother to look up to see his tormentor go. She had probably got bored with waiting for a reaction. He closed his eyes against everything and everybody. Let go. He would never be with her in the flesh again. If Kat wasn't there, he could have that final dream of her. If something had happened to her, perhaps they would soon be together again. Heaven or hell, which did it matter? Anywhere with her would be heaven. Vaguely he was aware of a guard shaking him every so often, trying to force him to drink or eat, then less so.

It was William's voice, shouting, that finally roused him. That and Lissy screaming "Dadde" over and over. He looked up dazed. William had the guard shoved up against the door frame, and no, it wasn't George or John.

"I don't give a fuck what your orders are. They can't be to let him die. That wouldn't be 'legal', and 'legal' is all your lot care about. Get someone from the infirmary down here NOW. And take the child with you, she shouldn't see her father like this. Margaret in the infirmary will look after her for the moment. Bess is there too."

He lay dazed, listening, and trying to work out what could be happening. The guard had picked Lissy up, she was crying and fighting the man. He felt he should go to her, but he didn't have the strength to stand. William was kneeling by him.

"For fuck sake, Thomas. What's happened to you? I thought you were alright to leave, that Kat had found a way to be with you. Can you even hear me? Why *now*? You've only four weeks left, but that oaf says you won't eat, don't even drink anymore. My God, what a state you're in."

Thomas tried to focus, to speak, to let William know about Kat. His tongue felt dry and swollen, and it was strangely difficult to get the words out.

"Something's … happened … to Kat. She *wouldn't* break her promise, but she hasn't been here since you all left and there was no-one, no-one at all to find out what was wrong."

William was quick to reassure him.

"Stephen will find out. He's gone to Ilfraycombe with Thom, to try to get Alice to talk to him. I persuaded him to give it another try. What in the name of God will starving yourself do to help Kat? She'll never forgive me if I let you die in here! And I won't forgive you for giving up. Just four fucking weeks and you can go yourself to find out why she hasn't come to you. Or is that what you're afraid of?"

"Edith Hawkins … she was down here. She said they weren't going to let me go … ever. I'll go mad alone here without Kat."

He felt his voice give out. Then he could recollect nothing until he found himself manacled to a bed in the infirmary, someone washing him, a needle and tubes in his arm and no strength to get up, which he needed to do, to find out about Kat.

"Take the fucking manacle off him!" William was yelling again, this time at someone else. "The man's dying! He's not going to run off anywhere. He's due to be freed in four more weeks. What the fuck does your savage little rule-book matter, when you've all left him to rot in that sadist's hell hole you pretend is a prison? So much for your superior race. You're as cruel and vindictive as the worst of us humans are. What did Thomas ever do to your precious community, other than trying to keep his wife and child safe? You'd better hope he's well enough to be released on time. I'll be sitting here waiting to take him home." William's rage was comforting, the words heard from a distance. He tried to focus on telling William to go and look for Kat.

"Have you heard from Stephen yet? Should you go after him? Leave me here and find out about Kat." While his voice was almost non-existent, he summoned enough strength to grab William's hand.

"I'm not leaving you." William was fierce. "These bastards are trying to kill you, and I won't let that happen. Stephen will come straight back if there's anything wrong. You, on the other hand, need to be ready to leave as soon as we know what's happening. The second your sentences ends, I'll have the paperwork here ready and a horse to get you to Kat, or at least somewhere you can find out answers. They won't be able to stop us. You need to get yourself strong enough to ride."

William turned to glare at someone – a guard – who had appeared beyond Thomas's shoulder. The guard sounded nervous.

"I've just come to take the manacle off. I've authority to do what's needful to get him back into shape. He's allowed to use a cleansing room and have fresh clothes from the store."

"Oh great! Finally. More humane treatment now he's too ill to enjoy it. Don't worry, just get someone here – preferably someone with an iota of kindness – to help me wash and dress him. And continue to get fluid into him. Perhaps pottage as well later, try to get his stomach into digesting food again."

He smiled, for the first time in days, it was an odd feeling. William sounded just like Kat, ordering people around, doing the right thing, as she and her father saw it. And, no matter how worried he was, it felt so much better to be clean, and then to have Lissy and Bess fussing around him, stroking his hands, whispering loving things to him, trying to get him to take a mouthful of liquid and mushed food every so often.

"As soon as you're freed, and in a fit state to travel, we'll all go to find out what's happened – whether Stephen is back or not. I'm sure there must be a simple explanation. Perhaps Kat's had a fall, broken her leg or something. She wouldn't be able to get to you then, would she?"

"I'm sure you're right. I know I stupidly overreact." Then he smiled, remembering, eyes half closed. "But at least I got to Kat in the floods. Saved her and Lissy from the water and the Thornes. Sometimes overreacting is needful; I could just have trusted she'd be fine. I hope she doesn't need me right this moment. I have to wait until they free me. Kat won't forgive me if I get locked away again for running out early."

"Believe me, from that very first moment in the sea you've done a much better job than me of keeping Kat alive. I'm glad I didn't kill you, back there in the cave." William tried to inject a note of humour, and he guessed that Kat's father was trying to distract him from his worst fears. "You'll get to her in time, whatever's wrong now. I feel it."

Chapter 19

So, Thomas, painfully thin, but walking and clean and with some food inside him was well enough to ride, thankfully, away from the complex on the due day. He didn't look back. More than almost anything he'd ever hoped for before, he hoped never to be in that evil place again. Lissy was in his arms, warm and comforting, ahead of him in the saddle. Bess was with William, riding alongside. Stephen hadn't returned. Not wanting to, but not daring not to, they checked all along the cliffs, looking down onto the rocks, just in case... Nothing. Thank Heaven.

Then there was nothing to do but head for the inn where Kat and Alice were or had been staying and hope that there were answers there. If only Joan had still been with them. It was his fault. Because the children were no longer there, she'd returned home. He should have insisted that his girls stayed with their mother and kept away from him.

His heart was thumping as they approached upper Ilfraycombe. Surely now he would be with her – but an aching fear in the depths of his body told him that she would not be there. He tried to keep upbeat. What had William said? A broken leg ... Lissy snuggled against him. *"See Mamma soon?"*

But at the inn there were no answers, only Stephen and Thom and more questions. Stephen, looking nearly as bad as he felt, grabbed him, almost gabbling in his rush to explain.

"I didn't know whether to come back and warn you, but I couldn't let the trail go cold. Neither of them has been here for weeks. The inn was about to let the rooms go. I've paid to keep them on. They're our only link. Look for yourselves – all their bags, everything is still here. As if they had only gone to the market, or down to the harbour for fish. Alice's hairbrush, just dropped on the bed, a warmer cloak …"

Stephen's voice choked and he looked wild and panicked. Then Thomas saw him abruptly pull himself together, recollecting Thom, and pick the boy up to hug him. "We'll find Mamma, Thom, don't worry, I'm sure she's alright."

Shock took his strength from him and he slumped down on the bed, holding both his girls close to him, Lissy on his knee. They clung tightly and he could feel how frightened they were, could read it in their faces. However much he'd feared it, nothing had fully prepared him for her to be so completely and inexplicably absent. If only he'd been with her … it was where he should have been, instead of being tormented in a prison cell alone. If he'd had any sense at all he would have been. They should have run away as soon as they'd escaped the floods, like William and Elizabeth had done all those years previously. But 'if only' didn't help. So much for having promised that he would always be there for her. All fucking pride. No fucking use.

"Mathias is here too." Stephen sounded a little more in control. "He came to see Kat, to tell her the latest about the militia. Now he's out, trying to find someone, anyone, who saw them."

As if he'd heard his name, Mathias walked in as Stephen spoke.

"Thomas!" He rushed to him and hugged him. "Stephen said they had you in the cells at the complex. I was out of touch for a while, I'm sorry. You look fucking dreadful. I came to comfort Kat and

Alice …" He looked pointedly at Stephen. "But there was no-one here. One of the women from the inn, the one who's in charge of the kitchens, she said that the two of them were walking down to the harbour, must be eight or so weeks ago, she isn't sure exactly, and they never came back. I think she's convinced I'm a man, she took to me and got quite chatty." Mathias paused for breath.

"Anyway, she said they had no travel bags, and they'd promised to bring her back some fish in any case. She said the darker-haired one – that must be your Kat – was always indoors by early afternoon because she went out on her horse later. The only odd thing she said was that she thought there was a big man hanging about, quite giant-like, but she thought he followed Kat each evening. Surely, though, if he'd intended to harm her in some way, he would have done something when she was on her own?"

The thought of a 'giant-like' man at once brought an image of the enforcers to mind. A cold shudder ran through him, and an ugly old pain twisted inside his guts. But there was no-one answering that description anywhere to be seen when he and the others all went back out to look.

For thirty more days they all combed the town, despairing, trying to get some sense of where Kat and Alice could have gone. They all listened to what was said, and the exiles listened as well to the human minds for what might not be voiced. Going out separately increased the scope of their coverage of the town, and they shared their information each night. Each of them had picked up thoughts of pirates, and a big man watching, but it got them no nearer to finding the women. On the thirty-first day, Alice came back.

He had offered money for any word brought to them at the inn and made sure there was always someone there to receive it and pay up. So, when Alice was found, blind-folded, stumbling around, hands tied behind her, there was someone only too happy to take her back to them and get paid. A dishevelled Alice, but otherwise unharmed.

Fortunately, Stephen and Thom were the ones who had stayed behind that day. When he got back, Alice and Stephen were in so tight an embrace it was almost impossible to see where she ended and he began. They were both crying, Thom too.

"Kat!" he yelled, running in, with hope in his heart. It was short-lived. Alice looked away from him, unable to meet his eyes.

"The pirates brought me back, they took both of us, but Kat fell and hit her head as they shoved us into the boat. They weren't really looking for her, they wanted someone like me to look after one of their own on Lundye. He was badly injured but I was able to help him. They wouldn't let me near Kat. Oh God! Thomas … Anstey was there … not dead at all."

"Where is she now?" He was still shouting, crazy at the thought of it, shaking Alice, throwing Stephen's restraining arm off. "What has he done to her?"

Alice made no attempt to struggle with him, meeting his eyes with the bleakest of looks as she fished a note out from her clothing. Alice and her notes. But he could see this one wasn't from Kat.

"The pirates that brought me back, they said Anstey gave me this for you." She handed it to him reluctantly. It was addressed to him, alone.

Dear Mister Alban,

I thought you would wish to know that I have rescued your Katharine from the rather unpleasant pirates who infest this place. Unfortunately, she suffered a nasty fall when she tried to prevent them taking Alice Derricott. As you will be aware by the time you read this, I managed to secure Mistress Derricott's release, but the pirates objected to letting Katharine go free as well. As a ploy to save her from them I have said that she is my daughter and that my companion Giles Donnett — you probably remember him, I think you made his intimate acquaintance when I was in charge of the complex and you were imprisoned there — is her husband. This means that they won't ship her off to the slave markets, though it cost me a certain amount of gold – well worth it.

What is amusing though is that she believes this fiction. Her amazing mind powers seem to be gone. She is rather a mindless and obedient little creature, helped by an interesting drug I managed to bring with me from my private collection on our home-world.

The three of us share a room. It is rather distracting for me. As I write this she is kneeling by the bed and Giles has her skirts around her ears while he fucks her. I'm hoping he might make me a 'grandfather,' he's certainly dedicated to trying. It is rather difficult to make him stop.

Did I say how pleased I was to hear that you survived, Thomas? I truly did not believe you would, we had such delightful fun with you, but this day would not be anywhere near so good if you had not.

Yours,

Richard Anstey

He stood motionless, unable to prevent the paper from falling from his grasp. His fingers, like the rest of him, had stopped functioning properly as his world stopped yet again and, this time, shattered into razor sharp fragments, puncturing his heart, his lungs, his mind and body.

Silence. There were no words left inside him, no breath to utter them. Vaguely, he registered that the others were watching him, but they were so very far away. With a remaining fragment of mind, he understood that they were afraid to reach out and touch him. Not that they didn't want to. Then he was all action. By the time any one of them had picked up the note and read it, he had buckled on his sword, added a dagger and the mind-stun device, picked up a pistol. Richard Anstey and Giles Donnett were dead men, perhaps he was too, so let them join him in hell.

Chapter 20

It was well after dark when Adam surfaced from his swim and edged, dripping wet, from the water onto the rocks. The fisherman was long gone, not wishing to tangle with the pirates, but he'd been true to his word, and very glad of the money. Adam had liked him, a friendly sort, and the man hadn't asked any awkward questions.

Despite thinking of little else since the women were taken, he wasn't at all sure how to proceed. Of one thing he was absolutely certain: Anstey was alive and behind the kidnap. That being the case, Anstey might believe him a friend – he could just show himself and say he'd heard rumours that Anstey was on the island and wanted to join him. On the other hand, pirates might kill him before he had a chance to contact the director. Perhaps it would be better to stay stealthy and try to spy out the lay of the land. If he arrived dripping wet, though, that might give added strength to his story.

In the end he decided that knowledge was essential. If necessary, he could get wet again and pretend he had just arrived. If he was going to protect Thomas's Kat, he needed to find out what had happened to her, what Anstey might be planning. There would be no way that Anstey would pass up the chance of revenge on someone who had been the ultimate cause of his defeat.

Time was moving on. He needed to find a safe place to hide, or to hide Kat and the other one if anything went wrong and the cliff had to be scaled while it was still dark. The climb was difficult, and it made him think of Kat, struggling down the steep pathway to be near to Thomas. They must have been able to talk, mind-to-mind. That must be something! He'd never been close enough to anyone to do that, but he'd heard about it. The humans were the only ones who never closed their minds against him and he kept his own tightly guarded. Humans had no idea at all what vulnerable creatures they were.

Not far into the climb Adam had a stroke of luck – there was a small cave. It looked as if it was well above any waves, however high they might reach in a seasonal storm, and when he explored further it was deep. There seemed to be nothing dangerous living there, just a few of the inevitable rats scurrying away from him in the darkness. With so many puffins nesting near he guessed that it must be a tempting landfall to any vermin foraging from the pirates' own and any captured ships.

Adam sat shivering in the sheltered entrance to the cave and offloaded the pack he'd managed to strap to his back. The pack itself was wet. Fuck, that had nearly sunk him on the swim. But he was pleased that he'd risked it and brought it ashore safely. From the inside he drew out a long coil of rope to hide at the top of the climb and then, wrapped in oiled cloth, his two long daggers and the belt to fasten them to. Strapping them on over his wet clothing, he left the pack to dry and continued his climb, noting anything that might guide him back to the cave, including the easiest route if he had to make the trip with one or both of the women accompanying him. The rope would help.

Near the top Adam grew very cautious. A crumbled area, with deceptive scrub making it seem more solid than it was, created the ideal place to mark the start of the climb down and hide the rope. To make sure it would stand out to him he broke back a piece of one of the branches, tearing it to leave a bark-free scabbed surface that should be relatively easy to spot, but only if you were looking for it. Keeping low to the tufty grass that barely covered the rocky cliff-top, he headed toward an area of denser darkness. About half-a-mile away he reckoned, and it looked as if it might be habitation. Lucky the island was so small since there was virtually no cover to be had anywhere. As soon as it was full daylight, he would be completely exposed to anyone on look out.

Two men emerged from one of the buildings as he crept nearer, briefly silhouetted in the light of a fire burning inside. They were clearly not expecting anyone to be there and Adam kept back in the shadows, listening for their thoughts. It was their voices that reached him first. They were noisy and slightly drunk — and out for a piss.

"Captain's pleased with the white-haired witch. She's worked a good spell on Sam, looks like he might recover after all. Thank God he's not screaming anymore."

"Yeah, think he'll let her go if Sam does get better?"

"Maybe. That fucking evil rich bastard that hangs around him has agreed to buy the other one if he does."

"The shorter one? She's a bit lacking, wouldn't fetch much in the slave market. That knock on the head seems to have scattered her wits, or maybe the drugs he feeds her, and she doesn't even know her own name. I think the old man wants her as a whore for his servant or sidekick or whatever he is. The big silent one. I've seen his greedy eyes light up when he looks at her. God help her if he gets it up her. Have you seen him piss? Never saw such a massive cock on a man. Can't imagine it primed for action. Still, not our concern."

"He's better suited to the witch, though she'd probably make it shrivel and fall off if she didn't take to him!"

They finished off, still laughing as they walked back inside.

That was Thomas's wife they were talking about. His fists clenched and his stomach curdled at the thought of how Thomas would feel. But it sounded just like Anstey. He must know Thomas was alive. To have that monster Donnett (and from the description it had to be him they meant) fuck the girl would be Anstey's view of heaven, made complete if Thomas found out, if he saw… If he could just find her first and stop it happening.

He needed a human pirate to tell him where everyone was. And in a hurry. Reading random thoughts would not be sufficient – he had to direct his victim to the specific information needed.

It was a long time since he'd mind-wiped a human, but he reckoned there wouldn't be a problem if he could grab someone who wouldn't be missed while he extracted the necessary details and left the man none the wiser. Stealthily moving nearer the doorway, fate played into his hands yet again, when one man left the same building on his own and crossed a courtyard area. The man's mind told Adam he was thinking of his bunk and sleep. Seconds later he was taken completely by surprise when Adam's dagger was at his throat and Adam's hand was over his mouth.

"Keep your mouth shut or I'll slice your fucking throat." It was so helpful to read the man's complete compliance in his thoughts. Adam dragged him through the darkness and out of earshot of the settlement, in case he did yell. It was pitifully easy to get a picture of the whole layout of the buildings from the human's mind, together with knowledge of the place they were holding the witch – more a room than a cell, not bad for Lundye – and, importantly, Anstey's rooms and the cell where Kat was currently imprisoned. Kat was in a cell on her own, alongside the one where the pirates held the captives they were about to sell on. Interesting that they'd separated the women. The witch seemed to be quite safe; he suspected they might well let her go. His efforts had to be concentrated on saving Kat.

Focussing his thoughts on the man's mind, he wiped away the

image of a man with a dagger at his throat and forced in another altogether – of the man on his own falling over in the dark, bumping his head on the stones. He hit him in the appropriate place to match the image and dragged him, semi-conscious, back to the courtyard, tripping him and leaving him on the ground where the man's head was now telling him he'd just fallen. Stupid human. Nasty fucking mind. He did *not* like pirates, especially when they were slavers, well not that one, for sure.

He crept on through the shadows, looking for Kat's prison, needing to get to her before Anstey bought her. But in this his luck failed him.

There were three of them there with Kat in the cell, the door was open, and Adam could hear every word. The human was the pirate captain, looking at, and thinking of, the bag of gold in his hand.

"Come, my dear Katharine." Anstey's hand was patting Kat on the head. "I know you've hurt your head, but I'm here now, your father, and look who's with me … your husband! We've ransomed you from these pirates. You'll be safe now that we're here for you."

Donnett shuffled forward and Adam shuddered. "Big Oaf. Oh God, the look on his fucking face, and his hands on her already." He couldn't think what he could do, there must be some way to disrupt them. Common sense made him wait and listen for a moment. It would be better to let Anstey and Donnett get her away from the pirates and take her to their room. That would improve the odds: the pirates were nearly as bad as Anstey and Donnett, and Adam doubted he could deal with all three at once. He might still manage to persuade Anstey he was a friend … before killing him for what he had made him do to Thomas and all the other evil stuff.

"I'll let the witch go tomorrow or perhaps the next day or the day after. You can wait 'til I'm sure that Sam's properly mended. There's no getting your hands on this one until that's all sorted. If anything happens to Sam, you'll need to negotiate some more. I'll take good care of your money in the meanwhile, and I'll make sure she's given that drug you've brought so that she doesn't get her senses back anytime soon."

"We're not trying to cross you," Anstey said. "We could take good care of her in our room. Her husband here is very anxious to have her safe with him again."

"I'll bet he is," the captain observed dryly.

Anstey sounded annoyed but backed down when the refusal was repeated. It was clear that the pirate captain very much doubted the truth of Anstey's pretence, but didn't really care, other than letting the fiction reward him with as much profit as could be gained from the situation. He was surprised that Anstey didn't try to influence the man's mind, but Anstey was looking old and weary. Perhaps his powers were less than they'd been. Perhaps the debauchery was catching up with him or his wounds had taken a toll.

No matter how tempting it was to think of removing Kat from the cell, he was sure that it would be a mistake. There was no way that he could contend, on his own, with a mass of pirates coming after them. As soon as 'ownership' had been transferred, the pirates would have their payment and put Kat out of their minds. At least it would be easier not to have both of them to rescue at the same time. Once he could be sure that the infirmary woman had been freed and was on her way to the mainland he could concentrate on Kat. A first step might be to make himself known to Anstey. There was no reason that he could think of for Anstey to suspect him. He should be in a good position then to spirit Kat away before Donnett got his hands, or any other part of his anatomy, on her.

Chapter 21

The man who says he's my father and pretends to be kind, he frightens me. But not as much as the other one, who is supposed to be my husband. He makes my skin crawl, the way he looks at me. But I do know them. I'm sure I do. Could it be possible? Why would I have said yes to him? Perhaps the old one forced me to. Why don't I know what's happened to me? There's so much nothingness, but somewhere I feel there's something, someone I should remember. My head hurts so badly and I feel sick all the time – that's a memory in itself. I remember feeling like this before, but not when or where.

The 'medicine,' the drug the older one leaves for me. I think it makes me worse – dizzy, disoriented. The last few lots I've managed to tip away. The other ones who are keeping me locked up don't care if I take it or not. I will pretend to feel its effects though, while I try to find out what is happening.

I can hear voices, and now that I'm freer of the drug, I think I can hear minds. Does everyone? I can't hear the two who have bought me, but all the other rough ones I can. They call themselves pirates, and they trade in flesh. That makes me shudder, but I'm learning things from them. They don't believe the other two are related to me, even though we have the same funny markings. They think the big one wants me, and their thoughts are graphic. I see what they think he'll do to me, and pretend it is his right. Not one of them knows *my* secret though: I can feel there's a child already growing inside me. Of one thing I'm completely certain – the baby has *nothing* to do with the man who claims to be my husband.

Oh, dear God, I'm crying again. I'm such a pathetic creature, I could have agreed to marry that man. Perhaps I needed a father for this child. Should I be nice to him? Close my eyes and pretend I'm not there while he does what he needs to and I pay whatever price I must for keeping us both alive. The child and me. I'm surprised the big man wants me. I stink. At some stage I've wet myself and worse, probably more than once.

I wish I knew my name. It would be a comfort. The old man says I'm Katharine Donnett, but I'm sure I'm not. My name is shorter. Deep inside me I believe … I hope, that someone somewhere is calling me by it. Waiting for me to come home. But I'm still muddled with the effects of the drugs and strange surges of something else inside me.

There's a lot of fear and panic in the ones in the bigger cell. They don't have markings. The pirates captured them too. They know they're going to be sold in the slave markets – I wish I could help them, they're so frightened, particularly those with children.

*

Adam debated the likelihood that she might hear him if he tried to speak to her mind. Was it possible given they were not bonded in any way? There was nothing to lose by trying, and the drug Anstey was feeding her, it might make her more open to his inner voice. For himself, he felt he knew her so well, knew her through Thomas's feelings and through their shared love … of Thomas.

Leant against the wall in the shadows he tried it, whispering inside himself: *"Kat, Kat, can you hear me? I've come to save you. Your Thomas sent me, him and your little girls."*

It was a strange feeling. He had to try a few times and take his own defences down – as alarming as that felt with his shameful past at risk of discovery and knowing how close Anstey and Donnett might be. Then there was a vague, faltering whisper in return.

"Who ... who are you? Who is Thomas? Am I Kat...?"

"I'm Adam, you don't know me, but I've been watching out for you and now I've come to save you, to get you away from the pirates and from Anstey and Donnett too."

"Anstey ... my father?"

"Anstey isn't your father, never believe his lies. Your true father is William and your true husband is Thomas. Wait for me. I may have to pretend to be nice to them before I can find the right moment to help you escape. With luck I'll be able to get you away before the big one gets his hands on you. But I can't promise you that I will be able to save you from that. Thomas will love you and want you back no matter what happens, I promise you."

"Adam ... safe ... Anstey not my father."

He moved away, not sure whether she had absorbed his words, but afraid to keep trying for the moment. Now to convince Anstey he was a friend.

It wasn't as difficult as he'd feared. In truth he had been unnecessarily cautious – Anstey welcomed him with open arms. His burnt hand was a badge of honour, his capture and banishment, which he quickly recounted, more than sufficient to ensure a warm welcome. He laid it on thickly – his relief at hearing Anstey was still alive, the way he'd bribed a fisherman to bring him out there, the swim. He was open about bringing his weapons, and, indeed, Anstey seemed pleased that he had, confessing that it was wearisome keeping the pirates in line and how much easier it would be if he had two enforcers to guard his back. Nothing was said about Kat, and he pretended ignorance, waiting for Anstey to tell him about her presence on the island.

There was time to settle in, Anstey trusted him alone in the room. He was less sure about Giles Donnett. They had never been particularly drawn to each other, but as long as Donnett didn't actively suspect him, he felt that he could take him by surprise when it came to the point of rescuing Kat. He did scout around amongst the pirates – Anstey had told them he was a 'friend.' Relieved, he located the armoury, and found that he could easily acquire a brace of pistols and ammunition to supplement his own knives if necessary.

Evidently Sam was taking longer to recover than they had anticipated. The Captain didn't budge from his position with regard to Kat, so he had longer to spy out the land and plan. After dark one of the younger pirates was friendly and accommodating. Attracted, he allowed himself to take his pleasure. It didn't feel unfaithful to his thoughts of Thomas since it might well help him in rescuing Kat. What it did reveal, however, was that Anstey maybe didn't trust him as much as he pretended. One of them, whether Giles or Anstey himself, must have been checking up on him. After the first time with the young pirate, it was obvious that Anstey had discovered what had happened when he nudged Giles and said:

"There, you see, Giles, you don't need to worry about competition for the girl. That isn't Adam's particular interest, is it?"

Giles just grunted but Adam could tell that it had been a worry of that sort, rather than suspicion, which had coloured Giles's behaviour towards him. It was always Anstey who was the crafty, suspicious one. It made him even more cautious about approaching Kat, since he wasn't supposed to know of her existence. Yet he had to keep her aware that she did have one friend to trust. And he wanted to take every opportunity to remind her of Thomas. From his snatched mind-to-mind communications with her he could tell that she still had no recollection of the man who loved her and Adam worried that she might have forgotten that she loved Thomas so much. He thought of her lonely nightly vigil on the beach by the complex, after braving that difficult climb. She did love Thomas. He wouldn't rescue her if she didn't, Thomas didn't deserve any more heartache.

With all that going through his head he did have the presence of mind to rise to Anstey's bait.

"Girl?"

"Someone you'll be very pleased to meet! The one that destroyed your hand!"

"What! Here?" Adam remembered, just in time, not to use Kat's name. He probably wouldn't know it, if he hadn't stayed in touch with everything Thomas and his family did.

"Do I get to make her suffer … get the satisfaction of personal revenge, or have you two got a prior claim? I guess that nothing that happens now will mend what she did to me, I'm sure anything you can think of inflicting on her will satisfy me if I can watch." He hoped his acting would be sufficiently good to fool Anstey, but his words sounded a bit stilted, a bit forced to his own ears. However, Anstey seemed too busy gloating to notice.

"We might save you something, once Giles has finished enjoying himself. I'm sure he'll let you watch to see if she screams. All I want is for Thomas Alban to arrive in time to see his wife suffer. You remember Thomas, don't you? I think you've already had the pleasure. However, we've all got to wait, the pirates are playing games and there are too many of them to risk pissing them off."

He feigned a certain level of disinterest, having pretended to agree with the general idea of Kat being punished. Anstey was unlikely to be particularly bothered whether it was Donnett or Adam doing the deed. Plus, Anstey knew that Adam wouldn't revel in it like Donnett. The anger that Anstey, that fucking devil, must have briefly glimpsed in his face, anger he hadn't even tried to disguise at the appalling thought of the man's sadistic plans for Thomas, would be bound to be interpreted as directed against Kat rather than Anstey himself.

Sick, deluded Anstey would never understand anyone thinking and feeling differently from the way *he* did. Fucking depraved bastard.

It wasn't until a few days later that Anstey alerted him to imminent action.

"Adam, the first stage of our revenge against the Albans is upon us. The pirate scum has decided to release our Domum-Orbis compatriot Alice."

"Alice?" He pretended surprise at the name. "She's not the one who burned my hand. I think she's the one who patched me up in the infirmary. I don't have anything against her, but I could stop them if you want."

"No! Don't do that! She's part of my plan. The pirates kidnapped two of them, Alice and Katharine. As soon as Alice goes free, I get to have the other one … Thomas Alban's Katharine. She's the one you should be interested in. And I've written a note for her husband. It's not the total truth, but I've created a pretty picture of how things are, just for him. I'm only fractionally in advance: it's a scene that will shortly be happening in reality. Enough detail in the note, I think, to make him come rushing as soon as Alice has delivered it for me. His poor lacerated little heart will be breaking. Here, you can take the message to where the pirates are getting her ready for departure. Make sure she has it somewhere safe and knows to deliver it to Alban, and him alone. I wish I could watch his face when he reads it."

Reluctantly, he agreed. He would have preferred to check on what Anstey was doing while he was occupied elsewhere with the man's errand. It looked as if Anstey, and Donnett (judging by the latter's anticipatory grin), were off to collect Kat. The rescue was now or never, but he still had to make sure that the two were unsuspicious so that he could take them by surprise. There was no way around it, he had to deliver the note first. While he didn't know exactly what Anstey had written, he could guess. Anstey and Donnett had to be dealt with before Thomas arrived and before they had a chance to do anything too terrible to Kat. Thomas would be in total torment and prepared to risk anything. He was determined that Thomas would find two dead bodies rather than confronting two living and potentially lethal enemies.

When he arrived in the cove, the white-haired one was already blind-folded and being helped into a boat.

"Wait! Anstey wants her to take a note." There was some resistance, but he was getting better tuned to manipulating the pirates' thoughts and they sullenly moved to allow him to put the note in Alice's pocket.

"A note for Thomas Alban, and no other." He told her, unsure if it was the wisest thing to do. It hurt him to think of Thomas reading it. But at least if it brought Thomas, Adam could help him get Kat away and remain himself to hold off any of the pirates who objected. As long as the fucking monsters from Domum-Orbis were destroyed before *he* arrived, he should be able to keep Thomas and Kat alive and safe.

Delaying as little as he could in returning to Anstey's room, he raced back via the stores. It was easy to knock out the solitary pirate standing there, from behind, and no-one else attempted to stop him as he liberated two pistols from the pile he had spotted earlier. He felt so much better when they were loaded and shoved securely into his belt. At close range his left hand would be fine. One for Donnett. One for Anstey.

By the time he returned to the room, Anstey and Donnett had Kat securely in their power. Anstey was telling Donnett that he could only do it to her once, then he would have to wait until they caught Alban attempting a rescue, all so that Thomas could be made to watch. Donnett was making the most of it, he had torn off her clothing and had his cock out, starting to force it into her. Kat's wits might be dazed, but she was screaming, loudly.

There was no alternative, despite the inevitable noise, no point in delaying. He shot Donnett in the head from close range – less chance of survival – blowing his brains out. Anstey turned to him in shock and horror. By the time the man was facing him, Adam had the other pistol pointed straight at him, and a second later Anstey's brains were similarly splattered across the room. Shoving Donnett's dead body off Kat, he grabbed Anstey's cloak. Wrapping the girl in it, he flung her over his shoulder and left the blood-soaked scene.

What he didn't forget to do was to keep up the tenuous mind contact he'd achieved with her. He didn't want to sap her sanity any further … he couldn't imagine what it must have been like for her … that monster starting to rape her, and then seeing two men with their heads literally blown away. She'd stopped screaming and was silent, but he kept up a litany of soothing words, telling her that Thomas would come to save her soon, that he, Adam, had a safe place where they could hide until Thomas arrived. She was crying, he could feel her chest heaving, but it was noiseless now, and she made no other sound until he had negotiated the appallingly difficult climb, carrying her, and had gently set her down in the cave.

She looked surprisingly calm, drawing the cloak around her nakedness. It scared him briefly when she rushed at him and hugged him, but her voice, when she spoke, remained reassuringly steady, even matter of fact. He hadn't fully realised that she could speak coherently, up to that point, and to hear her use his name was also a surprise.

"Thank you for killing them, Adam. You saved me." Then her voice turned wondering, "I felt something, some power in my mind growing stronger, but even if I'd been able to deal with the one, I doubt I could have got both. In all of this fog there's a sensation of repetition in my memory that tells me I've tried to kill them before. Thank you for making their deaths so … absolute … so beautifully definite."

He saw her shudder, but then smile, an exultant smile – more than relief – deep satisfaction. He decided she was more like him than Thomas. Thomas might hate, but death would never bring him joy. Thomas believed in redemption. Thank God.

Meantime, Kat had turned to more pressing issues.

"It's time for you to tell me, slowly and clearly, everything you know about me. My head … this terrible void … I must know. If this power the danger has woken up is as strong as it feels, and I already read the pirates' thoughts and those of their other captives, I must be careful not to hurt anyone who may come to rescue me, and I must make sure that they don't hurt you."

He was shocked, in a good way, at how well she was coping. Giving her a brief embarrassed hug in return for her more enthusiastic one, he encouraged her to sit down so that he could begin the tale.

Chapter 22

I know who I am, yet at the same time I don't. Yes, I know how silly and contradictory that sounds. Adam has spent endless time patiently telling me as much of my life story as he knows. The person I really do know now is Adam – how kind he is, that something in his past makes him ashamed, that he loves me in a gentle brotherly way, and that he loves the mysterious Thomas in an absolute, unchallengeable kind of way. Does my husband return his love?

But my mind stubbornly fails to tell me anything about the real me, the real Thomas, the real baby I gave birth to. To me the only real baby is the one I'm carrying inside me now. Somehow, I can tell Adam anything. I've told him that the baby has been inside me since before I hurt my head. He, I'm sure the baby is a he, is a constant presence, and there's something in me that's afraid for him. Someone will be hurt and angry about him, though I don't know why. Perhaps this Thomas is more frightening than Adam lets on. Perhaps Adam only *thinks* that Thomas loves me, because he worships Thomas. I must be sure before I let this stranger, this man who is my husband, into my head. I can't risk being in anyone's power. I still shudder at what that monster was doing to me. What if Thomas is like that too and Adam is deluded by loving him?

Adam is the only person I trust in this whole world. He looks after me, he's the one who saved me, he's brought me food and clothes, takes me down to the sea to piss and get clean – he tries not to look and never makes me uncomfortable. He has promised me, faithfully, that we will set those people in the cells free, even if it makes the pirates angry enough to attack us.

Funny thing, I do remember someone else now, but it isn't Thomas – I think the one I remember is my mother, but I think she died – Adam thinks she did too. But it seems as if there's a piece of her inside my brain. I'm a baby in her arms, and she's telling me things, whispering to me. I'm not sure that I've ever remembered this before. Not even when I had my full senses.

I've told Adam that I remember it as if it was *me*, but that I'm sure it must be a memory of hers planted in me. I can only re-live it because I am her daughter and she has willed it so. In the memory I feel as if I'm opening an *ostium*…? Holding time and space in my mind, piercing it, making a way through for the man who was Anstey. I remember that he was the one to smash the ostium, once he was safe, and I feel her anger inside me because it was before she was ready. She did something illegal for him and he betrayed her. But more importantly I remember … not just remember, *know* … exactly how it was done. The opening, I mean. I am absolutely certain that I am able to do such a thing myself.

Adam believes in me. He says I can do anything; he says I already have. He showed me his burned fingers when he told me what I did. But he has forgiven me because he deserved it and he can use his other hand as easily. There was something very bad that he did. He won't say what it was, only that he did it to Thomas and he's so very ashamed and sorry. Forgiving me and looking after me is part of what he does to gain, in turn, Thomas's forgiveness. But I think it isn't only for Thomas. I think he cares for me too now, in an odd, kindly, unthreatening way.

*

Adam was worried about Kat, cold and alone in the cave, while he was warm and sated and held by someone who had feelings for him, more feelings than he should have let develop. Being with Mark was not a betrayal of his love for Thomas. Thomas wasn't his to betray in that way, and never would be, even though he would always love Thomas more than anyone else. In any case he was doing this, well at least in part, to ensure that there was someone among the pirates who would look out for their interests, his and Kat's, and alert them to Thomas's arrival.

There could be no doubt that Anstey's note would bring Thomas and the thought concerned him greatly. How could he keep Thomas safe if he charged in, intent on killing Anstey and rescuing Kat, two things that he, Adam, had already accomplished? Ideally, he would have liked to have taken Kat home before Thomas had a chance to do something crazy, but Kat was surprisingly stubborn and wouldn't move without helping the other captives to escape the pirates. It was too late anyway. They would have had to have left as soon as Alice had departed for the mainland with the message, and that would have meant tangling with the pirates in the wake of noisily killing Anstey and Donnett.

Sighing, he held the human closer to him, warm in his arms. He was sure that he had impressed on the young man's mind the need to keep constant vigilance in looking out for Thomas, and probably one or two others. There was always the hope, too, that Thomas would also be able to read from Mark's mind their location in the cave, together with the knowledge that Adam was not like Donnett, that Adam was only keeping Kat safe and was no danger to her himself. Mark had yet to be instructed in all these details, in truth he hadn't sorted everything out in his own mind yet, but it would have to be done soon. Fortunately, their relationship was proceeding quickly, at least as quickly as Adam judged to be wise. It was a lot to hope for though and depended on Mark thinking the right thoughts and Thomas stopping to listen, despite being likely to be mad with fear for Kat. Was it right to use Mark in that way? He was young, but not too young, early twenties perhaps. The pirates had kept him back from one of the batches of captives when he had just been a child. Now he was someone else that Adam wanted to protect.

Moving reluctantly away from the young man, he started to dress quickly in the dark cold of early morning to return, guiltily, to Kat. He felt eyes on him. The human was awake and watching him – looking sad that he was leaving. He wanted to reach out and stroke his face. On the spur of the moment he took it as a sign that now was the time to reveal his and Kat's hiding place. Leaning forward he kissed the human gently on the lips.

"Come with me, I've something to show you," he whispered in his ear. Mark eagerly rose and dressed with speed. So young, an endearing puppy … but it was more than that. His heart gave an uncomfortable lurch. Maybe, after this was all done with, he might help the young man to escape from his life as a pirate and take him to the mainland. He had kept some of Anstey's money for himself, enough for them to be able to set up together. Just the two of them, and no more deception between them, however dangerous such a relationship would be.

So far Mark had established to Adam's satisfaction (while remaining unaware that his thoughts were continually being read by the man who shared his bunk) that the pirates were unconcerned – possibly even pleased – that Anstey and Donnett were dead. A trip back to the main buildings to take some money from the dead men's room and to raid the pirates' stores for warm clothing for Kat had been essential, but he had been canny about it and left sufficient money to make the pirates (who had no idea how much Anstey had secreted away) think they had profited handsomely from the deaths.

In the matter of the clothing, the pirates had so many unopened chests of stolen cargo in the store that they were probably unaware he had even been there. They were always much more concerned with the profitable human cargo the captive vessels provided. It was easier to convert lives into gold rather than attempt to sell cargo. There was nothing in Mark's mind to suggest that there were any problems. His efforts to make the pirates forget about Kat's existence were paying off. Food was the greatest difficulty, but the pirates had accepted his presence and seemed perfectly willing to provide him with food and drink. Always in their minds was the thought that he would be bound to join with them before long. Hardest was transporting some of the provisions to Kat, but he did his best.

It wasn't altogether surprising to him that Mark was not overly enthralled to meet Kat. Alert to the likely difficulty, he managed speedily to reassure him that she was another like the white-haired witch and would help the two of them to escape together. Impressing on Mark that the man he was looking out for was the girl's husband and lover, he confessed that he was only keeping Kat safe to deliver her to Thomas because he owed the man an (unspecified) debt. Kat, he noticed, was kind to the young human too. It was something of a relief to feel more certain that the affection she showed him personally – something which had alarmed him in the beginning – was not an affection of a type he might need to discourage. There was always that unfulfilled wish though – uncomfortable between them – why could she not begin to show at least some remembrance of Thomas? If he could only read her thoughts. But, despite the curious ability to speak silently mind-to-mind with her, the rest of her thoughts were deeply hidden from him. Mark's thoughts weren't hidden. Mark loved him.

Chapter 23

Thomas practically ran from the inn, intent on searching for any vessel that might be available to take him out to Lundye without delay. The others all rushed after him, as he'd guessed they would, trying to dissuade him from any action before they'd had the chance to plan properly. Whilst he wouldn't have listened to any of the adults, Lissy, held in Alice's arms, was screaming hysterically for him to stop, and Bess was calling out to him and crying. Torn in two, he found that he had to wait long enough for them to catch up and mill around him. William touched his arm tentatively.

"We got organised before, when Kat came after you. It's the best way to do it. We won then; we can do it again."

"But you've read what he's doing to her! The monster's fucking her."

Oh God, what was he saying, he'd blurted that out in front of his children. He rushed on, hoping they might not have realised what he was talking about, finishing on a whisper.

"How can I leave her even a second longer to endure that?"

"Please Thomas, I feel as you do, I'm her father for God's sake, but think for a moment. *If* the note is true, we're far too late to save her from rape, but I think, I pray, that Anstey is goading you. I'm positive that he'll keep Kat alive until you're there to see what happens to her. There's a chance that the drugs he talks about will protect her mind at least. You survived when it was the other way around. She can too. She's my little girl, but she's powerful, she'll do something. Think how she killed that human lout, how she killed Richard, how she blasted those infernal devices of theirs. If *you* go out there unprepared, he may even use you against her."

He hugged Bess and reached out to take Lissy from Alice's arms. Holding his children tight, one in each arm, he allowed the others to lead him back to their rooms. There were so many tears with the girls cuddled up to him that his own were unnoticeable – for which he was grateful.

The men were all adamant that they would accompany him. It seemed natural to include Mathias in their number; Margery had gone forever. Alice wanted to go too, pointing out that she, alone out of all of them, had been held captive on Lundye. It was folly for them not to take her, she insisted. Who better to take than someone who knew the island and knew where the pirates kept their prisoners? Her husband was equally adamant that Alice was on no account to go. Thomas had no doubt that Stephen was simply trying to protect his wife from further danger, but that didn't mean that he wasn't making good sense as he tried to persuade her.

"Kat and Thomas are banished from the complex still. If either of them should be injured, who is there, apart from you, who could treat them properly? You have to keep yourself safe, you're the only one outside the complex who has the knowledge and the skill."

Mathias seconded Stephen.

"Stay Alice, you're completely hopeless as a fighter, but utterly indispensable as a physician and surgeon. I may be able to get some others to accompany us. Even up the numbers. All my human friends are eager to get at the pirates, and the merchants are supporting us."

It wasn't mentioned, but there was also the thought that someone would need to stay with the children. If Kat was there, she would back Alice to go with them; Kat was always angry if she was shut out of anything. But Kat wasn't there, that was the whole point. He didn't take sides, waiting for the argument to be done. Alice conceded fairly rapidly, but on balance he found that he was sorry she had, he'd come to regard her as more dependable than Stephen. Though it was true that she wasn't a fighter – at least, not with the weapons that were available to them.

Stephen and William both gripped his shoulders; bringing him back to the moment.

"We're with you." And Stephen added, so low no-one but Thomas could hear, "I'll never let you down again." It sounded like something he might have said to Kat, and it made him feel guilty.

*

The assault took less than a week to prepare, thanks in great measure to Mathias, living fully as his new self for the duration of the action, or perhaps forever. Thomas learned that Mathias had encountered little difficulty in persuading some of his more hot-headed friends to organise a swift skirmish, intending to engage one or more of the pirates' ships and draw them out from their land base. Some of the fishermen from Clovelly had also offered support and were co-ordinating with Mathias so that the two actions were simultaneous. He told Thomas, gleefully, that both his own group and the fishermen had chafed at the long delay while the legally sanctioned operation was being planned. Thomas tried to connect with Mathias, with his enthusiasm, but his heart was too fearful, thinking of Kat. So many dangers, and no guarantee that he could save her. He might already be too late.

Concentrate on the practical. As a first step, he paid a generous sum to hire a merchant bark, a fairly small two-master, with a reliable crew (he and Stephen had vetted the minds of the sailors very carefully). The plan was for William and Stephen to sail out to Lundye with him, where they were to wait off the coast of the island until the action against the pirates began. Then the crew would land all three as covertly as was possible and wait offshore for a signal to come and pick them up again – with Kat. He had to keep believing…

The week continued to be total agony for him.

Half his time was spent persuading the children that their mother was safe and doubtless hiding somewhere, having killed Anstey and most of the pirates with her mind powers. Lissy was determined to believe that was what had happened, having been brought up on his whispered stories of her mother's prowess. Bess agreed, but he wasn't sure that she really did. There was always the feeling that she was trying to make *him* believe it, rather than herself.

The other half was spent trying to suppress the hideous images of what might actually be happening to Kat, images that were depriving him of sleep and threatening his sanity again. If he was to stay sane and rational, he could not afford to give into them. If he was to survive this, he could not, would not, be too late.

Although he felt like a complete nervous wreck by the time they were actually at sea, he was certain that adrenaline would kick in when it came to a fight. Inside him he kept up a continual prayer to the God of his home world and the God of this place, hoping, believing they were one and the same, begging, pleading for Kat to be safe. The nearing outline of the island, as the wind blew consistently in their favour, and the sun striking sparks from the inky sea, as their wake churned the water, raised his spirits. He *would* find her; he *would* save her.

Once in position, lurking off the far point on the ocean side, rather than the channel side of the island, it seemed they were waiting an age, but, at last, there it was, the sound of cannon fire. He hoped it was Mathias and his friends getting a first shot in. Whoever was firing, the action was happening and their hired ship drew back in towards the channel, close enough for the three of them to jump into the water and semi-swim and wade ashore. All three had swords drawn and stun weapons ready by the time they reached dry land; Thomas regretted their lack of pistols, but there had been no way to prevent such weapons from being wet and useless by the time they were landed.

At first there seemed to be no-one around as they emerged, dripping, onto the rocks, but then a young man appeared, running down toward them, waving his arms in what appeared to be a greeting, and shouting "friend!" at the top of his voice. They came to an uncertain halt, weapons still out and ready.

"Is any of you Thomas?" The young man asked the group randomly. "We have Kat safe, me and Adam, and Adam's killed Anstey and Donnett for you."

He had no idea who the young man, or Adam, might be, but a wave of sheer happiness washed through him when he heard Kat's name.

"Where is she? Take me to her. How near is she – can I signal the ship to come back in for us?"

"I don't think she'll agree to come with you yet. She's in a cave a way up from here, but she and Adam are plotting how they might rescue a crowd of the pirates' captives, a load being held for transport to Salé. Adam says you're bound to help me get away from the pirates too. I'm Mark. I was a pirate but Adam says to explain that I'm reformed."

The young man sounded cheerful and confident, but Thomas couldn't get his head around any of it – he just wanted Kat, he wanted to see her, hold her in his arms, have her safely away from this place. He didn't want to wait for anything or anybody.

"Take me to her," he demanded. The young man shrank back a

bit at the ferocity of Thomas's tone, and his voice, when he replied, was less hopeful and less friendly. Thomas felt slightly guilty, but he couldn't help himself, consumed with the need to see that Kat was alright.

"Follow me, but don't hurt Adam, he says he looks like one of the bad ones, but he isn't. I know he isn't; he's been looking after her, your wife, making her safe."

Mark, no longer cheerful, sounded anxious and suspicious. It could be a trap – the young man's thoughts were jumbled, as if he was deliberately trying to think certain things. There was always the possibility that Anstey was manipulating him. Without any reliable answers available in Mark's head, he was still bewildered as to why Kat might not want to come back straight away with him. William and Stephen held back, waiting for his lead, but Mark was all they had. He managed to nod brusquely to him and the three of them followed the young man on a steep climb up from the rocky landing place.

It was a difficult ascent, though Mark climbed confidently and quickly. In the end Thomas and the others were forced to sheath their weapons in order to grip whatever handholds they could, relieved when Mark stopped abruptly on a ledge part way up.

"They're in the cave, shall I go in first and let them know it's you?"

He couldn't wait for that and rushed in; he felt his heart would leave his body it was thumping so wildly. Then he saw her, he moved towards her. His only initial thought was that she would race into his arms, hold him, but instead she shrank back, actually shrank away from him, to stand closer to a big man who was alongside her. She was … clinging to *him*. That other man. Thomas found himself struggling to breathe. He called out to her, but she just looked bewildered. He tried to reach out to her with his mind, ready to tell her how much he loved her, but it was closed to him.

The man she was clinging to tried to edge her forward.

"This is Thomas, your husband, I told you about him. Don't be frightened, he's come to rescue you. I promised he would." She made no move to leave the man's side.

The man looked embarrassed.

As he watched them, together, Thomas saw what he hadn't noticed in his rush to be with her. Her hand was curved protectively over her belly. He had seen her like that before, when she was carrying Lissy. She was expecting a child. He thought of how long she had been held, so much time while he was still imprisoned. She must have thought he had abandoned her – he should have moved heaven and earth to escape that first evening when she didn't come to him. Now she was with that other man, he was sure of it, and, despite the joy of knowing she had survived, the pain of knowing she had found someone else was completely unbearable. To be shut out from her mind. He remembered that *he* had inflicted such a thing on her once … that hideous pain … now he knew exactly how bad it was. No wonder she had chosen to forget him. And now *they* were about to be a family. Kat and this man. He knew he should be thanking the man who had saved her, given her love. What he wanted to do was kill him. Sword, knife, bare hands, it didn't matter.

William moved forward, perhaps trying to ease the awkwardness that everyone seemed to be feeling and squeezed Thomas's arm reassuringly. But Thomas could read in Kat's father's mind that he was thinking the same thoughts about Kat and that man.

"I think Kat is still confused and suffering from memory loss," William reminded Thomas, in even tones before turning to his daughter. "There's all the time in the world for you to remember us … don't struggle with it now. All you need to know for the moment is that I'm your father, Thomas is your husband, and Stephen is a close friend. You're completely safe with us. Stephen's wife Alice was kidnapped with you, but they freed her and she's back at home with your two children, Bess and Lissy, and Stephen's own son Thom.

She's told us all about it."

Kat moved hesitantly forward. "That man, the one Adam saved me from, *he* said *he* was my father, that the one who … the other one … was my husband. I don't know who I am. All I can remember is a time when I was a baby, and someone I think was my mother."

She looked at William, half-smiling, as if she was aware of him in her past, and he smiled back at her. Thomas badly wanted to smile at her too, but his face was frozen. William was talking again then, telling her about her mother and that Anstey had ordered Elizabeth's death. Kat turned toward the other man. "I'm glad you've avenged her, Adam; you've done so much for me and now it seems that you've done so much for my father too."

She hugged him … Adam … and kissed his cheek, and Thomas couldn't decide if it was red-hot knives or ice-cold shards that stabbed him. Either way the agony was the same and equally ferocious. Then she seemed, reluctantly, to recall his own presence. She reached out a hand toward him, apologetically. He couldn't take it, not without dragging her into his arms, and he knew that would frighten her, and, when it did, her rejection of him would destroy him all over again.

"I'm sorry … Thomas … I'm sure I will remember you soon, you and our daughters. Give me a little time. But first we have work to do, people to free from the pirates." Her voice was placatory, as if he was an unpredictable stranger to keep sweet.

"Of course," he heard his own words and how stiff they sounded. Feeling panicked and alone, all his senses were telling him that he'd lost the fight before it had begun, and he had absolutely no idea what he could do to change things.

Chapter 24

Adam led Mark and the other three on the treacherous climb to the top of the cliff, trying to focus, solely, on the job they'd been sent to do. Why the fuck had things gone so badly wrong back there in the cave though? Adam couldn't understand how it had unravelled. He'd told Kat as much about Thomas, about her and Thomas, as he'd known. But everything he'd done to make Thomas happy, by keeping her safe, was just dust now. Why had she been so distant from her husband? He knew she loved Thomas – those nights when she'd sat on the beach, the climb she'd risked, so many times, to be near him. Surely her memory of Thomas should have preceded all else. Adam had the oddest feeling it was something to do with the baby as well as Anstey's drugs. Some hidden memory that was connected to Thomas. Had Thomas not wanted it? Hadn't he known?

They still had a job to do – Adam registered gloomily how difficult the climb was and remembered carrying Kat. How were they going to get so many frightened captives down to the cave? It was all fucking impossible. Yes, he felt sorry for the humans, but it was all falling to pieces, and now Thomas and Mark might lose their lives in attempting a rescue that *she* had ordered – instead of going to her husband and making him happy again. Adam sighed. He felt a great affection and sympathy for her. But she was difficult, and very determined. Thank God she'd stayed behind in the cave, ready to open the ostium – if indeed she could do such an incredible thing, though she'd sworn she could – and help them all get off the island.

As they approached the buildings, Adam could see that all attention was focused out to sea, where a fierce battle seemed to be raging. Cannons, flames. Most of the pirates were involved, only a handful were left on land to guard their stronghold. Adam shook his head in warning, motioning the others to avoid engaging with the remaining few pirates. He didn't know how Mark might feel about killing any of them. Why kill when they could probably achieve the rescue unseen? Well, that might depend on how noisy the captives were.

Once they had crept inside the nearest building – silent and apparently deserted – Thomas motioned Adam to his side. Adam was wary. He had felt the surge of hatred from Thomas when Kat had hugged him and kissed his cheek and he had the feeling that Thomas had recognised him … from before. Now was not the time for explanations, not that Adam had one to give, other than to assure Thomas that there was nothing between his wife and her rescuer, however much her actions seemed to suggest the contrary. But Thomas's friend Stephen, standing alongside, was drawing his attention to a curious device on his hand, one that resembled Anstey's mind weapons. Adam looked down, quickly, at his burnt hand. Surely such weaponry didn't exist anymore, did it? Stephen saw the direction of his gaze and obviously realised what was going through his mind.

"It's alright, these are new, they only stun. Explain to the young man. We'll only be knocking the pirates out. We won't be killing anyone. It may be necessary to stun some of the captives, if they don't trust us. You'd better be the one to explain to Kat if we carry any of them in unconscious."

Adam reflected morosely that even Stephen had noticed Kat's

total trust in him. Whatever they thought of him, however, Stephen and Thomas both had the same kind of weapon, so he took another from Stephen to use on his left hand. William didn't carry one, Adam guessed that they might not work for humans, and didn't ask for one for Mark. He did quickly whisper to the young man that these were strange devices, partial weapons that incapacitated but didn't kill.

This was all wasting time. Adam sighed with frustration. At any moment the battle at sea might end. The pirates would surely race back to their rocky stronghold if they felt they were losing. He took charge again, leading them to the cells, where the human captives — men, women and children — were huddled dejectedly.

"It's alright, we've come to aid you." He kept his tone even and low to avoid alarming them. "The woman who was in the other cell has escaped with our help, and she sent us back for you."

Adam could tell that Thomas and Stephen were joining their minds with his in exerting as much soothing reassurance as they could muster. Their combined strength seemed to be having the desired effect. Once the lock was broken, the humans all moved out in a surprisingly orderly fashion. Children in arms, men and women helping each other. Adam reckoned there were around ten adults, four children, and his heart sank when he thought how long it might take to get them all safely to the cave.

As they moved to leave the building, Stephen motioned quietly to Adam.

"You lead, the way is more familiar to you. Thomas and I will bring up the rear and stun anyone coming up behind us. Fast as you can."

Perhaps Stephen was concerned that Thomas might attack him if they were left together. Adam was certain Thomas wouldn't, no matter how much he might want to. Thomas might get angry, but never, never would he kill unless driven to in an actual fight. Besides, if Thomas did want to kill him, it was only right and fair for him to do it, after what he had done to him before, and now for failing to return Kat's love to him, intact. As long as no-one hurt Mark.

But misery couldn't be allowed to interfere with what they were trying to achieve. Adam led the way.

*

I must be ready, I can feel power building, but I fear it too. Once upon another time, in the void, something bad happened to me when I used it. I feel my belly, reassuring the child in me that I will keep him safe. Can I split the power? Use half to open up a way through and away from here, use the other half to protect my child from the way I know the power will surge through me when I'm ready. Divert it around him. Clearer memories of my mother tell me that she never achieved such a feat. She avoided her power while she carried me. Later, the continuous use of it, to protect my identity, to hide herself and my father from Anstey's notice, destroyed any brother or sister I might have had.

I can feel some stirring of memory of my father. It might be my imagination. The other man, Thomas, he is awash with emotion and I can't sense whether he is angry or upset or both. I don't remember him, I don't trust him, I fear he is an enemy to my baby. My priority is to help all these frightened people – the children especially. Adam will help me. He's strong and dependable, he killed the monsters; he will make sure we are all safe.

Chapter 25

Thomas waited at the top of the cliff, a rear-guard. His choice not to lead. He'd whispered it to Stephen, mainly because he was afraid to be alone with Kat in the cave. Alone in the sense of no-one else from their home-world, other than the two of them, being there. If there was no Adam, he might not be able to resist kissing her, holding her tightly, and it would scare her. His stomach knotted with the tension of seeing her and being unable to reclaim her. He wanted, so very badly, to crush her to him, hear her laugh with him, tease him about her ribs. There was a time he might have risked it ... before ... but he wasn't that man any more.

He watched the others struggling to shepherd the humans down. Adam had a rope; they'd fastened it at the top and it was at least helping with the exodus. Fuck, he was disgusted with himself. Everything Adam succeeded in achieving made him hate the man more – as if they were on opposite sides instead of working together to save lives. What kind of sick, jealous bastard was he? He was ashamed.

At some point, if Kat managed to open an ostium, someone would have to stay behind to signal the ship that was waiting offshore for them. He had decided it should be him. The others would all work together better in his absence.

He was facing away from the path when Stephen ascended for the last time.

"Everyone is ready, Thomas. You need to come down."

"I'll see you all safely away, but I'll stay to signal the ship."

"I can do that."

"No need, I'd rather. Make sure they all get away without any problems. Do you know where Kat will attempt to go through to?"

Stephen hesitated, before saying, quickly,

"Adam knows a cave near Ilfraycombe. He's shared the location with Kat, in her mind. I think he's lived there when he didn't have money for lodgings. It's been a difficult time for him since the banishment, his damaged hand prevents him from taking on a lot of work."

"Well at least he wasn't hanged," he couldn't stop himself from saying bitterly – ashamed the moment he'd uttered the words.

"Thomas! He saved Kat! Surely you wouldn't have preferred to come here and find Donnett raping her, with Anstey watching!" Stephen sounded shocked, rightly so. Thomas didn't understand what was happening to him either.

"No! No…!" He felt sick. "I couldn't have borne that. I *am* grateful to the man. I truly am. But to see him with *her*! *My* Kat. And it looks as if he himself has been doing what Donnett wanted to do. Didn't you notice that she's pregnant!"

"Yes, of course I did. But her feelings will change when she remembers you and how much she loves you. How do you know it's not yours anyway? Perhaps before you were taken to trial at the complex."

"Kat always used contraception. She knew how frightened I was of another pregnancy."

"Maybe she forgot."

"I don't think so, she hated to worry me." For a moment he tried to clutch at that straw, but, after losing their first, Kat would have told him if that were the case. He shook himself and focused on facing unvarnished reality. "I'll see you people off and then leave on the boat."

Stephen put a hand on Thomas's arm.

"Don't give up. She'll love you again – I nearly lost Alice by being stupid. I know this is nothing like that, but please don't just let your marriage slip away. Give her time. Think of the girls if not of yourself."

He looked at Stephen, pain in his heart.

"Your daughter and mine."

"Bess is your daughter. She always will be. She chose you – I'll always be second best for her."

"And Kat's chosen Adam."

"For the moment, maybe. Do *not* give up."

Then Mark was scrabbling his way back up to them.

"Come ON." The young man was excited. "She's ready."

Stephen headed down; he followed more slowly.

Everyone was waiting in the cave. He had no idea what they'd told the freed humans, but there seemed to be no panic. Those from Domum-Orbis going through would help erase the memories of any of the humans who didn't cope well with the idea of travelling in such a fashion. There should be no panic at all – assuming Kat could actually do as she'd promised. How could she remember something from when she was a baby and not remember him ... them?

Kat, looking magnificent, was standing very straight and alone. She was so brave, so beautiful. Just like she had when Anstey's weapons were destroyed. She raised her hands.

For a split-second he didn't want to share the warning that sprang into his mind. Then he had to. Just because she didn't love him, it didn't alter the fact that he loved her.

"Be careful, Kat. You don't remember, but you lost our first child because of using your power. Our Thomasin. Please be careful. I can see that you … that you have a baby in you now."

She turned to him with a real smile, one that reached her eyes. Oh, she was breath-taking… "Please, dear God, don't let her be lost to me forever. I'll do anything," his mind whispered.

"Thank you, Thomas. I do truly appreciate your warning. I *will* remember you and Thomasin and our other girls, I know it, I promise. For now, I think I've found a way to prevent the surge passing through my womb."

Then she turned and gestured at the wall of the cave with her arms. None of the humans there had ever seen an ostium, apart from William, but no-one was in any doubt that they were seeing one then. The rock shimmered and seemed to dissolve, leaving a strange cloudy film that rippled like water on a shadowed lake.

"Go through … now … quickly. I have no idea how long I can keep this open." Kat was gasping and shaking with the effort, and Thomas doubted she was able to protect the baby from such a surge of power. Stephen and Adam were sending the former captives through. William and Mark were watching Kat, in wonder, as they joined them.

Then they were all gone and the familiar, burning scent of the power was easing. Kat turned to him. He was surprised she, too, had not already gone from him; he assumed that she could close it from either side.

"Are you coming?"

"I have to contact the ship. Will you be able to close the ostium straight away once you're through? I could stay here for a while, make sure everything is alright. I'll see you back in Ilfraycombe."

"Back in Ilfraycombe," she repeated softly as she passed through and the cave wall slowly returned to normal.

He was left alone. More alone than he had ever been. There was the time she had left him when he was angry, the time when Anstey had held him prisoner and she'd been so ill, then those hideous weeks in the cell when he didn't know what had happened to her. But she had never chosen to be with anyone else rather than him before, as she seemed to have done now. He'd always had hope. At least he did have a smile to hold on to. Perhaps she would remember him in the end. He would be there for her if she wanted him, take her on any terms she might impose, regardless of whatever had happened between them, Adam and her.

Slowly he made his way back to the top of the cliff and took his shirt off to signal: ready for the sea voyage back, and his next chance to make Kat remember that she loved him.

Chapter 26

I think I may have been wrong to fear Thomas.

Everything I'm told makes him appear to be some paragon of impeccable virtue: brave, self-sacrificing, and blessed with moral certainty in all his actions. A man such as that, with such inner confidence and a compulsion to do what is right, no matter the consequences, would surely have known not to fall in love with me, whoever I am. That's why I shut him out in those first few moments when he rushed toward me.

Yet everyone tells me how much he loves me; how much I will discover I love him when my memory returns. But I can't shake the feeling that my pregnancy bothers him. If we are … were … so much in love, surely this has to be his child too. At first, when he seemed fierce and angry, I couldn't imagine why I had aroused such negative feelings in him and he seemed repelled by my pregnant body. Yet just now he warned me of danger to the child. Perhaps I have misread him. Perhaps he is only worrying about us. I'm glad I smiled and saw such relief in his eyes. But why did he stay behind, when I know his friend Stephen would have willingly done so? Perhaps that kind of gesture is what makes everyone feel that he is self-sacrificing. But while it might make him admired by friends and those around him, it must make life unbearable for anyone wanting to be the first and only person in his life. I'm not sure that I could cope with loving Thomas Alban. I fear such an emotion might destroy me.

At least I have succeeded in saving those poor forlorn captives and Adam and the one called Stephen have altered their memories. They all dispersed happily enough, believing they had sailed back from the island, liberated by part of the force that was attacking the pirate fleet. Mark's image has been imprinted on them as one of their rescuers, in case he might be accused of being a pirate at some stage. I'm so glad that he and Adam are together. However, they have warned me how dangerous it would be for anyone to suspect their feelings for each other. I am resolved to stay silent and trust no-one, not even Thomas, with their secret.

For now, Adam and Mark have said goodbye to the rest of us. Adam is using some of Anstey's gold to procure lodgings for them, the most unlikely 'brothers' you might ever see. The lodgings will have a lock and key, and their love will remain hidden. It's sad that Adam is banned from this complex they speak of. From everything I've been told about the place, he and Mark could have lived together openly there.

Stephen wants me to talk to Alice, his wife, who is looking after my children and is good at talking people through what he calls 'traumas' such as mine. William, I mean my father, believes that I should travel back with him to my first home. He thinks that recalling my mother ahead of anyone else might mean that my memory will unfurl in an orderly fashion, oldest memories first. I think he is planning to take me on a trip through all the places that have been significant in my life. He will exclude the complex: apparently, I am banished from there for some reason.

I don't know what I want. I keep thinking of Thomas Alban and hoping he will sail safely back to Ilfraycombe. He looks so tired and ill … serious and somehow stern. But he is my husband. I feel awkward and shy. What if he wants to resume our life together without waiting for me to recall what was between us? No doubt he will feel he has rights, but I don't want him to see me unclothed and with this pregnant belly, especially if his feelings surrounding the child are ambivalent. All I can think of when I am driven to contemplate nakedness and sex is Donnett – triumphantly stripping me, pushing into me with his hideous appendage – then his brains oozing out over me and my savage, savage satisfaction in his death. I will always love Adam for what he did for me.

I make a decision and explain very carefully to William, I mean my father, and Stephen. I will go with William first. Before I even see my own children. I don't, in any case, know what they look like. How is it they can be so totally excluded from my recall? My father may be right about my memory, and I can only imagine how terrible it would be for my children to see me when I can't recognise who they are or respond to their love. What if they should hug me and try to speak inside my mind? I can't let anyone but Adam there at present. It doesn't seem safe. I almost let those evil men inside my head when they pretended to be my nearest kin.

Better to go now, straight away, before I have to share Thomas's room and bed and risk rejecting him irrevocably if I am unable to get beyond my current memories of all that Adam saved me from. I shudder when I think of someone touching my body, my markings.

Stephen will tell the children that their mother is unwell and has to go somewhere with grandfather to be made better, but that she will be with them very soon. I leave him free to judge what will be the best thing to be said to Thomas. I hope I'm making the right decision. There is a tiny sliver of feeling inside me that tells me I want to be with Thomas, right now, that I want him to show me how much he cares, persuade me of our love. But I have to *know* it, deep inside me, not just be told about it. For now, there is a life growing that must take precedence.

*

It was a horrible shock to Thomas to arrive in Ilfraycombe and find Kat already gone. All the way back on the boat, he had convinced himself that she would be with the girls when he returned. She might have forgotten him, that he could believe, but Bess and Lissy – surely there was no way. He hadn't realised how much he had banked on the thought that seeing the children might open up some channel to her inner mind. The picture he'd been nurturing, of her turning to him, seeking his arms, kissing him and telling him she remembered him and loved him faded away to nothing. Leaving only a void, one that threatened to engulf him.

Instead the girls snuggled in his arms, Bess was really way too big to do that now, but it didn't stop her. They were both crying to think that their mother was unwell and away from them. He hoped they didn't realise that he was beginning to doubt whether Kat would ever come back willingly. Perhaps the thought of having to be with him would even keep her away from her daughters. At least William was with her. Or would they lie to him about that? Suppose she had gone away to be with Adam. Suppose William didn't want him to know in case he went after them. Suppose she didn't want *his* children, only the one she was carrying, which was surely Adam's. A horribly clear picture of the three of them replaced the one with him in it. The image of Adam, Kat, and a tiny boy, the spit of his father, drove another shard into his already mangled heart.

He did so love his girls, but was it right to hang on to them if in doing so he made it difficult for them to have a relationship with their mother? How could he deprive them of her? Doubtless she would have come here to be with them if he hadn't been here too. Could they share the children? But how on Earth could he live if he had to give them up too? Yet, Kat shouldn't have to see him if it was unpleasant for her, not if it stopped her wanting to be there for her girls. Alice and Stephen would be bound to help by bringing the children to visit him from time to time. Feeling sick, he realised that he wouldn't even be able to end his life. Kat and the children could never be made to feel guilty about any of this.

They were standing there now, with Alice and Stephen, who were looking at him with concern on both their faces. He hoped none of them could see that he was trying not to cry. It would be safest to put the girls to bed before talking to Stephen. Bess helped him with Lissy, and then waved him away, back to his friends, independent as always.

Stephen had wine poured for the three of them when he returned, so far nothing had been spoken of Kat, other than hopes for her speedy return to health, in front of the children. Thom was there too, but he was fast asleep already, curled up, with a cloak over him in one of the far chairs in the second room. The child was unlikely to wake and overhear. The time his father was away on the rescue, though short, had been frightening for the boy and he hadn't slept while Stephen was absent. He understood. Thom's mother had left him alone with his father for weeks on end, now his godson was afraid to trust either parent to remain with him.

With a return to despair, he realised that almost none of this would have happened if he hadn't agreed to return to the complex with Robert. Most of it wouldn't have happened either if he'd had the sense to run away with Kat the first moment there was any suggestion of being put on trial for his actions in the flood. No wonder Kat had turned to Adam. While his own choices damaged everyone around him, Adam simply marched in and killed Kat's foes for her. And the amazing ability in her, the ability to create an ostium, no less. That had never surfaced while she was with him. It was as if her mother had implanted the memory, but warned her baby daughter that such a gift must never be revealed until she was safe with a special man from Domum-Orbis, someone who would care for her and protect her while she worked such miracles for her people. He was a failure – not the one awaited. Early on her power had frightened and angered him; he had consistently failed to be there for her, maybe he'd even been envious of her self-sufficiency. Now Adam was her chosen saviour.

Becoming aware that Alice and Stephen were still regarding him anxiously, he tried to find enough of a voice to speak sensibly to them and prevent them from understanding how far his thoughts and plans for the future had progressed.

"Did William say how long they might be gone?"

"No, I think his intention was to be led by Kat and how much she remembers. He's starting at their first home, going on to the derelict house near the complex, then to Barnstable. James says that your house there is ready when you want to return. I don't think you want to say to Kat that the Thornes's bodies were removed from your upstairs room when the flood waters receded."

"She's had enough horror in her life. I'll just say they perished in the flood if I ever get to talk about that time to her."

"Why don't you ride after them? You could help William to recollect all the places that could mean something to her. William would like that, I'm sure."

He thought of taking Kat to the cave again, how good that had been for them – both times. For a brief second, he was tempted. But no, what if she remembered nothing, or worse, turned from him in disgust at the thought of ever having lain with him there. Fuck. *Fuck*, he was going to cry again. A whole childhood of not allowing himself the luxury of tears, and now look at him – he seemed to be crying all the time. The choking lump in his throat prevented him from swallowing properly, but he tried to hold it together. He wouldn't break down in front of his friends.

"I don't think riding after them will help. I suspect that Kat would prefer not to be with me at present. I frighten her. Look, I'm sorry, I don't think I can talk about this now. Maybe tomorrow."

They were reluctant to go, but he made it as plain as he could that he wanted to be alone. As soon as Alice had returned from Lundye they had transferred from the inn to the shop and lodgings Alice had taken on. They seemed reconciled and he found it in him to be glad for them. Stephen drew Thom into his arms without waking the boy. With evident reluctance they took their leave, promising to return the next day. He didn't particularly encourage them in the idea. Being alone left him free to grieve without shame.

When the door shut behind them, he turned the key in the lock and went back to his chair. With no one to see him he cried himself into an uneasy sleep, ridden with nightmares. Not the old ones. Brand new ones in which Kat was running from Anstey, running from Donnett, while he stood still and did nothing as she called to him to save her. His legs wouldn't move, his voice wouldn't work. Then there was Adam, killing the monsters, and Kat in Adam's arms, while he looked on, *still* fucking frozen. In the morning he discovered that he must have cried out loud. Bess was sitting on his lap, trying to soothe him. Like long ago.

"Let me and Lissy go after Mother. I can show her things in my head, I've done it before. She does love you; I know it. Even if she doesn't remember it herself, she'll love you all over again if she sees us together as a family. I don't have all your memories, but I think I have enough. I think Lissy can show her things too. She needs to see it all, experience it and not just be told."

"Who would go with you? I don't want to frighten her by forcing my company on her … I mean while she's unwell."

"I hear things, Father, I know how it is, what's happened. You talk in your sleep. Don't forget how old I am now. I could go alone, I'm big enough to care for Lissy. Or maybe Uncle Mathias could go with us, or Uncle James. We could travel to Barnstable and wait for her there. Grandfather is bound to take Mother there."

He hugged his big daughter.

"Let me think about it. At the moment I couldn't bear to be without you, either of you. I'm going to be selfish for a while. Hold you and Lissy close to me while I still can."

Bess threw her arms around him and kissed him.

"Love you Dadde."

"Love you too."

It was balm to his pain to hear her voice in his mind and the affectionate childhood address, *Dadde*, that he thought she'd grown out of. He could see that she was thinking carefully. She hugged him tightly again.

"How about if you share? Only for a short while. You keep Lissy with you and I go to Mother and bring her back to you, to us."

"I'd be afraid of you not coming back. It would make me sad."

"I've always come back to you before. You've often let me go off with Grandfather, to stay with Aunt Cecily and Uncle Edward. I'm probably even fourteen years old now – old enough to be married! I didn't let you down when you were in gaol, how would I not come back to you now?"

"I know, I know, my special girl. I trust you to come home, but with everything that's happened I'll always be afraid that something, someone might prevent you. Wait a while, let your mother recover some more – you never know, she might be back with us in a few days." He wished he believed it.

Over the next few weeks, with Kat still absent and no word from William, Bess wore him down. He decided that if she was determined to go looking for Kat, he'd prefer her to travel with James. Mathias was too busy having dangerous adventures and he didn't want Bess to be involved in any of those. She was already too brave and too independent. He wrote to James, explaining, and Stephen, when he next visited, volunteered to deliver the note, taking Thom with him. It struck Thomas that he could have sent Bess with Stephen in the first place (and that Stephen knew it). More proof of his jealous nature. He didn't want to think of Stephen and his Bess. He would be alone soon enough.

It was a relief in more ways than one when James arrived in immediate response to his letter. James insisted on staying for a couple of days before taking Bess to find her mother, and when the girls were in bed, he again insisted, forcefully, on making him talk. Thomas found that he was not the only one suffering from guilt. James and Robert still blamed themselves for everything that had happened.

At first, he would admit nothing, share nothing about that awful moment when he had reached Kat on the island and known she no longer cared for him. But once he started to talk, he found he could hold nothing back. He confided in James that once he was sure Kat and William had moved on from Barnstable he would go there himself … live there alone, hoping to see the girls from time to time if Kat wanted them with her, or have them living with him if she couldn't remember them or bring herself to care for *his* children.

The most difficult part was telling James about Kat and Adam and the baby. It made the picture in his head more real.

"I can't blame her. He did everything I should have done; I'm not surprised she doesn't remember me. And once they have a child. What chance is there of her coming back to me? It's better for her not to remember me, but the children need her to remember them. I feel that she's ready to begin a new chapter in her life, and I won't hold her back or make her feel guilty or miserable. I will give up the girls if that's what it takes to make her see them and love them again."

James groaned. "You don't know for sure about any of this. Don't rush into leaving her before you know it's what she wants. You don't know the child is this Adam's. She's grateful to him. Of course she is, who wouldn't be? That doesn't mean she loves him. You've created a whole story out of nothing."

"What else am I to think? I was ready to rush to her, but she shrank from me and let him hold her instead. She kissed him. It must be his child; she was on the island with him for all that time when I was imprisoned and couldn't get anyone to find out what had happened to her. She remembered nothing about me, why wouldn't she turn to the man who saved her? I don't think she would be so protective of the child if it was Donnett's – he's the only other possible father."

"Stephen tells me that the man is one of the banished enforcers. His hand is burned. Forgive me, but he's probably one of the men who did those appalling things to you. Are you sure he's a fit person to look after your wife?"

"I remember him. He *was* one of them – I remember each and every one ... their faces as they came for me. I see them ... waking or sleeping ... I always will. But they didn't know what they were doing, they were too high on Anstey's drugs. Afterwards, that last time, when it became an uncontrollable orgy and I was so badly damaged inside, he carried me back to the cell in his arms, and the others teased him for it, for not dragging me. I think he felt remorse, even then. I won't hold the past against him. But if he hurts Kat, then I might find it in me to kill him. I don't believe he will though, he's kind and tender with her. I watched him. I don't believe he'll let her down. But on the island ... Oh God, I wanted to kill him so badly. But how could Kat ever forgive me for doing something like that, after what he did for her."

"You voted for him not to die. Don't you regret that now?"

"No! Though I did, just for a moment. But if he hadn't been there to save Kat. It doesn't bear thinking about."

There was a wail from the other room. Fuck, Lissy was having nightmares too.

He hurried to her and picked her up – thankfully Bess was still sleeping. Cuddling Lissy, he carried her into the room where James was waiting anxiously.

"I want Mamma," she was sobbing quietly.

"Dadde's here Lissy, Dadde loves you, Mamma will be here soon, I promise." But he couldn't console her, it was Kat she needed. It made his mind up for him.

"Take both girls with you. Bess, I keep forgetting she's grown up now, will look after Lissy and you can guard them both. They need to find their mother, I'm not enough for them. If you have a chance to talk to Kat, ask her … beg her … to let me see them sometimes."

"Don't do this! Give Kat a chance to come back to the three of you. Don't let your mind create these pictures that may or may not be true. Have faith."

"If it was just me, I would wait forever on an off chance. But I can't deprive the girls of their mother. She's much more likely to let them back into her life if I'm not around to complicate her feelings. Take them both with you. It's damaging them to be apart from her. How can she not remember if they're both there to tell her they love her?"

He closed his eyes. They felt raw. The sooner he let his daughters go the better – too much delay and he wouldn't be capable of doing it.

Chapter 27

William, my father, is a kind man. I trail around after him, hoping I might remember something, I know how desperate he is that I should. William is determined that I shouldn't go back until my memory returns. I don't know what he suspects I might do. I think he hoped, perhaps still hopes, that Thomas would ride out after us. However, my head is full to the brim with thoughts of the baby. He, the child, is my only reality at present. Riding is getting uncomfortable. I'm not that big, I don't think anyone realises how near my time is.

We stay at William's house for a while, and he talks to me about my childhood there, takes me to see my mother's grave. There's an embroidered wall hanging, with the name of Thomasin on it, in the house. Apparently, I did that when we were living there – when I was pregnant with Thomas's daughter – in memory of the child Thomas and I lost. I remember none of it. Someone must have helped me; I don't see myself as a sewing person. Should I be making clothes for the baby? There's no-one else to do it.

I don't remember Cecily and Edward or the boy. They seem nice enough, and happy living in my old home. They seem to love my father. I did notice that Cecily cried when I didn't know her, which made me sad. Friends I have no recollection of. What name shall I give my baby?

We move on. William takes me, I think he's reluctant to go there, to a derelict house near that man Anstey's complex. It looks forlorn, but brings back no bad memories, something my father says he had feared. No good ones either. William tells me I killed someone, a man who was trying to rape me, in the fields outside the house. Using my power when I was threatened. Then he takes me down to the bay. I had been hit on the head then too, but apparently Thomas saved me from the waves. I shiver, imagining as I look out to sea what it would feel like to have the waves close over me. It makes me grateful for Thomas's kindness. It would have been a horrible way to die. My baby would never have existed.

William lets me see the outside of the complex. He explains that I'm still banished. We sit on the hillside and look across at it. William takes a very long time telling me all about what happened there. I try to focus. He tells me that Thomas suffered badly at the hands of Anstey and his men, he can't bring himself to say how, exactly. Perhaps he doesn't know the details. Then he tells me we lived there for a while, when my first full-term baby was born. I can tell he loves her … Lissy. I hope my father will stay in my life, even if I don't remember him and that he will love this baby too. I can't find a name for my little boy that seems just right.

My father is angry and bitter now, he tells me that uncaring people have taken over the complex. He tells me they hate Thomas, and he tells me what they did to him. It was why I was alone when the pirates took me. Well, me and someone called Alice, Stephen's wife, the one he said he wants me to talk to. She helped me when Lissy was born. Perhaps she will help me this time, even if I don't remember her. I will find her and talk to her.

Then William frightens me. He wants me to look into his mind. He tells me I can because he's human. He's done it before. He did it with Thomas. I panic, I don't want to; if mind-power is involved it might harm the baby.

William is soothing and persuasive, he takes me to a cave, hidden by the river somewhere.

"Please," he begs me. "Please. You not remembering is breaking Thomas's heart, and he's been through so much. I will hold all my memories of you and Thomas in my mind, available to you. You can go where you choose."

He kneels in front of me and I put my hands on either side of his head. Darkness swirls around me. William is trying to open a door for me.

"NO!" The effort is breaking into the protection I've woven around my baby, separating him from my power, protecting him from it. I let go and run outside.

"I'm sorry, I can't do it. Not yet. Leave me to go back to Ilfraycombe, please. We've been away so long that Thomas will have given up on us anyway."

I see the defeat in my father's face. Tears in his eyes. I can tell how much he cares about his son-in-law. They all seem to.

"You don't want to go to Barnstable? You and he were so happy there before the floods. Won't you at least try that for him?"

But I feel that it is near my time. I must return to Alice, without delay, if the baby is to be safe. So, my answer to him is "no." And I won't allow him to come with me. That hurts him badly, but he respects my decision. He doesn't know what else to do.

*

Thomas sat alone. The weight of sadness pressing on him was a millstone taking away his ability to breathe properly. It was difficult to remember a time when his heart beat properly, his lungs could fully fill with air. When he had really smiled, and meant it. Before the children had left, he'd kept it all together – more or less. He had packed everything Lissy and Bess would need. Had waved goodbye to them as they went with James. Had even managed a fake smile for them. Seeing their two sad little faces was heart-breaking; it took all his resolve to go through with it.

But none of that had prepared him for the sheer emptiness of the rooms now that they were gone. There was no way that he could just sit there. The one thing he wanted to do was die – and he couldn't. So he didn't have the first idea what he might do instead. Where he might escape to. Work was in Barnstable, the one place he had promised not to return to, just in case Kat was there. James would let him know when it was alright to go back. Presumably when Kat returned to Ilfraycombe in a few months ... to have Adam's baby. He wondered, idly, what they would do to him if he returned to the complex. If he even cared ... other than that it would upset the children. But where else could he go?

He wandered around the space, filled with the memories Kat lacked. When the council's guards came for him, she had shouted at them, begged them not to take him. She had followed him, bringing Lissy, just so that he wouldn't be on his own with his stupid, stupid pride and a cruel regime, re-emerging from the dust of an old. Then, before that, those special weeks between escaping from the floods and the Thornes and being led away. He remembered Kat, making love with her, how it felt. If only she hadn't had the contraception from Alice, that might have been his child she was carrying now. She would remember him then. If it had been, he reckoned the child would be due shortly now. Alice would be on hand to help.

Endless, idiotic, and pointless thoughts. Life was as it was. Nothing he could do or say or think would change the past. His life with Kat had been fraught with anxiety and trauma, but he could never regret a moment of being with her. Now, however much he hated Adam, he had to free Kat, allow her to find whatever happiness remained to her. No hanging around there, like a spectre at the feast of her new love. There was no guarantee that she wouldn't already be on her way back, so he needed to be gone. She and William might meet with James and the children on the road to Barnstable, they might all return together. Or she might not be with William at all. No-one would have dared to tell him that.

Leave a note, that would be best, like the one she had left for him that time, the one part of their past he didn't want to remember and hoped she wouldn't recall either. Not like the words he had left for her when she was hurt so badly. Both times he had faced the prospect of life without her, both times he had been sure it was impossible for him. She was probably still kind-hearted, despite her injury and the drugs. If he pleaded, begged on his knees, would she pretend to love him, abandon Adam? He could live with bringing up another man's child. But he couldn't live with making her unhappy. A clean break, before he had time to think about it. That was what was needed. A clean break from everyone – leave his friends, his family for a while at least. He couldn't bear their pity. Dear God, help him, what would he do?

He had little to pack. It took him a far longer to write the note. A lot of false starts found their way into the fire.

Dear Kat,

It's clear to me that you don't remember me, and that you've moved on with your life. I won't hold you back. I can see that it's over for us and I don't blame you for that. Please, I beg you, don't abandon our girls, they still need you. If it makes it possible for you to spend time with them, I can give them up. I'm sure they are happier with you. Bess also has Stephen. Has anyone told you about that? Lissy cries for you all the time. I'm incapable of consoling her and I only want what's best for her, for them and for you.

I love you. I always will. I'm so very sorry that it has ended like this. Anstey finally had his revenge on us.

Your Thomas

Leaving it in a conspicuous spot on the table, he went down and paid for the rooms to be kept on, in case Kat returned with the girls and wanted to stay there for a while. Eventually Kat would want to be near Alice. He calculated from Kat's time on the island that the baby would be due in four or so more months. He hoped she would survive the birth; he was alarmed at how big she'd been at such an early stage. But Adam was a large man. No, enough, stop! Thomas did not want to think of him, them, in that way … ever.

He made his way out of the door and left the key with the human on the gate. The man, Thomas had forgotten his name again, promised to relinquish it to whichever of their friends arrived to settle back in. A nice man, one who knew them all by sight and had a list of their names. As long as someone was paying, the innkeeper wasn't worried about empty rooms.

Chapter 28

Adam had not intended to keep up his surveillance of Thomas and his family. He reckoned he'd done what he could for them. There was no future in his love for Thomas and he felt that, although his debt to Thomas could never be repaid, he had done enough to earn himself a new life with Mark.

Easier said than done. Adam could practically feel Thomas's misery from streets away as he fetched his horse; the children's misery when they left had been palpable too. So many unanswered questions, they made his head hurt. Why had Thomas sent them off with the other one to Barnstable? Why, most of all, had Kat gone off for so long with her father? She didn't remember William either, so why? Why had she not gone straight to Thomas? Adam suspected it was something to do with the baby, but he couldn't imagine what. Thomas was devoted to the children; he would be happy to welcome a new addition to the family … surely. She must suspect something was wrong with Thomas's feelings about the new child. Had something happened to her – was it not even Thomas's child?

He'd watched James head off on the Barnstable road. The older girl, Bess, was riding her own horse, with the little girl in front of her. James rode close, but he looked worried and unhappy. Adam guessed he was reluctant to take the girls away from their father. Presumably it must mean that Kat was in Barnstable and waiting for them there. He was surprised that she wasn't nearer Alice. From his reckoning the baby must be imminent.

Fuck, he needed to follow Thomas and just make sure he was alright. There was no way that he could just abandon him. Mark had agreed to stay and watch the inn in case anyone returned. Adam had finally confessed to him the terrible things that he and the other men had done to Thomas, and Mark had still hugged him and said he loved him. It was a miracle, and it meant Mark fully understood the weight of that debt and was willing to help. Mark loving him, such unconditional love, it was the best thing that had ever happened to him. He had totally revised his opinions on expendable humans. Some of them were warmer, kinder, more worthy of love than most of those from his home planet.

Worryingly, Thomas, who was riding quite slowly and aimlessly, didn't seem to have any destination in mind. He couldn't be visiting anyone Adam knew of. Alice, Stephen, and the boy were in their lodgings over the shop. James and the girls were heading for Barnstable. The reckless Mathias one had moved back to Barnstable too, ages ago, though he and his mates were probably still celebrating their famous routing of the pirates. Thankfully not Mark. He was struck by the thought that without Kat they would never have met, nor could he have kept Mark safe so easily without her and the ostium.

But, for now, William had not returned with Thomas's wife. Adam harboured some ill feeling toward William. Kat's father had seemed to be kind and thoughtful, but instead of leaving his daughter in Ilfraycombe to meet up with Thomas again, he had spirited her off on her own. It made him wonder if William still had the wrong idea about him and Kat. Why she had clung to him in the cave and then kissed him instead of her husband, he couldn't guess. They had all been watching, and the reactions that had provoked at the time had left him with the suspicion that William thought it would be a good idea for Kat to be far away from him, Adam, until her memory of Thomas returned. If it ever did. He reckoned it had been too long now and doubted it would. Anstey's drugs were mind-damaging. If William had left her alone, Thomas could have taken her to bed and straightened everything out that way. She might not have remembered her husband, but she could have fallen for him all over again. That would have been the right thing to do. It would have made Thomas feel so much better and he had suffered enough for one lifetime.

It wasn't high on his list of potentially comfortable conversations, but he decided it was time to find somewhere quiet to talk things out with Thomas. The man seemed hell-bent on complicating and ruining his life. Some kind of permanent fucking death wish. A certain amount of guilt still made him worry that Thomas had never, and probably would never recover from what they'd done to him. What *he'd* done to him. He wished to God they hadn't done it, prayed for forgiveness, but he couldn't change it. After that night he knew there would be a special place reserved in hell for them all. At least he'd killed Anstey and Donnett. Sent them on ahead. But now he was with Mark he didn't plan on joining them anytime soon.

They seemed to ride forever; he kept out of Thomas's line of vision in case he looked over his shoulder but was afraid to fall too far behind in case he lost sight of his man. It had started to rain, again. He didn't dare leave it too much longer to risk his approach, but he was afraid to make the first move and hadn't had time to plan. In the end, when he realised that he had no idea where Thomas was heading for, he took a chance on being attacked, rode closer, and hailed Thomas as he rode onto the Bedyford track. He found himself shouting to Thomas's receding back.

"Thomas! Wait a moment, I need to talk to you."

"I've nothing to say to you." Thomas obviously recognised his voice, but the reply was surly, strained, and didn't invite further conversation. Ignoring Adam, he continued riding at the same pace.

"Please Thomas, at least stop and listen to me. Just hear me out and I promise I'll disappear from your life forever."

"Taking my wife with you, no doubt." Now there was bitterness and hurt, but at least Adam knew the source of Thomas's misery.

"I have no idea where your wife is. She went off with her father as soon as we returned to Ilfraycombe. Why would I keep in touch?"

"Don't you care about her, about your baby?"

"*My* baby? *Your* baby, you mean. Has she had it yet? It must be due. She was a few month's with child before she was taken by the pirates and got her head injury." He began to feel more confident that he could make Thomas listen. "Look, come back to our lodgings, mine and Mark's, come back and have a drink with us, we need to discuss this. I think your father-in-law has the wrong idea too."

Thomas stopped dead and turned his horse, so that he was facing him.

*

I've been having pains at fairly regular intervals for a while now. I think it's the baby. I have a vague physical recollection now of how it was before. I have to get to Stephen's Alice if my son has any hope of being delivered safely. I'm glad I've come alone, I don't want my father here, or for him to know. He'll insist on fetching Thomas, and I'm not sure that I want him – yes, he's my husband but he's still a stranger to my mind – to share this with me. I keep feeling that I should avoid him being involved; I'm not sure why, but the feeling is strong.

I'm at Alice's door. I'm controlling my breathing pretty well but I need to be inside the house, with her. I said goodbye to William, I mean my father, some time ago now and I feel very alone. When we parted, he was reluctant to let me travel on my own, but he gave me the directions that have led me safely here. I persuaded him to go to

Barnstable and promised I would talk to Alice – as I mean to, need to – and then re-join him there. He had no idea of the rush I'm in now. For some reason he seemed to think there were months to go.

Stephen lets me in, takes one look at my face and shouts for Alice. My baby boy is on his way.

Chapter 29

And the world changed. A baby arrived and my whole being whirled back into place. I was Kat Wrenn-Alban, I was in love with my husband Thomas. Alice was my best friend, William was my father and my darlings Bess and Lissy had a baby brother, as yet unnamed, waiting to see his father and sisters for the first time.

Alice found it difficult to believe how easily the baby joined us. Lissy had been altogether different. She wondered if my mind-power had focussed on protecting this child and was convinced that the amnesia and Anstey's drugs had set my power loose to do what it wanted without me guiding or controlling it – something I had learned, at my mother's knee, to be frightened of doing. The ability to open the ostium had been part of the same hidden part of me, locked away from my conscious mind. It appeared as if I now had access to everything that I was capable of.

It was impossible to sleep with so many dizzying thoughts circulating in my head. Alice, Stephen, Thom, and *my* Thomas's baby son were all asleep. I had let Alice and Stephen persuade me to rest and they had promised to help me find Thomas in the morning. They weren't certain whether he and our girls were still at the inn. They knew Thomas had been planning to send the girls to Barnstable, but, if they hadn't already gone, they would not travel in the middle of the night. It surely made sense to wait until the morning, and I was exhausted and sore. The birth was easy, but not *that* easy.

Wide awake, in the silent darkness of early morning, I became certain that waiting had been a really bad mistake. Not only was I flooded with all the memories of our love, Thomas's and mine, it felt like a living thing inside me. And with it came guilt. I was shocked at the way I had behaved when I couldn't remember him, how I had clung to Adam. The irrational fear of him knowing about the baby, I was only now beginning to understand that it had arisen from a deep-seated concern not to worry him. When I was on the island, shut out from being me, I hadn't understood that I was fearful *for* him not *of* him.

Before I lost my memory, that anxiety for him had been particularly strong in my mind. When he had been imprisoned and I couldn't see him, when I had only been able to speak to him through his mind, I had been afraid to tell him about the baby. Contemplating anxiously how Thomas would react to the news, given that his actions had resulted in my being banished from the complex and unable to return to give birth there, my fears had seemed justified. I knew that, being my Thomas, he would have blamed himself for causing danger to me and not me for forgetting about contraception. He would have been alone in his cell for hours on end picturing me dying and it being his fault. The darkness would have descended on him with a vengeance – as it had when he realised that something had happened to me and that he was totally helpless to do anything about it. My father had shared those details with me, but it was only now, back in my own mind and body, that the impact of how much he would have sunk into despair fully hit me. Well, why should he suffer these extra hours before morning alone, when I could tell him everything and see the joy on his face when he saw our son safely delivered?

I crept out of Thom's truckle bed. Thom was tucked up with his parents and my son – my Thomas's son – was in Thom's old cradle.

My clothes were easy to find, and in no time at all I was in the street and heading toward the inn. Perhaps I should have waited, dawn was beginning to break, and it was cold. I felt dazed. But no, I was fixated on the thought that Thomas was suffering needlessly.

It was a shock to find that Thomas wasn't there at the inn, I had been sure he and the girls would be waiting for me. However, the man I spoke to, he was just unlocking the gates, reassured me that the rooms were paid for, and doubtless the family would return shortly. Thomas had told him my name, and described me, so the man was happy to hand over the key. Perhaps Thomas had left word for me.

Everything had seemed so happy, even joyful a moment or two earlier. I had thought that at last our lives would be mended, that we would all be together. Thomas's note was like having an ice-cold bucket of water poured over me. I couldn't stop shivering, not only from the cold, and I had no idea what to do. I had left it too late. What point was there in recalling all the faulty decisions I had made. He'd written that it was 'over between us,' I didn't read beyond those cold, pain-filled words. I had lost the man who made my life worth living. For a while, how long I had no idea, I sat there frozen. In the end the silence of the room, the absence of my husband and children, became unbearable.

Outside, my first instinct was to return to my new-born, but the thought of seeing the tiny replica of Thomas without his father standing beside me was like a knife in my ribs. Pain I wasn't ready to face. I decided to walk for a while. Calm myself down. Try to breathe. I couldn't think straight, I couldn't face anything or anyone. I couldn't quite bring all the words in the note back into mind. It was crumpled up, left lying in the room. Was Thomas saying that we couldn't even live together for the children? Would my presence deprive them of his? I wished I'd brought the note with me to check; I hadn't really read beyond the first few devastating lines. My actions had forced him to break our bond, I couldn't deprive him of his children as well. He deserved better.

As I walked, I thought how the future might be for him. Of course, he would think of me and of the children first. He would put himself last. But I could see him, with the three of them. A much-loved father with his two daughters and a new-born son. Being together, as a family, might heal him and them in time. A wet nurse could easily take my place. I had betrayed them, denied them. Not a fit wife or mother.

Having no idea where to go or what to do, barely noticing my surroundings, my feet found themselves on the path to the complex, the cliff-top path I had ridden all those evenings when I went to sit on the rocks and share Thomas's mind. I wasn't particularly intending to go there, but the sea and the complex were the only places I knew to head for. It was as good as anywhere. Wandering without aim or purpose was marginally worse than following a track to somewhere I didn't especially want to travel to. All I wanted was to be with him, to be in his arms, and that was never going to happen now. How I regretted all the time I had wasted since he had first arrived on the island to rescue me. It could have all ended well, but I had stupidly messed everything up, and nothing would ever be right again. How could it be right without him making it so?

A question for the philosophers. Could one open an ostium in time only? Return to a moment in the past, a moment before the wrong decision was made – go back and have a second chance. Life couldn't be that easy. Those of us that could do this strange thing with time and space … You just had to know that there would be a limit on what could be done. No-one would be allowed to live such a safe life, trying one decision against another. Forcing personal second thoughts on those around us. Even God would choose not to use such a power, if it existed. It would definitely not be available for one such as me. But how I did wish it was. So very tempted to try – even if it led to nowhere and nothing… Nothing to lose.

*

At last Thomas finally understood how utterly wrong he had been. They had returned to Adam's lodgings and Adam had explained it all, even told him about Mark. They had enjoyed a conciliatory drink together. He felt guilty for all that hatred he had felt. They had only just finished speaking when Mark arrived.

"I've been looking everywhere for you both to let you know! I didn't realise you'd returned already. I was watching the inn, but I saw your wife, Thomas, entirely alone, and thought I ought to make sure that she made it safely to wherever she was going."

"Kat! Where did she go?"

For a second, he was terrified she might have gone to the inn and found his note, with all the rubbish he had written when he'd thought she was with Adam. But Mark was able to reassure him that Kat had gone to Alice … ages ago … Mark had then ridden after him and Adam, unaware they'd turned back.

"I think she may have been in pain. Alice is the one who cures people, isn't she?"

"Oh, my dear God! The baby! And she isn't at the complex. I don't know how Alice will be able to help her without all the equipment they have there. She could die! I must get to her now!"

A new fire burned in him – racing for the door, he was heading for Alice's house before anyone could stop him. He vaguely registered the amused glances Adam and Mark shared, but he didn't care and nothing was going to get in his way. He wasn't sure how Alice's and Stephen's neighbours would react in the morning, but he banged on their door, pushing it open without a care for the noise. Alice and Stephen appeared on the landing blinking sleepily. And then there was the sound of a baby crying, the mewling wail of a very new baby. Alice disappeared back into the bedroom, reappearing with a puzzled frown and that very new baby in her arms.

"Here Thomas, your 'mini-me' son. But your wife has disappeared. I see she's not with Adam, as he's with you. Could she have gone in search of you?"

For a few moments he was mesmerised. The tiny boy had stopped crying and had looked up into his eyes, with his eyes.

"My son …" he whispered in awe. Then the rest of Alice's words penetrated. "No…! She wouldn't have gone to the inn, would she?"

"I'll fetch the horses; we can search for her more easily if we're mounted. I think yours and mine are still saddled and bridled. We were remiss." Adam was as ever practical.

"I'll get them," Mark said. "You stay with Thomas. It looks as if he's going to need you."

He was in a daze, again, looking at the tiny child in his arms. "My baby. Our baby. Oh, if only I'd known, why didn't she wait here for me?"

"It's my fault," Alice said slowly, thinking as she spoke – in a considered Alice sort of way. "She remembered everything. As soon as the child was born it all came back to her. Almost a brainstorm. She wanted to go straight way to find you, but I persuaded her to wait until the morning. She'd only just given birth, and I thought I might be able to talk to you first – I knew what you thought. I wasn't sure if you would look clearly at the child and see that he could only be yours. She must have left to find you a short while ago. We were asleep, or I might have felt her making the decision. Her mind has been in such turmoil."

"The inn, she mustn't read my note. She'll misunderstand. I must find her before anything else happens to separate us."

Reluctantly, he passed his son back to Alice.

"Take care of him, please. I'll bring his mother back safely, I really will this time."

He and Adam headed toward the inn; they could think of nowhere else Kat might have gone. What had Master Shakespeare said about 'star-cross'd lovers'? The man at the gate was able to tell them that Kat had been there, had rushed up to their rooms and had been there for a very short while, before coming out slowly and heading off somewhere on foot. Of course, the man had no idea where. He tried to draw the picture from the man's mind and could tell Adam was trying to do the same.

"The path, the way she used to go to the cove near the complex when she went to speak mind-to-mind with you. I followed her so many evenings. It looks as if she went that way."

Mark arrived with their two horses at that point. If Kat was on foot, they should catch up with her easily. He wasted no time and mounted straight way. Mark shared the other horse with Adam, evidently reluctant to be left behind, and he abstractly registered the extent of Adam's feelings for himself, and how vulnerable that made Mark feel when he and Adam were together. The young man was so unsure of himself, such an innocent, and amidst his own fear and anxiety he took time to hope that the two of them would achieve a happy life together. He owed an immeasurable debt to Adam for saving Kat, and more again for the hatred Thomas had felt for him when he'd so badly misjudged the relationship between Adam and Kat. Comparing that with the night of Anstey's orgy, when Adam had been only one of the many and not as bad as most, he judged that Adam had more than repaid his side of any debt between them, if such a thing could be weighed on scales.

But thinking of Adam and Mark was simply a distraction. His heart felt as if it was in a vice. "Please, oh please let me find her, let it all be alright this time." Neither he nor Kat had a God-given right to happiness, but oh how he prayed that this time it would work out for them, for their tiny, vulnerable family.

They were almost to the complex, when Thomas thought he

could see a small figure in the distance. She was walking along the cliff edge, and he was afraid to shout out to her, whether aloud, or mind-to-mind, in case she should startle and fall. It was almost as if she was sleep-walking. Adam drew abreast with him.

"It's very near here that she used to leave her horse. I hid in the thicket over there, only wanting to make sure she was safe. Look she's started the climb down. I was terrified each time that she'd fall."

"Hold my horse for me. I daren't risk frightening her. I'll be as fast on foot."

He sprinted forward silently on the soft turf. Below him he could see Kat on the path. His heart lurched as she lost her footing and grasped some scrub growing in crevices. And she'd done it, over and over, just to talk to him. He should have had faith that her love would return.

It wouldn't be wise to start down after her until she was safely on the rocks and sand at the bottom. Then he could risk his own neck and run. With the right momentum, it was almost a better way to tackle it. He remembered running down such a path to rescue her from the sea … a lifetime ago, or so it seemed. She reached the bottom and he thought she was going to stop there, she hesitated, and he wondered if that was where she had sat when she saved his reason, night after night in his dark solitary cell. He cursed the pirates and briefly imagined her coming to meet him as he was freed; having spoken to him every day, as she had promised.

As he raced down the steep path, he saw that she had moved on, walking across the shore toward the water. The tide was out but starting to turn. She still seemed to be unaware of him being there. Or of the danger. Reaching the bottom, he yelled out her name. And reached out to her mind. She didn't turn or even break step. He ran harder then, as she walked forward into the water.

"Kat, Kat! Please, Kat, I love you, I misunderstood. Please take no notice of that stupid note," he was crying and yelling and running at the same time. If anything, she was moving faster, and he could see the water draw back, as it always did before racing forward as the tide turned. He tried for her mind again.

"I love you Kat, wait for me! If you can't bear life as it is, wait, and I'll come with you. We'll go together. But think of the children too. Don't leave them alone without either of us, because I can't, I won't survive without you."

She hesitated and he re-doubled his pace, then he was in the shallows, almost up to her as a surge of water hit them both from the side. He made one last desperate lunge and grabbed her, while the strength of the water threatened to rip her from his grasp. Then they were choking together as the waves broke over their heads. Using all his strength he wrested her from the current. Then other hands were there, Adam's and Mark's, somehow, between them they dragged themselves and Kat back onto the shingle above the lowest rocks. Neither Adam nor Mark waited to be thanked.

"We'll see you at the top, by the horses." A debt finally paid in full.

He held tight to her, but silently; he was so afraid she might shut him out if he spoke into her mind. She was wet through, they both were. He was shaking, but something had to be said.

"Kat, please … I love you. Forget that stupid note, I couldn't ever give you up. Please, Kat, please, what can I say? How can I make you see that I love you beyond life?"

And then she looked at him and smiled, back in her right mind, and clearly in his head he heard her laugh and say:

"Did we go back through the ostium after all? You're breaking my ribs, Thomas, like before, you don't know your own strength."

And then he was kissing her, and she was kissing him back, and her voice, even in his head, was both weary and happy.

"I love you Thomas. I'm so very sorry that I took such a long time to

remember. Let's go home, wherever that is now."

He found that he was laughing too.

"We have a cliff to climb first – tell me you didn't do this all on your own, in the dark as well, just to talk to me."

She said nothing, but rested against him, wet and icy cold. He cursed himself.

"Sorry, I forgot to take my cloak off before chasing you into the waves, I've nothing to get you warm. We'll ride back to Alice, as fast as we can, and she can patch us both up."

Adam and Mark were waiting at the top with the horses. Both had been wise enough to take their cloaks off before rushing down to assist in the rescue. Adam insisted on bundling Kat into his and passing her up to Thomas as soon as he was mounted. Mark arranged his own cloak around Adam and himself once they were on the other horse.

"We'll go on ahead, and home. Are you two alright on your own now?" He couldn't decide from the words if Adam was amused, exasperated or relieved; probably a mixture. He grinned anyway.

"Thank you both, the debt is all ours, mine and Kat's, now. Stay in touch, I'll talk to James about the possibility of getting your banishment rescinded – although I can't promise anything. It would be much easier for the two of you if you were safe in the complex. Oh, and by the way, I hope you won't mind, as long as Kat is in agreement, we'll be naming our son after you, Adam."

Adam laughed with surprised delight, "Thanks! I'm honoured."

He heard Kat's heartfelt assent in his mind, and he called out to Adam: "Kat says 'yes'," then they were riding, his favourite sort of riding, a gentle pace with Kat cuddled close in his arms, telling him how much she loved him as they headed back to Ilfraycombe. All would have been perfection if they weren't both soaking wet and shivering with cold, but then one couldn't have everything.

Chapter 30

Although I took a lot of reassuring, I trusted, in my heart, that Thomas really did love me. I was sure I had never, at any stage, forfeited that. My faulty reading of Thomas's note – how had I missed him saying 'I love you'? – and my post-natal, post-trauma muddle-headedness had been the only problems. Almost as if I'd been in a trance. I was glad he'd later uncrumpled the note and underlined the words for me – it made me aware of how much *my* note, offering him *his* freedom, all that time ago, must have shaken Thomas. We were both so prone to overreaction, and so quick to believe ourselves unworthy of each other, which was obviously utter nonsense since it couldn't possibly be true for both of us at the same time. I decided that I really didn't care what had happened, what he had believed, why he had believed it. He loved me, I loved him. Fairy-tale ending. No more to be said or apologised for. I could scarcely believe that I had just walked out into the sea and nearly killed us both. Had I been looking for that time-only ostium?

It did mean, however, that I wanted him near me the whole time, making up for the weeks we'd spent apart. We had moved back into the rooms in the inn, and a note had gone to James and William, who would bring Bess and Lissy back to us. We had wanted to go for them ourselves, but Alice had advised against travelling while baby

Adam was so tiny.

Unlike our shaky time when Lissy was born, Thomas was drawn closer by baby Adam's presence. I would sit and feed him, and Thomas would sit beside us with his arm around me, apparently entranced, occasionally running his fingers down my swirls and kissing my hair, my neck, and our baby's soft, downy head. I was sad that his fear and depression had deprived him of moments like this when his Lissy was small. I couldn't wait to see the girls, but I was scared too.

"Do you think they will forgive me? I'm afraid they'll feel I rejected them."

"They're both special people, Kat. We must make certain they understand. If they can do that then I'm sure they will forgive," Thomas smiled wryly. "They're probably used to how stupid the two of us can be. You have no idea what an embarrassingly pathetic misery I was when I thought I'd lost you."

Thomas looked down at his baby son, kissed the tip of his own finger and touched it lightly to the baby's cheek. I could feel the awed sense of a miracle in his mind.

"It's amazing to think that the birth went so easily for you this time. Could you do that thing with your power again?"

I puzzled over the question for a few moments; back in my right mind, I was no nearer to understanding my power than I had been in the beginning.

"Who knows? I think, for the moment, I'd rather trust in Alice's contraceptive drug. One child in arms at a time. And I warn you, Thomas Alban, I don't intend for us to abstain from our love-life to ensure that end." I snuggled closer to him.

"I want us to be back in Barnstable and working together again. As soon as Adam is a few weeks older, we can return to our home together."

The thought of Barnstable made me frown, I had other relationships to sort out. "There's William too, I need to beg my father's forgiveness for misleading him. I still don't know why he dragged me off. He was so keen to tell me how special you are, but it would have been better if he'd let me talk to Alice. She at least knew I was with child before going to Lundye, it was unfortunate that she assumed you did too."

"Your father must have suspected the same as me, that you were Adam's lover – only because you didn't remember me, of course. You have no idea how much I wanted to kill him – Adam – even after everything he had done for you. I was so grateful that he had annihilated Anstey and Donnett, but that got at me too. I always want to be the one to do everything for you."

I put Adam down in his cradle, but Thomas remained seated, and pensive. I stood in front of him and cradled his head against me, kissing his hair, his lovely soft, dark, rumpled hair.

"Why do you torment yourself? My love for you is beyond everything. It isn't something that makes me go to bed at night totting up what you've achieved for me during the day."

Thomas grinned up at me. "I'm glad to hear it, I can think of other things to do in bed at night." I could see that happiness was making Thomas unusually light-hearted and silly and I was deeply glad of it, after all I'd put him through.

"Shush now, I'm being serious. Don't interrupt with tempting suggestions." I teased him. "Now, where was I? Oh yes, I know. Fate hasn't always been kind to us – *stop* grinning at me, Mister Alban, you're putting me off – but it did bring us together in the first place, it did give us the gift of loving each other and at least we have our happy ending. I said stop grinning, Thomas, I'm saying something important. Anyway, what I mean is let's keep it that way, the happy bit I mean, and forget the bad bits of the past, other than knowing we have to trust in ourselves and each other more. I'm really sorry I acted stupidly, I have no idea what possessed me, walking into the sea like that. There, end of pompous bit, promise." I finished triumphantly, at full gallop.

"It's not just you," Thomas was serious again. "I nearly did something like it too, when I was so hopelessly mired in depression. You're right, we must be honest with each other, share our feelings, good and bad. I promise I'll tell you about it, the thing I nearly did, one evening when we're back in Barnstable. At least what *you* did — not that I'm recommending you do it regularly — has given me a good memory of saving you from the waves again to set on the plus side of the balance when I can't escape from the numbness and the dark. That's three to me and none to the sea — or river — or water in general. *You* may not be totting things up, but a dark side of me does. I'd like to say I've conquered it, but I fear that's a lifetime's work. You're my life-line."

Thomas sighed and grasped me around the waist, pressing closer. I hadn't re-laced my bodice, so he took advantage of being able to nestle against my breasts and sighed again, this time more contentedly. He nuzzled his nose into the dip between them.

"I envy my son," he murmured. "But now we need to get ready. I can hear horses in the courtyard and very familiar voices. Our family is back."

Chapter 31

I started to rush toward the girls as they entered, but my father, looking serious, put his hand up to prevent me.

"Bess has asked me to say that they, she and Lissy, want to talk to you both before we do all the hugging and kissing."

I stopped and grabbed Thomas's hand, feeling him squeeze mine tightly.

"But it's been so long! I can't wait, please let me hug you both."

Thomas put his arm around my waist and drew me closer to him.

"Let the girls speak, we owe it to them."

Bess stepped forward, with Lissy holding tight to her hand. Her face was very serious, they had obviously given it all a great deal of thought.

"I promise we'll hug as soon as I've done. Remember that not seeing us was your own choice, Mother." That really hurt, and I heard Thomas draw his breath in and tighten his grip on me. Bess pressed on regardless. "Just let me say what I have to – and it may take some time. Grandfather has told us a lot about everything that happened. He knows that he was silly and suspicious too. He had the first telling-off." Her face softened as the tightness in her jaw unclenched a little. "But first, please get it through your silly addled brains that we love you both very much. We're not saying we don't, we just want to be listened to. And please don't cry, either of you, we won't be able to say what needs to be said if you do."

Lissy looked at us both, a little in awe of what her big sister was daring. "Love you. Promise we do," she said quickly.

"We understand, we'll listen. We know we've put you through so much lately. But you do know that none of this was your mother's fault. Anstey's drugs have bad effects." Thomas spoke quietly. I nodded agreement to the listening bit and was grateful for his attempt to excuse my actions. For myself, I said nothing. The 'not crying' bit was a lot easier if you didn't speak.

Bess cleared her throat awkwardly.

"As I said, we love and need you both, we're a family, we want to be together and we want to be happy. We haven't been happy for what seems like a long time now. One or other of you keeps shutting everyone out and coming close to destroying us all. Hurting each other worse than Anstey did. That man could hurt our bodies; you can hurt our hearts. You always *mean* well, but you both think you know best. You're so intense! All the time. Talk to each other, stop hiding things, share your thoughts more honestly with your family, instead of doubting each other and us. We should be working together, sharing decisions, talking about our feelings, stopping to think and figure out solutions. How can we possibly expect to help our wider family and friends – and I know that's what father wants and needs to do – until we can work together? You can't always protect us from knowing about the bad things that happen and sometimes you use *us* as an excuse for doing really silly things."

She turned to Thomas: "Father, you've saved our mother time and again, yet you brood over not being good enough for her. Why? How can you even begin to think she doesn't truly love you when the evidence is in front of you all the time? No, don't interrupt, I intend to tell you both off, give me time, I'll get to Mother in a moment."

Bess frowned at Thomas, as he tried to say something. He subsided and Bess continued.

"Then, when she's hurt and can't remember you, you stay away from her, imagining some silly scenario that she loves someone else. How could she possibly fall for someone else when she already has the best man in the whole world, even if *he* won't admit it?" She glared at Thomas as she emphasized the 'he.' "Any fool could see that she was bound to be grateful to the man who killed Anstey and Donnett – you can't imagine how grateful *I* am, I've dreamed of ending Donnett so many times, over so many years, but it doesn't mean that I want Adam as my father. I know you would have killed them for us if you'd had the chance – two evil men are dead, what can it possibly matter who did it in the end? Oh, and stop trying to live with the memory of what was done to you locked away in some cobwebby prison in your mind. We all, well most of us, need to talk about that too at some time in the near future."

Bess paused and looked at Thomas. This time she let him respond.

"I know you're right, Bess," he said, meekly. "With all that's happened, I'm afraid that I've been fighting off something of a mental breakdown for a long while now and I've been ashamed to admit it to any of you. Hiding from you all and locking memories away to fester has been part of that. I wanted to be some kind of hero for everyone, instead of understanding that you love me for who I am, not who I dream of being."

I squeezed Thomas's hand again, and risked Bess's wrath by kissing his cheek. She looked as if she wanted to kiss him too and smiled at him, clearly appreciating his honest admission. But then she went back to looking stern and turned to me. With a pang I realised that she would always love him more than me, and I couldn't blame her for that.

"And you, Mother, you're as bad. You always try to protect father and end up making things worse. But let's start with the way you undervalue yourself. Why do you imagine that those exiles who were brought up in the complex are looking down at you, that they think you're not good enough, when no-one there can do a small part of what you can with all that power in your mind? If anything, it's likely that they're afraid and envious. Why do you blame yourself for failing to kill Anstey and Donnett, when you did more than anyone else could possibly have done? Of course Father loves you and doesn't regret marrying you; how can you even begin to believe otherwise?" She glared at me, and I tried not to notice Thomas hiding a grin.

"Where was I? Oh yes, about trying not to worry Father and ending up worrying him more. You admitted to me that you were wrong not to tell him about your first baby – so why did you not tell him you thought you were with child this time? He would never have dreamed up this stupid idea of you being in love with Adam if he'd known it was his child you were carrying. And why on this Earth did you let Father go back to the complex with Uncle Robert? Why didn't you just stop the two of them and explain to Uncle Robert the cause of the nightmares? Have you any idea how upset Uncle Robert is about what happened, and how angry Uncle James was with him? They very nearly split up. And why did you pretend to Father that it was you who didn't want to live in the complex, when it was your concern for *him* that caused you to insist on leaving there?" Bess paused for breath; I could see that all these questions had been seething in her mind for quite a while. She had been a silent spectator for a long time and we had ignored her. Now we were paying. She returned to addressing both of us and her theme.

"Why don't you talk to us about things? Lissy and me. We've had to get this information from so many different people. We could have told you that it was stupid for you to trust those wicked people that are back in power in the complex. We would have insisted that you find another way. We hate what they did to you, Father – have you any idea how frightened Lissy was when she saw you collapsed, nearly dead, in that cell after the Edith-witch told you all that rubbish?" She sounded exasperated. "Oh! I could go on and on. Lissy and I cannot escape knowing that you love each other beyond reason. It's different from the way you feel about us children, that's not to devalue your love for us in any way. Your love …" she searched for the words. "You're way, way too old for the comparison now, but you're a bit like Master Shakespeare's *Romeo and Juliet*. Did you read that yet?" Thomas and I looked at each other, eyebrows raised. Being told off by your own children hurts! And, surely, we weren't *that* old!

Bess was oblivious to our discomfort and continued on, winding up … hopefully. "You need to trust each other, and us. Maybe we can't solve everything, maybe things will hurt us all, but nothing is worse than being shut out, and you two do it to us 'for our own good' all the time. Oh, and I do know that Uncle Stephen put a baby into my mother and that the baby was me – Thom told me about that, we children do have ears – why would either of you imagine that it would affect my relationship with my true father, the father I chose – I'm not so shallow. Now there's three of us children – we'll allow this new one to join our little group – and only two of you. You're outnumbered, get used to listening to us. Now, can we see him? We know you love us and we love you. But Adam Wrenn-Alban doesn't know he has us to back him up yet."

Lissy was looking wide-eyed at her big sister, but she raced for Thomas and me as soon as she saw permission granted. Somehow, she managed to get an arm round each of us and administered a stranglehold hug. It hurt us both to see her cry and know how much we were responsible. Bess went straight to the cradle, letting her sister have us first. All the noise had woken Adam up, so Bess eagerly picked him up and jiggled him gently, to his apparent delight as he waved tiny fists in her direction.

I could see that my father was trying to slip out quietly and leave us all together. Not a chance: I called to him.

"Wait! no running off, you are family too, you know. If you want to do something useful, you could get a meal sent up. We've been waiting for you to arrive to order it," I hurried over to him before he could leave.

"Your wish is my command. Glad to have you back, bossy little daughter. I'm pleased to see that your own children are ordering you about, just as you did your mother and me. I'll collect my hug later." Seeing that Thomas was involved with the children, he added quietly, "By the way, I'm very glad that you and Thomas have survived … again. I had begun to doubt it this time. After our shaky beginning, I confess that I would have hated that. I've come to love him too."

He didn't have to wait for his hug.

Around the meal table, later, we began to understand how much careful thought Bess had given to our precarious position in this dual world. I could appreciate the difference between her level-headed, and to some extent confrontational, ideas of planning for the future and Thomas's and my solitary plotting. Ours left us rushing belatedly to rescue each other as each new trouble engulfed us. He and I were very emotional people, living from moment to moment, easily victim to doubt and to the fear of losing each other – with us it had grown to be almost an obsession. Bess was suggesting that the real dangers we faced were out in the dual worlds we were trying to hold together. We had to plan better, together, in order to contribute to that struggle without ever risking it dragging us down completely. To trust in each other.

"We all, and I'm including the Aunts and Uncles, need to be much more active in the affairs of the complex once your period of banishment is ended," Bess lectured us. "And I've had an idea of how you can work in the complex without being trapped in it at night. But only, ONLY, if we can make sure you're properly protected, Father. Uncle James will help with that. You should really take it as a compliment that the current councillors hate you, just the way Anstey did. All the good people admire you and they're making their voices heard. Uncle James says that Anne Gomfrey is in bad trouble over what she tried to do to you. She's being investigated." Bess looked seriously around the table as she came to the substance of her plan, pleased that we seemed to be listening to her. And her idea was ingenious, nothing like anything I'd ever have thought of. While Thomas and I reacted, Bess thought forward and around things.

"I think that we should move back, as a family, into your parents' old house, Grandfather. It was above the floods in the valley, I heard it was one of the few places that survived. Didn't you take Mother there when she was trying to remember?"

We were all staggered by the thought. The meal table went eerily silent. Yet I was immediately struck by the perception that the house was only so unwelcoming to us because none of us had ever *wanted* to be there. The house was neglected and unloved … by us. There was nothing wrong with the house itself.

Thomas and my father looked at me, remembering what had happened there. The attempted rape, my first kill. But for me the idea was somehow tempting. Thinking my way through it, I said, slowly, "We would need to exorcise the ghosts and the bad memories, but if we could bear to do it, we would have somewhere outside the complex to return to at night, near enough to influence our fellow refugees and yet remaining in the relative safety, for us at any rate, and warmth of the human world."

I could see the logic and gave a cautious assent to the idea, turning to my father for approval. It was, after all, *his* house, the one his parents had left to him. He had only returned to it reluctantly, persuaded by my mother, and he had seen her dragged away from there on the first stage of the journey that had ultimately led to her death. He slowly nodded his consent... and if he and I could do it... The idea was inspired, Bess had just tossed it out to us and moved on, leaving us to work out the practical details of how it might best be achieved. We let her continue, while the ideas were taking root in us.

She next informed us that she intended to study to be a Domum-Orbis notary and a human lawyer, like Uncle James and Uncle Robert. In future, she insisted, she would be able to protect her father from any misuse of Domum-Orbis laws. Clearly Bess had decided that the Wrenn-Alban family needed a single voice to lead us forward, and that it was going to be hers. Not a bad choice. She was determined that no-one would ever be in a position to treat her father so appallingly again.

My father, still slightly bemused, confided that Bess had got hold of Master Shakespeare's *Complete Works* from the Future-Earth Library, the one I'd been reading, and that her favourite character at that moment was Portia from *The Merchant of Venice*. She didn't deny it, and I could just see Bess silencing the council as she gave Portia's 'quality of mercy' speech. Perhaps she might even have prevented them from doing what they did to Thomas. Perhaps not – if my memory served me correctly Portia hadn't succeeded with the words of mercy; it was her attention to the tight legal wording of the contract that had saved Antonio's life. If Thomas's enemies had imprisoned him in some more humane way, they could have made their point without coming so callously close to killing him. If they hadn't banished me, I would have been there with him instead of fighting for survival on a rocky island twelve miles out to sea. Pitiless pursuit of the law was a harsh foundation for a new-born community such as ours to build upon. Added to that, there was too much scope for malign misappropriation of power. If that foundation could be manipulated and usurped, so quickly, so easily, by a mixture of egotistical administrators and inflexible traditionalists a grim future beckoned to us. I focused my attention back on the room, feeling guilty about letting my thoughts drift away, but the complex had nearly destroyed Thomas and me and it haunted me. The why of it was never far from my thoughts.

Bess was still speaking, reassuring us. "I do know not to discuss Future-Earth books with humans who don't know the truth of us. I haven't yet been to one of his plays" (she must still be talking about Shakespeare) "but I had heard talk and that was what sent me to look for them. I did a lot of reading when Father was locked up." I was glad that Bess continued to be well aware of the need for some secrecy in our lives – but then I thought of her, alone in the library, reading as she waited for her next opportunity to be with her father, to comfort him while I was prevented from doing so. My Thomas could not have asked for a better oldest child.

She had talked about honesty; I was grateful and relieved, however, that she didn't share everything with the two youngest children in our family – not that baby Adam would have taken much notice. It was only later drinking wine (Bess's watered) and sitting by the fireside – long after the little ones were sleeping and my father had insisted on going to Alice's and Stephen's for the night – that Bess went on to speak briefly of 'grown-up' matters to Thomas and me. All three of us had suffered Donnett. Thomas's and Bess's experiences had been so very much worse than mine, I thought with a shudder, and *she* had been a child. Bess suggested, calmly, that we needed to find some way to properly mind-share in the near future. As she pointed out, it was poisoning Thomas. Even hidden away it ate at him inside. Going to him and throwing her arms around him, she spoke passionately about it and hers was the right to do so.

"Father, Dadde, you won't begin to heal, I feel it, until you've fully shared the pain of that evil, evil night. I saw you when they brought you back. Megs, me, the other girls, we all thought you were dead. We were so frightened for you. You need to share your memories of it, and you would be safe going there together with us, with Mother and me."

Thomas went very quiet and very pale – I didn't know, couldn't guess what he felt about her words. We had never thought of mind-sharing outside the hand-fasting ceremony, where there were two people, not three, and I said so. She countered by saying that just because it hadn't been done before that didn't mean that it couldn't or shouldn't be. And, of course, she was right, but only if Thomas could survive the memory. "Please, oh please don't break, Thomas, not now, after everything," my thoughts whispered. He had already drawn back from us, just an infinitesimal amount, and wouldn't talk about it, but he did promise to think on everything she had said.

Much later, tucked up in bed, I watched Thomas in his night clothes surreptitiously using the chamber pot – why it still embarrassed him I had no idea – before clambering back into bed with me. We had Adam in the cradle, Bess in the truckle bed, and Lissy in with us, so we were being *very* circumspect, but Thomas still cuddled up to me, sharing his cold hands and feet more than I appreciated, and whispered in my ear. "I don't think you're old at all."

I kissed the tip of his nose, which was also cold. *"And you are exactly the right age and have a very fine young body, Mister Alban. I'm looking forward to exploring it some more, when we have a room to ourselves."* Then I clung to him, afraid to let go.

Chapter 32

The banishment was legally over. We were in the process of moving back into the old damp, damaged house. Anyone we spoke to, humans at any rate, thought it would have been better to knock it down and rebuild. Or build alongside and forget the wreck. But we were making a point to ourselves – hoping that Bess had been right, hoping that it would be possible to reclaim the place. Not so much the physical house but the atmosphere inside it, an atmosphere so heavily charged with unhappy memories that the dust – and there was a lot of that, along with dirt – even seemed to crackle with it.

Other than our children, who had never lived there, each of us had our fair share of those unhappy memories. As we entered the forlorn building for the first time, I vividly recalled the men who had taken my mother away and my fear when I was deserted, or so I thought, by my father. And how could I ever forget being dragged out by the men who had attacked me, the blood spurting over me from the one I had killed. My discomfort increased when I remembered turning my back on Thomas, writing that misguided note, and leaving in response to him being so angry and then so cold to me. Moving through the hall, my mind conjured images of John Dinley dying from the injuries he had suffered during the escape and I started to miserably revisit the thought that it had been an escape which I alone had made necessary. But, thinking of Bess's words, I reminded myself that it was all, ultimately, down to Anstey. His fault, never, ever mine. Dead Anstey … thank you Adam.

For my father, I guessed that his memories were of my mother, his Elizabeth, being taken from him and the shock of finding that in rushing to save his wife, he had abandoned his daughter to life-threatening danger. On this, the first day of our return, he shut himself in his former study to deal with the pain on his own, despite all Bess had said about sharing. He didn't want us to see what was in his mind. But that was my father's way. I hoped it wouldn't, ultimately, be Thomas's too.

With his arm around me, Thomas told me that the worst of his memories of the house was the pain of reading my note, believing he had lost me through his own senseless and ill-controlled anger. He confronted once more the shock of Edith's crazy accusations, and then, like me, he was anguished at the memory of John's body and the knowledge that he was, with me, partly responsible for his friend's death. This time, when we finally brought ourselves to discuss it, he talked to me, honestly, about that sense of guilt. He blamed himself for the deaths that had resulted from our hasty, ill-planned departure from the complex, and I trembled to think that some part of him might always see our love – well, to be more crude and accurate, him fucking me – as him achieving his own personal desires at the expense of his friends' well-being. I missed no opportunity to remind him that Anstey was the one responsible. Not him, not me. Any attempt to hold himself responsible inevitably attached the guilt to me as well, and I hoped that he was reluctant to do that, where I was concerned.

Towards the end of the first full day, we held hands as we walked around outside. From our hand-fasting, Thomas recognised the surrounding fields, seen first-hand for the first time in daylight. His arms moved protectively around me. Holding me comfortingly tightly, ever his way. I rested my head against him and he bent his head to nuzzle against my hair.

"You were so powerful, my love, I wish I'd been with you to help."

"Too many bodies. You'd have killed them all. How would we ever have got away with that?" I teased, turning to look up at him. "But, seriously, in a sense you were there. Having you present in my mind at our hand-fasting, showing you what happened, put it all into perspective for me. I was afraid that what I did to that man would make you angry with me. It was such relief when I knew that you understood!"

"Do you think Bess is right, about sharing again?"

"I don't know, my love. How did you feel last time?"

"Last time it helped. I was afraid that you would turn your back on me in disgust, because of what I did to my parents, to that poor girl … Afterwards, when you still cared about me despite everything that I revealed to you … well I saw things from a different point of view, I began to admit to myself that you were right, that Anstey alone was to blame."

"So? Does that mean that you could give it a try?"

"This is slightly different. It's more that I don't want you to have my memories in your head or in Bess's head. If it makes *me* sick to think of it, to see it repeated over and over in my dreams, how can I inflict that on you. And Bess is scarcely more than a child."

"If you remember what happened to her, you can't think of her as a child. Sometimes she is, but rarely. Donnett stole that from her. She, more than anyone else alive, is capable of understanding. In the absence of really knowing, our imaginations, hers and mine, supply us with the very worst details possible. And she saw you immediately afterwards."

I couldn't confess to him what Alice had shared with me – he might not forgive her – but the logic of my argument was weakened by the knowledge that what had actually happened to him was probably worse than anyone's imagination could conjure. I rushed on, anyway. "Besides that, we can't bear for you to be living with something so terrible that you won't let us shoulder a part of the burden."

"Oh Kat – sometimes I wonder how it would have been if I'd ridden up that very first morning, killed those who were harming you, and we'd run away together. I was strong then. Not weakened like now. I could have done it. With your power too, *we* could have done it. Where would we be now?"

He kissed me, possessively, one arm holding me and the fingers of his other hand gently reaching beneath my ruff to stroke my neck tenderly, feather-light touches following the patterns in my skin downwards. My physical response to him – so easily awoken, I couldn't resist him – silenced a boringly prosaic voice inside me, a voice which would have reminded him that, even if we'd survived that first fight, I would have died giving birth to Lissy. We wouldn't have rescued Bess and the others; Anstey would still be running the complex and a lot of innocent people would have continued to die. And Thomas would never have forgiven himself for deserting his friends. I sighed, even as my mouth opened to his kiss. Some fantasies were best shared, some truths were better left unsaid. I mustn't become too boring a person to dream. Pressed firmly against him, the two of us together, I knew exactly what he meant – the spirit of it – and abandoned myself to his love instead of speaking. It reminded me of my fantasy of a different kind of ostium. One through which we two might step into an eternal time that was just ours … alone … together.

*

Thomas looked around him as he chose pieces of timber from the barn for his indoor building project. No, it might not be the best house in the entire world, but it was a lot more than most humans

255

had throughout their entire lives. He *was* appreciative … it was only the thought of what lay ahead.

James and Robert had made sure that they were well provided for from the Barnstable profits. They'd done well. A significant part of him would much rather have returned to Barnstable and consigned the complex to hell. But he had a responsibility that couldn't be shelved. And now Kat's father, sharing this house with him, had insisted on gifting the tenant-rent income to him. An undeserved relief, but too many incomeless weeks in Ilfraycombe, first her, then him, had badly drained their resources. Physical and, he couldn't help adding, mental. It was impossible to avoid the cold quake in his gut at the thought of his time in Ilfraycombe without Kat. Another sore place inside him that wouldn't quite heal over.

He hefted a few pieces of the prepared wood on his shoulder and took them inside.

Anyway, they weren't in Barnstable – they were here. Making the most of it. He owed it to Bess and Kat, who were trying their best, and, for once, family and duty weren't opposed. When it came to the practicalities of their new set-up, Kat had already organised a year's contract with two friendly local people, arranging to have them start work straight away in preparation for when she and he would be away each day in the complex. He was kind of coasting along in her wake. Everyone treated him so carefully; as if he was about to disintegrate. They meant well. He supposed. But there was a residual resentment inside him that he was aware of and tried to squash as unfair.

Trying not to think too deeply about the future, he reviewed the latest arrangements in his head. The workers Kat had hired were married and saving to have their own place, which was nice. Jane was a very good cook, a relief – Kat was a bit haphazard – and Jane had also taken immediate charge of the neglected but now newly stocked hen houses and pig pen. Gregory was nearly as competent as Thomas's father-in-law's John. A good man: well able to look after the horses and take care of all the day-to-day concerns of the house and its grounds, together with rent collection from the estate. And they were getting along well. Like now, when Gregory was helping him with the house modifications. Easy company.

He put the wood down and checked out the drawings he'd made. Gregory was on his way up with more.

Being truthful, he was disappointed that it had been so easy to find them. Jane and Gregory. He had come close to suggesting to Kat that he could stay home and do those jobs while she went to the complex to keep an eye on things there. Got as far as rehearsing the arguments he might put. But that would have been wrong. If he didn't do his share in the complex, he wouldn't have a voice in the elections. And that would mean letting Bess down and admitting to her and to Kat how frightened –shit scared – he really was, despite all the legal assurances he'd had. There was no way he'd survive even one single night in that fucking cell if they dreamed up something else to accuse him of. He felt his gut gripe at the thought.

Why couldn't he just be with Kat and the children – let the rest go fuck themselves! No-one forcing him to be what he wasn't. Even his own family. He wasn't sure who was bossier – Kat or Bess. He tried not to care. They meant well, and in this hiatus, before he started back to technical work, the women's organising skills left him a lot of free time to play with his small daughter and infant son. They never did anything but love him regardless. Immensely satisfying, particularly seeing Lissy smile more.

Perhaps the best thing, no, not perhaps, definitely the best thing about this time was the enjoyment of as much glorious, safe, sex with his wife – who wasn't ever too busy for that – as the constraints of family allowed. After everything that had happened, he hungered for her – all the time – which wasn't easy in a crowded house. Please God that wouldn't change when he was back working in *that* place. He was all too aware that this was a brief enough interlude, before he would need to face his fears. But only God knew how much he ached to swoop Kat and the children up in his arms and run far away with them.

"Where do you want these?" Gregory had returned with some more smoothed panels of wood, interrupting his reverie.

"Upstairs, the end of the upper hallway please."

"Any more needed?

"Just a few more. Look, I have the drawings here. It's going to be a small prayer room. Screened off from the open corridor. It's not ideal, but it just needs to be a private space. Away from the racket in the rest of the house."

"You mean baby Adam," Gregory said, grinning.

Thomas groaned. No words needed.

It was good to have friendly help. Male help. Made the job easier being able to chat – a million miles away from all that intensity and pity. Someone who didn't look at him and see a pathetic wreck. The others, they all meant well, but they knew far too much about him and he hated that.

By evening the shell of a room was ready and he was pleased, more than pleased at the progress the two of them were making. Dealing with their mental and spiritual issues, his, Bess's and Kat's, was his only working priority connected to the house. James had helped with the early details at the drawing stage, and now, with physical assistance from Gregory, Thomas began to feel that it would be possible to create a very real sanctuary room. Like a small chapel, his plan was that it would be dedicated to the memory of Anstey's victims – in particular Henry, John, and Kat's mother – a gift to them from Anstey's survivors. Located here, deep within the house itself, it would be a very private space.

And then, once it was completed, he needed to make that final decision about the mind-sharing with Kat and Bess.

*

A month or so after moving in, Bess, Thomas, and I took a collective deep breath one late evening and braved our triple mind-share in the sanctuary Thomas had created for us. Lissy and Adam were asleep, and Jane was keeping an ear open for them so that we might be undisturbed. Bess was certain and assured. We couldn't let her down, but I could tell that Thomas was sick with fear, nearly reneging more than once. I thought to myself that it was probably the bravest thing, in a lot of brave things, that he had ever done. There was even a certain amount of fear in my heart too – fear that my behaviour when I hadn't remembered him might have finally broken his spirit and been instrumental in this acquiescence. I was very scared too but unwilling to be the one to let the others down. James had brought the drugs to us: after my Lundye experience, I think I feared that aspect as much as anything. But he understood and was an amazing support – staying in the outer room and promising, faithfully, to bring us back if anyone was too distressed to continue. Once Thomas agreed, what more could be said? It was both agonisingly heart-breaking for the two viewing and cathartic for the one sharing and revealing. I was surprised at how much it helped that there were two of us entering the shared mind-space.

Thomas and I were together, clutching each other's hands and hers, to share Bess's horrific experience. Ready to hold her older self in our arms as we cried together after each revelation – grateful that she had let the barriers down and was allowing us to comfort her. I had been there before, she had once shown me what was done, but then I had been too weak to help her cope. Now it aided her to be part of a family, with Thomas's and my joint strength beside her. And, beyond that, there was her knowledge of Donnett's death. When she'd shown me before it was moments after she'd seen him escape, after I'd failed to kill him.

She and I, holding tight to each other and crying scalding tears as we burned with fury, saw the appalling, unspeakable things Thomas had suffered. I had thought the detailed infirmary report was bad enough, but to actually see what they did, hear their taunts, until he'd lost consciousness, was worse. But I had to forget my perspective, this was for him and it meant that this time he didn't suffer alone. We were there to hold him and to let him know that there was nothing about it that shamed *him* – to let him know how much he was loved and admired and honoured. But it was a bad and unexpected shock to both Bess and I to then see him on the cliff-top and to know that, without Alice, we would have lost him. Neither of us had been aware of that memory, nor how close it had been.

Thomas and Bess shared my memories, which also gave them a satisfying glimpse of the demise of their tormentors. They saw my fear and comforted me. I hadn't fully realised, with the idea of mind-sharing being so new to me when Thomas and I had first ventured into that shadowy mind-world, that this was not some one-off visit to another's memories. Those who travelled left some part of their presence there. Ever afterwards, when I remembered lying there with Donnett inside me and his brains spattered over my bare flesh, I remembered from the perspective of an observer. I felt their tangible love there with me too, strengthening me, holding me in the light, diminishing the darkness. Both Thomas and Bess told me they felt the same way.

Later, in our bed, Thomas whispered to me that flashbacks to the scene of his torture, re-living it in all its sickening pain and terror, had been a continual part of his life ever since it had happened. A treadmill with no reprieve. He confessed that his feelings of shame and humiliation had mentally magnified the agony of the extreme physical violation he had survived … just. And he allowed himself to cry with me. Just the two of us alone. But he spoke in more detail of the new sensation that Bess and I were there with him now. And, while we couldn't protect him from that suffering, the certainty of us loving him, rather than despising him, bridged the pit of despair that always threatened to drag him down. He was no longer that mangled creature lying naked and helpless, he was the mature observer, recognising at last that it *was* all Anstey's sin, the perpetrators' sin, and all this while held safe in the arms of the two who loved him and never thought him diminished in any way. With his arms tightly around me he told me that, while he would never be completely free, in his undying memories he would at least never feel such terrible shame and never suffer entirely on his own again.

Bess had cheered us earlier when she told us how much Thomas, Megs, and the other girls, had already helped her all those years back, and the immense satisfaction she felt now at actually seeing, through me, her tormentors blown to pieces. Definitely *my* daughter in terms of being bloodthirsty. Now that she was privy to the full story of all that had happened on Lundye, including Adam's and Mark's love affair, she resolved to spend some time with Adam, letting him know how much she loved what he had done for her and trying to legally get his banishment rescinded, so that he and Mark could enjoy some of the comforts of the complex. I speculated (to myself) that Mark might be very favourably impressed with the showers, if he ever got to share one with Adam. The memory of Thomas and I enjoying ours was on my list of 'best but all too brief' memories. Followed by one of the worst: discovering Richard to be a traitor and killing him.

The deed was done, and we had signed up for our future positions in the complex. Returning had been made safe for Thomas. It was now up to us to work to change the inertia that had allowed things to go so very wrong. There would be new elections shortly. And I would soon be teaching, again. I knew how happy that would make Megs and the others. Anne was too busy with council work, assuming she kept her post after the official reprimand, and I didn't trust her with the minds of the very young. Too many secrets surrounded the excuses that had been made for the maltreatment of my husband. It would have killed him if my father and the others had not stepped in to protect him. Thomas was intending to pursue some scientific project and also secretly planned to re-engage with examining the mind-sharing drugs. A lot of us were still hoping that the ban on mixed hand-fasting would be re-visited. Thomas didn't want to share progress on either idea as yet but promised that the overt project would be something harmless and unlikely to arouse any further ire on the part of the council. Like Bess, he was also working with James and Robert to get Adam reinstated for his services against the pirates. We were very, very cautious, checking that we stayed on the right side of the letter of every Domum-Orbis law and tradition. It helped that Alice and Stephen had, at least partially, returned to the complex with Thom, that Mathias called in regularly and that James and Robert were there most days.

It remained to be seen if we could survive this return without being plunged back into the nightmare of our previous time in the settlement.

Epilogue

A full day working in the complex, his first, a late afternoon playing with the children in the house, bedtime stories, and now time alone – just the two of them.

Thomas lies with his wife, kissing her, holding her close against him. Her fingers reach out, gently touching the swirls that curl down from his shoulders under his skin. He touches hers, following them, fingers lingering, down to her breasts. Kissing them. He wants to make love to Kat; he is roused, ready, and he presses her closer to him. They look into each other's eyes. Whisper love in each other's minds. *"Keep your eyes open, look at me,"* they say to each other as he eases gently into her. And then he's not so gentle, and neither does she want him to be, as in the half-light of a mid-summer evening, staying in the current moment, they reclaim each other, safe in their own home, from the horrors they have shared. In the way they know best.

If you enjoyed *Anstey's Revenge: Will Love be Enough?* look out for *Anstey's Legacy: No Greater Love*, the final book in this 'Anstey's Kingdom' Trilogy.

ABOUT THE AUTHOR

Susan Hancock, PhD, is a former University Lecturer who has written and published non-fiction over a number of years. She gave up teaching in order to concentrate on her battle with a cancer which is now fortunately dormant. Fingers crossed.

In a totally surprising move, she became obsessed with the idea of writing an adult novel and ended up writing three, the 'Anstey's Kingdom' sequence. She has discovered that characters are hard taskmasters, determined that their stories should be told. It isn't uncommon to find her in tears at the laptop when something dreadful happens to one or other of them. But they and she understand that some things can't be changed.

Why not visit her website for information on Book 3 of the 'Anstey's Kingdom' trilogy: *Anstey's Legacy: No Greater Love,* and details of future books: https://www.susanjenniferhancock.com.